MW01462867

MY UNEXPECTED TREASURES

MARIE DIAS

Copyright © 2023 Marie Dias

All rights reserved. No part of this publication may be reproduced, distributed, or transmitted in any form or by any means, including photocopying, recording, or other electronic or mechanical methods, without the prior written permission of the publisher, except as permitted by U.S. copyright law.

The story, all names, characters, and incidents portrayed in this production are fictitious. No identification with actual persons (living or deceased), places, buildings, and products is intended or should be inferred.

To Jesus Christ, the lover of my soul and the keeper of my heart. He has patiently guided me every step of the way, not only in the writing of this book, but in every season of my life. He is the Treasure in every darkness.

I will give you the treasures of darkness,
Riches stored in secret places,
So that you may know that I am the Lord,
The God of Israel, who summons you by name.
—ISAIAH 45:3 (NIV)

CONTENTS

CHAPTER 1: The Explosion	1
CHAPTER 2: The Search Begins	13
CHAPTER 3: Do We Have a Cohort?	27
CHAPTER 4: Reality	39
CHAPTER 5: Christmas in the Country	48
CHAPTER 6: Closed Doors	61
CHAPTER 7: Goodbye?	80
CHAPTER 8: A Bigger Hurdle	89
CHAPTER 9: The Big Break	109
CHAPTER 10: Back in Atlanta	145
CHAPTER 11: DFACS	177
CHAPTER 12: I Couldn't Stop Myself	188
CHAPTER 13: Becca's Research	196
CHAPTER 14: Melinda	223
CHAPTER 15: The Adoption	243
CHAPTER 16: Where Is My Baby?	253
CHAPTER 17: Jerry's Story	271
CHAPTER 18: The Answers	287
CHAPTER 19: Upheaval	297
CHAPTER 20: Justin	305
CHAPTER 21: Baby Girl	319
CHAPTER 22: The Inevitable	326
CHAPTER 23: A New Season	341
Afterword	353
About the Author	359

CHAPTER ONE

The Explosion

Tina pulled her Ford Escape into the last empty parking space, shut off the engine and sat staring out of the front windshield. She had just completed a late afternoon photo shoot and returned home to her one bedroom apartment a few miles outside of downtown Atlanta. The usual letdown after a demanding shoot descended over her as she took down her messy bun and let the red curls fall wherever they wished. Photo shoots were exhilarating and strenuous all at the same time. She took off her glasses, laid them on the dashboard, and slowly massaged her temples to relieve the built-up tension.

With a long sigh, Tina leaned her head back

against the seat to relax for a minute. Living in Atlanta was exciting in many ways but more demanding than she had expected. Her career as a photojournalist was starting to show profit and she was thankful for that. Her name and reputation for creative shots combined with compelling background stories were slowly gaining recognition.

She sat up, gathered her things, put on her glasses and pushed the door open with her left foot. A sudden, loud explosion and the tremor of the earth knocked her back into the car with a jolt. The rumblings continued to rock the car. In the distance she heard someone screaming. It took a minute to realize it was her. The initial shock subsided and she sat shuddering, listening to the rumbling and growling in the aftermath of the explosion. People yelled and sirens began to scream from a distance. Tina was slow to raise her head, afraid to look at what just happened. Spasms shook her body and she could not stop shaking. As though from far away she heard someone knocking on her car window. She looked up to see the face of the man who lived across the stairwell from her apartment. She did not remember closing the car door.

"Are you OK?" he was yelling through the closed window.

"Yes, I'm alright. What happened?"

"An explosion across the highway. I'm going over to help. You need to get inside."

"OK . . . OK . . . no, wait, I'm going with you."

Tina threw down everything except her camera, jumped out of the car and ran along behind him. Struggling with the already blackening air burning her eyes, she held one arm over her mouth and followed him across the highway. A few cars were moving slowly forward while others had pulled over onto the shoulder. Some people were honking their horns and yelling at the slow moving traffic, while others poured from the cars and ran towards the excitement. Tina and her neighbor began working their way across all six lanes of I-75/85. They dodged and jumped then ran quickly to avoid being hit. After several close calls, they reached the grassy area beside the freeway. Together they jogged down to the parking lot of a large hotel. The site before her was incomprehensible. Smoke, particles of ash and debris, people running, crying, police and fire trucks with sirens and horns blaring were approaching from several directions. There was total mayhem. The twenty-story hotel was literally collapsing as she watched.

She placed her camera up to her eye and began snapping as quickly as possible. After a few minutes, he interrupted her.

"Barry."

"What?" She looked up briefly with an annoyed expression.

"Barry. That's my name, Barry. I live across from you."

"Yes, I've noticed you. I'm Tina."

Before they could continue this awkward conversation, a young woman carrying a small child and leading another by the hand stumbled out of the smoky rubble and came straight to them. Barry immediately reached out to help her with the child but as he did so the woman began to fall. Tina was trying to catch the baby while Barry grabbed at the mama as she collapsed at their feet. The young boy beside her stood motionless, staring at nothing, while tears mixed with dirt ran down his small face.

"My Baby," was all the lady said before losing consciousness.

Tina sank to the ground cradling the baby with her free hand while Barry held the woman's head and tried to revive her. The little boy stood still and quiet. The baby wailed and flung her arms, reaching for her momma and trying to break free of Tina's grip. After several minutes of trying unsuccessfully to revive the lady, Barry worked his way through the crowd to the closest EMT.

Tina tried to calm the baby, speaking softly in

her ear. "It's OK, sweetie. Mama's gonna be alright. Shhhh . . . shhhh. It's OK, you are alright." The boy continued to stand and stare at nothing while Tina continued to wrestle with the screaming baby. The smoke was choking her and burning her eyes. She wondered how in the world the kids could stand it. Finally, two EMT's followed Barry over to where she waited. After checking the lady, they looked up at Tina.

"Is she family?"

Tina shook her head. "No, I have no idea who she is. She just walked up and handed me her baby when she started falling."

"So, the baby is hers?"

"I guess. She was carrying the baby and holding the little boy by the hand when she stumbled out of the fire. I have no idea why she walked towards me. I really don't know anything about who she is."

The EMT's glanced at each other as the guy continued taking her vitals and attempting to bring her around. The lady EMT was searching the woman's pockets looking for identification or anything that would give them her name. Finally, she sat back on her heels and shook her head. "Nothing." She looked up at Tina, "Did she have a pocketbook, a wallet, phone, anything at all?"

Tina shook her head, "Not that I saw."

The EMT looked towards Barry, "She's not coming around, we're gonna need to transport her. I'll get the gurney. Be right back."

Tina and Barry stood helplessly, still holding onto the children. Barry spoke up and asked where they were taking her.

"Grady Hospital. You can check in with them as soon as they assess her. Well, perhaps not, since you do not know this woman."

The lady EMT returned with the gurney. She looked at Tina and asked the obvious. "What about the children? We need to hand them over to The Department of Family & Children Services (DFACS)."

Tina involuntarily hugged the baby girl closer and looked up at Barry. About that time, Barry spotted one of the Fire Chief's and pointed towards him. "Hey, I know that Chief. Should we get him to find the social services people for us? I know you guys are slammed here."

The EMT's strapped the lady on the gurney while Barry jogged over and shook hands with the Fire Chief. The Chief looked their way and gave a thumbs up, indicating he would take it from here. Tina looked down at the little boy who still stood silent. It was strange that he didn't cry when they took his mama away. He appeared to be about two or three maybe. Surely old enough to know she was leaving. Still, he was in shock and may not have realized what was happening. His baby sister had cried herself into a stupor and just lay against Tina's shoulder. Her eyes had that empty, staring look.

After a few minutes, Barry and the fireman walked back over to where she was standing. "Tina, this is Tom Evers, a good friend of mine. He is the Fire Chief of Gwinnett County."

Mr. Evers looked at Tina with a soft expression. "So, I understand you have no idea who these two children belong to, is that right?"

"Yes Sir. Their mom collapsed at our feet. We barely caught the baby before she dropped her."

"I see. Well, I wish I had an answer for you. The only thing I know is that Social Services had some agents here earlier. They rounded up the children that were alone and took them over to the Union Street Mission."

"But . . ."

The Chief held up his hand to stop her. "I know what you are thinking, M'am. It's a traumatic time for little ones like these. The shelter is not ideal, but it's going to be dark soon and these children need to get somewhere safe and away from all this. The Mission is a safe place for tonight. They have a special house for women and children. They will clean them up and feed them and tomorrow DFACS will begin sorting things out."

Tina's heart dropped to her toes. She looked down at the terror stricken face of the little boy. He had attached himself to Barry's leg. And the baby had finally accepted that Tina was not going to hurt her and settled her head on Tina's shoulder.

The Chief sighed and started again. "Did anyone see you help the lady? Anyone at all that may know her or the children?"

"No sir. Not that we know of. She was only here for a minute."

He stood with his arms crossed over his chest, staring at first her and then Barry. Finally, he spoke softly. "Look, I know it's a hard call. I get it. However, the shelter is a good place. It's clean and the workers are trustworthy. Tonight it will be overrun with extra children. That's for sure. Still, you can relax about them if you take them over." He looked intently at each child before speaking again.

"Look, we all know that they would probably be a lot more comfortable at your place for the night." He looked at Tina and continued, "I have known Barry for years. If he is willing to stay with you . . ." His voice trailed off. "We never had this conversation though."

After a few seconds of heavy silence, he continued. "What I must tell you is that it is completely outside protocol for you to take these children. Even overnight. Even if you took them down to DFACS first thing tomorrow morning."

After another sobering silence, he continued, "God help us and these babies. Look, I have my hands full here. I have to get back at it. Whatever you do, these kids will need a lot of attention tonight. And most likely for a long time. Right now, they need to get out of this smoke. You guys need to as well. A traumatic event like this can cause long term issues if not handled properly."

With that, he touched the tip of his hard hat, nodded and trotted off.

Barry and Tina stared at each other for several minutes. Now she was a bit in shock herself. Take the children home? To her apartment? Even for a night was too much to consider. What in the world? They could get arrested for kidnapping. They could be mistaken as child abductors. Sex traffickers. She could not do this! There was no way on God's green earth she was going to do such a thing. Still, the little guy was holding onto Barry's leg with all his might. And the baby had finally calmed down. *Dear Lord, what should we do?*

Finally, Barry spoke up. "Look, Tina, I don't

know you, but I know Tom. He has been a good friend for a long time. I realize what we are thinking of doing is basically illegal. It could end very badly if someone at DFACS got the wrong idea. However, Tom would stand by us. It is a critical situation and sometimes we have to make drastic choices. And, remember, the mother chose to hand them over to us. Out of all the people here, she came straight to us. Technically, she left them in our care."

Tina was literally shaking. Her mind was going a thousand miles an hour and getting nowhere. "He said you would have to be willing to stay with me. I suppose because he doesn't know me. How could we do that?"

"Well, I will be willing to take the boy with me, but that would leave you alone with the baby. For your own protection, I guess the only way is for me to sleep at your place."

Tina shook her head sharply. "What??? No, no, no no. Are you crazy? I don't even know you!"

"And I don't know you. Either way, it isn't about us, is it? I do not like the idea of sleeping on a couch in a strange woman's apartment, in charge of two kids I don't even know. Come on. I don't like this any more than you do, but we need to make a decision quickly. Us or the shelter?"

"Of course. I'm sorry. It's just that I don't know

what to do here. My heart hurts at the thought of dropping these two at the mission. What happens if their mom doesn't come for them? We know she will be in the hospital at least tonight. The kids cannot tell anyone their names. How will they ever connect them if we just drop them off? At least we have an idea where they came from. And she did hand them over to us. The mom literally put them in our hands. Does that constitute leaving them in our care? WOW! I cannot believe I am even considering this. The whole idea is insane!"

Barry waited and watched her work through the emotions of all that was going down. Finally, she turned and looked at him. "OK, I am in if you are. Let's do this."

Barry shook his head in wonder and picked up the toddler. "Here we go. Coming ready or not." As they started towards the highway, Barry reminded her, "The first thing we need is supplies."

"Let me think for a minute. We could run to the store, but, with no car seat, one of us would be alone at home with the kids. That will not work. We must be a covering for each other at all times. There are some moms in the apartment building who will probably help. If we are really doing this, let's ask them first."

The freeway was temporarily closed off to allow

medical helicopters and other emergency vehicles a place to load. Thankfully, the traffic cop took pity on them and waved them safely across. Tina's heart pounded in her chest and her insides shook with the intensity of it all. *Dear God. Help us. What will happen when DFACS learns what we have done? Will they believe that we are really only trying to help? And how will we find their mother? We don't even know her name!*

CHAPTER TWO

The Search Begins

The early morning light filtered through the closed blinds in Tina's small apartment. Slowly awakening, Tina remembered she was not alone in her bed. The baby girl was snuggled close to her back, sleeping soundly. Last night was a battle for the baby. Finally, she inserted her thumb and sucked on it until sleep came. It now lay just at the corner of her open mouth, her puckered lips moved noiselessly as if still enjoying the slightly red thumb. Fuzzy little blonde ringlets lay softly on the back of the baby's head.

Tina eased out of bed and walked into the living room where she saw Barry on the couch, sleeping in his clothes from yesterday. Looking at the stranger on her couch, with the little boy lying close to his side, the stark reality of what had happened settled over her again. Chief Evers had better be a real good friend. They may just need him in court. "Oh, Lord!" she whispered.

Tina reached to click on the light then remembered the power was out. It probably would be for a while. She walked over to the front window and peeked through the blinds to the highway below. Morning traffic creeped along like any other work day in Atlanta. The hotel was burned beyond recognition and yielded up patches of smoke and a foul order that permeated the walls of her apartment. It was all too much to comprehend. "I need coffee," she mumbled to herself.

Last night many of the residents had gathered impromptu in the little clubhouse trying to determine what had happened. One man had a police radio that picked up a few details, but even those were inconsistent. They ended up hanging out in the small couch-lined room until almost midnight. There were two ladies with small children who gave her enough diapers, bottles, and formula to get through a few days. Someone loaned her two car seats that had seen better days but at least they were safe. She and her new-found responsibilities had finally fallen asleep sometime around 2:00 A.M. Sleep had been patchy after that, and this morning her head felt it.

The ring of her cell phone brought Tina back to the present and she searched her pockets and then back to her bed before she found it. Surprisingly, it had not awakened the baby.

"Hello," she answered in a whisper. The sound of her mother's voice brought immediate tears. She cupped her hand over the phone and cradled it close to her face. "Oh . . . Mom."

Tina walked out into the stairwell to talk. There was a slight breeze there, but it carried the putrid smell of burning debris. Which was worse, the awful odor and smoke or the steaming-hot apartment? She had called her parents last night to explain all that was happening and ask for prayer from her family in Chickpea. She did, however, leave out the part about bringing them home basically illegally. She may have watered that part down. Well, actually, she told her mom they had permission. Her mom would never understand doing something without authority. But then, she didn't see their little faces. Tina was in something way over her head and needed God like she had not in a long time.

Mom replied in a whisper as well. "How are things this morning? Are you OK?"

"You don't need to whisper, Mom. They can't hear you." Tina needed to lighten the mood or her mom would be headed to Atlanta.

"Oh, yeah, sorry dear. Anyway, are you OK?"

"Yeah, I guess. I just woke up and everyone else is still asleep. I hope they sleep for a while. None of us got much rest last night. The baby was doing much better until bedtime came. I think then she realized she was in a strange place and kinda lost it. It was heartbreaking to hear her sob and call for her mommy. By the time she fell asleep I was ready to cry and call for her mommy too! We finally went to sleep about 2:00 this morning after spending hours in the Club House. It was a weird way to get to know my neighbors. But some of them helped us out with bottles and such."

"Good. Do you know what your plans are for today yet?"

"No, not until Barry wakes up. And Mom, he is really something. He stayed right with me until bedtime and then slept on my couch with the little boy. He is still there . . . in his clothes from yesterday. Are you and Dad praying?"

"Yes, Dear, we have been and will continue. Do you want us to drive up and help you? How do you know this Barry is safe to have in your apartment? You just met him, for goodness sake!"

"I know, but he was a complete gentleman. There was nothing inappropriate and I really needed his help. Trust me, OK?" Her mom's long sigh let Tina know exactly how she felt, but amazingly, she didn't push the point.

She knew her parents wanted to be with her, but that would only add more people to her tiny apartment and further complicate matters. Tina was in this alone with a man she had only met yesterday and two children whose names she didn't even know. As she said goodbye to her mom and promised to keep in touch, her phone buzzed with a new call coming through from her neighbor and friend, Katie. "Hey Katie!"

That was all she got out before Katie launched into a thousand questions. "I just saw it on the news! What the heck? Are you OK? How is the apartment? Do I need to come home?"

Tina could not help but chuckle. "Hey, slow down. I am fine. So much to tell you, but our building is good, I'm good. But you will never believe the rest of it!" She launched into a description of all that had happened in the last 24 hours.

"Wait! Wait a minute," Katie jumped in the middle of her story. "Barry is the good looking guy across the hall from you? AND he is sleeping on your couch? AND he has a little boy with him? Tina! Good grief!"

"I know, right? It's been a crazy night. And Katie, he is a jewel. So caring and patient. He is helping with the kids. And I promise, he slept on my couch only to help keep the little boy calm."

Now it was Katie's turn to laugh. "I have no doubt, my friend. I know you too well to think anything else. I do find it interesting that it only took a hotel exploding, half of Atlanta shut down, you becoming a criminal and two orphans to get a man inside your apartment."

"Very funny, Katie. You're hilarious."

"But, seriously, do I need to come home and help you? I am ready to cut my trip short and get the next plane to Atlanta. Do you have any idea what to do next? I mean, technically you are way outside your rights, maybe even outside the law. I cannot believe you did that, Tina!"

"I know, I know. And no, there's nothing you can do. Barry and I have it covered for now. I am standing out in the stairwell, but I need to get back inside. The air out here is horrible. I'll give you a call as soon as I know something. Until then, no reason for you to come home. This may all be over by the time you could get here anyway. But thanks for offering. Enjoy the rest of your trip. I'll call ya soon."

Tina shut off her phone and stood for a moment pondering her situation. Her life had changed drastically in the last year or so, but this was another level altogether. Her background had not prepared her for anything like this.

She was a country girl, born in a little country town almost two hundred miles south of Atlanta. Her childhood was typical for growing up in a Southern town where everyone knew everyone. From an early age you are taught to mind your manners and your elders. It did not matter if it were your mom, your aunt or your best friend's mom, and certainly not if it was your grandma, the rules were the same. The only correct answer was, "Yes ma'am." And going outside the law, heck even the rules, was not acceptable. She shook her head in amazement at her current predicament.

Her parents still lived in the house where she grew up. Her two sisters and one brother lived within twenty-five miles of the home place. She missed the Sunday dinners after church which usually included the entire Brogan clan. Tina was the youngest of the family, and the only one not married, a fact which gained her great admiration in the eyes of her three nieces and two nephews. She was the cool aunt who spoiled them and played ball and took them skating. Did they miss her as much as she missed them?

However, as wonderful as life was in Chickpea, GA, the possibilities for a lucrative future there were limited. At twenty-two years of age, and fresh out of college, Tina had been ready for a change. The way she looked at it, if she was going to make a difference in this world, she had to bring something to the table—something uniquely hers, an input that could only come from her. She had to find her voice, her place and her purpose.

And so, early on a November morning, with a heart full of promises from God and encouragement from her family, Tina set her GPS for Atlanta and drove onto I-75 North. Along with the generous deposit her parents had made into her bank account, she had saved money from her job at Target. She was able to rent a furnished apartment and had enough money to get her through several months until she found work. A combination of excitement and fear had accompanied her three-hour drive that morning almost two years ago.

Photography had been her love since she was a small child and her Grandma Brogan had been influential in motivating her to keep learning and exploring the creativity that blossomed inside her. Her very first Kodak point-and-shoot camera sat prominently on the bookshelf in her living room as a reminder of how far she had come. "Grandma, I still remember our long talks on your porch when I would dream of traveling around the country with my camera and shooting on location wherever there was a story. One day, Grandma, it's gonna happen, one day."

For now she was living in an apartment on the second floor of an older apartment complex. Her new best friend, Katie, lived in the apartment just above Tina's. They had met one day on the stairwell when they both stopped to give a sideways once-over to the new guy moving in across from Tina. Once he disappeared inside his apartment their eyes met and they collapsed in laughter. And now that same guy was actually asleep on her couch! Since then, Katie had become as close as her back home friends. Of all times for Katie to be out of town for the week.

Tina stepped inside to find three expectant faces staring wide-eyed at her. Baby Girl was awake and Barry held her with one arm and with his other hand he patted the little boy sitting on his knee. As soon as Baby saw her, the wailing began anew. The little boy's lip started to quiver as he struggled to keep from crying, however, as soon as she spoke to the baby, the boy's tears began in earnest. Tina took a deep breath and fought her own tears. Picking up Baby and cuddling her close, Tina prayed again, "Dear Jesus, what am I supposed to do?" Barry wrapped both arms around the little boy and held him close to his chest. Over the heads of the children, Barry stared at her with frustration and pain in his eyes. She suspected his tears were very close as well. Neither of them felt adequate for the task at hand. After taking turns at a quick shower and change of clothes, they loaded up the children and made their way downtown.

"Listen," Barry began, "we both know what will happen if we take these kids to Social Services. How about if we try Grady first? If their mom is there and awake, we can reunite them with her and that will be that. What do you think?"

"I think that's a great idea. Wouldn't it be wonderful if she was awake and asking for her children. Or maybe a family member would be there visiting her and would see them. But, how do we get in to see her if we do not even know her name?"

Barry shrugged his shoulders. "I have no idea. But, I still think it's worth a try."

Grady Hospital was a mass of people and confusion. Barry talked with the clerk at the information desk and asked about a lady brought in by ambulance last night. The clerk looked at him like he was from another planet. Tina watched as he shuffled his feet and began again. The next time was even worse. Apparently, one needed information in order to get information.

Next they walked through several waiting rooms.

Most were filled with family members and friends of the victims. They walked slowly through each one in hopes that someone would recognize the children, but no one gave a second look.

A small prayer circle had gathered close to the vending machine. She could hear the sniffling and soft rumblings of people asking God for help. In times of crisis people return to their roots. In the Bible Belt that included calling on Jesus for help. Tina smiled and joined in prayer with them as she walked past. "Lord, I know you are listening. I know you will help each one of us. That's what you do. I hope it is soon, Lord, very soon."

After a while, they admitted that walking through the halls only added to the stress of the moment. The hospital was too traumatic for the children and since nothing was being accomplished, they gave up and made their way outside before another nurse stopped and asked them to leave. Afterall, children were not allowed in patient halls.

Barry buckled the little boy up and Tina secured the baby in the other car seat. It was extra hot in Atlanta and Tina closed her eyes and waited for the cool A/C air after Barry turned the ignition and started the car. The kids were quiet, Baby sucking her thumb and the little boy staring out his window.

"I wasn't prepared for that!" Barry sat behind the wheel without making any move to pull out of the parking space.

Tina was a bit embarrassed to witness his emotions. "Ahem . . . we should probably get moving huh?"

Next stop was Children's Services. Tina took the lead and briefly explained the situation. The young clerk was obviously in over her head as much as Tina. She explained that the nursery located on the bottom floor of the hotel was primarily for employees' children, but guests were allowed to use the services as well. Most of the employees' children had been reunited with family, but it was difficult to identify the small children of guests. In many instances, both parents were injured or killed. I suppose the computers and paperwork identifying the children is unavailable at this point. Most of it is likely destroyed. After her explanation, the clerk asked Tina to take a number and be seated in the waiting room. Someone would call her soon.

An hour later they were still waiting. Thankfully, Tina had thought to bring formula and a bottle. She opened the loaned diaper bag and pulled out everything she needed to mix up a bottle. Soon, she had the bottle filled, warmed under hot water and the baby was happily enjoying her lunch. It wasn't the best, but Barry located a vending machine and the little boy was munching on crackers and drinking orange juice.

Finally, their number was called and the four of them were ushered into a small cubicle along the back wall. An older lady who looked like she had been doing this for a very long time stood and shook their hands. "Hello. My name is Lucinda Mullins."

Tina and Barry each introduced themselves as they pulled the metal chairs up to the small desk and sat. Ms. Mullins looked like she had already had a long day, but her smile was genuine, even if it didn't reach her eyes. Tina guessed her to be at least in her late 60's and wondered how and why she was still dealing with displaced children at this stage of her life. She absently thought the lady should be home spoiling her own grandchildren.

Ms. Mullins reached over and patted Baby's hand. She spoke calmly to the little boy before she looked up at Tina. "So, I understand from the receptionist that you took these babies at the explosion yesterday?"

Tina nearly choked. "Oh no. No. We didn't 'take' them. They were given to us by their mother. We only kept them overnight because we didn't know for sure what else to do."

Ms. Mullins continued to search their faces. Tina

knew she was trying to decide if they were telling the truth. Finally, after what seemed like forever, she smiled and nodded rather uncertainly. Tina let out a deep breath and tried not to shudder. *She thinks we took the children! What if she calls the police?*

CHAPTER THREE

Do We Have a Cohort?

After an awkward silence, Barry launched into the full story of what happened. Ms. Mullins listened without making a comment, only occasionally reaching over to pat one of the children. Finally, Barry wrapped things up and sat quietly with the little boy on his lap. Ms. Mullins only replied quietly, "I see."

Lord, this isn't good. She doesn't believe us, does she?

After a moment, Tina spoke up and asked what would happen to the children at this point, "I mean, we know Social Services will find a place for them. But, how will you ever be able to reunite them with their mother? I mean, no one knows who she is. We couldn't even find her at Grady."

"The children will be fine. You let us worry about the details. We have protocols in place to ensure their safety. Thank you for stepping up and keeping them overnight. That was very kind of you, even if it was illegal." The smile that threatened to take over her face was barely held back. "Still, they appear to be well at this point. For now, we will find them a temporary foster home. As soon as we can determine who their mother is, we will research her home life, her health etc, and attempt to locate family members. All that will most likely take a bit, considering the lack of information we have at this point."

Tina's heart ached with the thought of what lay ahead for these kids. Still, she had no rights to them. Plus, she had her own life, her career and her own responsibilities. Glancing sideways at Barry, she assumed he felt the same.

Ms. Mullins stood and reached out her hands to take the baby from Tina. To Tina's surprise, the baby girl drew back into Tina's arms and let out a wail. "Shhh, it's OK little one. This is a nice lady who is going to help you." She patted her back and the baby settled down again until Ms. Mullins once again reached for her. About the same time, the little boy broke into sobs and wrapped his arms around Barry's neck.

"Well, it appears these two have bonded quite nicely with both of you. And you say you are not married? Right?"

Tina put her palm up and shook her head, "Oh, no. We just met actually."

The amusing look on Ms. Mullin's face was a bit annoying. "Seriously," Tina added.

"Well, no matter, just an old woman's imagination. I have been at this for a long time and it isn't ever easy to pull little ones away from people they trust. Obviously, these children have found a place of safety in you two. I will admit, I hate to pull them away and throw them into a temporary home, only to have to move them again in a few days. Chances are they will go through several homes before this gets settled. We will do our best, but it will be difficult for them."

The older lady sighed deeply with the pain of too many hurting children, too many dishonest and abusive parents and perhaps too little time left to help. "How would you feel about becoming a Foster Parent?" This was directed straight at Tina.

"What? Oh, I don't know. I have never considered anything like that. No, my life is very full right now. I have a lot going on."

Ms. Mullins concentrated on Tina for a bit before she smiled that sad smile again. "Yes, I suppose you do. You are young and busy. I understand. Still, it seems these children feel very comfortable with you. If there was any way you could consider becoming a Foster Parent, we could vet you and set things up so you could keep them until we find their mother. Is that a possibility at all?"

Tina looked to Barry for help. She saw the child sitting on his lap with those wide expressive eyes. She remembered the terror in those eyes yesterday and the way he had clung to Barry as his place of security. Instinctively, she snuggled the baby close to her chest and took in her sweet baby smells. How could she not do this? At least for a little bit? Just for these two, not for any other children.

Barry spoke softly, "I promise to help you in any way I can."

Tina broke out of her reverie and looked at Ms. Mullins. "Would there be a time limit as to how long I would have to keep them?" As soon as the words were out of her mouth, she was sorry. "I mean, if I agreed, of course I would keep them as long as they needed me."

Ms. Mullins smiled in that knowing way. The more she talked with this lady, the more she liked her. "We would need to put them somewhere until we can get your background check completed. That could take a couple of weeks."

Tina's heart dropped again. What a roller coaster this was turning out to be! "But, won't that defeat the purpose? I mean, once they get accustomed to someone else, they will need to readjust to me again."

Ms. Mullins stood and crossed her arms over her very ample bosom. The tension in the room was palpable. The sound of people talking in the adjoining cubicles suddenly sounded very loud. The older lady cocked her head to one side and leaned over with her hands on the counter. "Tell me, Tina, where do you live?"

What just happened? One moment they were talking of finding a temporary foster home for the children. The next thing she knew, she was filling out page after page of very personal information in order to become a foster parent. Next, that sweet old lady with the gruff voice and kind but sad smile had winked and ushered them all out the door. They were loaded down with supplies along with a promise to come by for a home visit in the next couple of days. What about the temporary foster home? Was she it? Well, yeah, she thought she was. Somehow Ms. Mullins had managed to look the other way for the good of the babies and let her bring them home. She and Barry rode in silence back to the apartment. Neither trusted their voice . . . or their thoughts.

Walking back into her apartment and finding the lights on and the air conditioning running was enough to bring the tears again. "Thank you, Jesus," was all she could say. Barry looked at her strangely but didn't say anything. Apparently, he did not understand who was really in control here. No matter, she knew and she was grateful for every little sign that He was near.

Oh Lord! I know, I know in my heart, that you just intervened for these kids. There is no way, ever, that DFACS would just let me bring them home. What in the world? It had to be you. You just do what's right, no matter what, but I didn't think you would overlook the law. Would you? I think you just did!

Tina turned on the TV to try and get more information about what had actually happened. She tossed the remote on the couch, and walked into the little kitchen. She pulled her hair back and wrapped it into a ball on the nape of her neck, reached into the fridge for the jelly and started making sandwiches. They had stopped on the way home and picked up peanut butter for the little boy, and ham and cheese for Barry and her.

Spreading the peanut butter on the bread made her think of her niece, Lottie, who loved PBJ's. Little Lottie was seven and Tina fourteen that first summer she kept her niece while her mom, Becca, worked. The two became fast friends and that had not changed over the years. Lottie was fifteen now and much more mature than Tina had been at that age.

Before taking lunch into the living room, Tina needed to check on the baby. She had fallen asleep in the car and was now sleeping peacefully in the middle of Tina's bed, her empty bottle close by. "Oh, baby girl," Tina whispered, "I am so very sorry you don't have your momma with you. We are trying to find her, really we are." Sighing, Tina turned away and walked into the living room with the sandwiches.

The local news was reporting the explosion was under investigation but first reports did not indicate it to be the work of terrorists. Police were cautioning people within a twenty-mile radius to stay inside as much as possible until the air cleared. That would most likely be a week at best, so masks were advised for anyone out and about.

The little boy finished his sandwich and promptly fell asleep in Barry's lap. He had cried so many tears in the last twenty-four hours; his eyes were swollen and almost shut. Poor guy. He was still too traumatized to speak or express what was going on in his little heart. Barry gently lay him down on the couch and whispered to Tina that he was going over to his apartment to make a few phone calls. Tina nodded and picked up the remote but as she started to press the "off" button, photos of the people killed in the explosion began to play across the screen.

> Elizabeth Ferguson, 34, wife and mother
> Aaron Jenkins, 26, survived by his wife and unborn child
> Melissa Bryant, 25, a law student
> Morgan Justice, 54, father and grandfather
> Alevia Thompson, infant daughter of Maurice and Evelyn Thompson
> Julia Lester, infant daughter of Todd and Marley Lester
> William Andrews toddler
> Alexandra . . . an infant baby girl with only her name tag from the center to identify her
> Jerome . . . a toddler with only a name tag

On and on the photos showed on the screen until Tina thought her heart would break. Her own tears flowed freely but quietly as she slowly began to grasp the enormity of what had happened.

After the photos of the deceased, the announcer gave the number of injured who were still hospitalized.

More than a few could not be identified due to extreme burns. Tina sank lower and lower into gloom as she realized her chances of finding the children's parents were slim. She was thankful her thoughts were private.

How selfish can I be? People are hurting and dying and missing and I am concerned about being inconvenienced. I'm sorry, Jesus.

The buzzing of her phone came at the perfect time. Katie's photo appeared on the screen and Tina gratefully answered. "Oh, Katie. Thank goodness!"

"I knew I needed to come home! What has happened?"

"No, no, you don't need to come home. But I do need to talk to you. Do you have time right now? The kids are both asleep and Barry went home for a minute."

"You still have them? Tina!"

"I know! It is crazy. So, we went to Grady. It was a waste of time. No one knew anything about the kids. Then we went to Social Services. And this is where it gets crazy. I mean really crazy."

As Tina related all that went down at DFACS, Katie kept interrupting her with exclamations and questions. Finally, she got the story out and waited for her friend's response.

"Oh, WOW, I don't even know what to think.

First you bring them home without permission and now you agree to being a Foster Parent. AND you have them without even a background check. Tina, that just isn't possible. Nor is it wise!"

"I know, right?? I am telling you, God is doing something crazy and amazing here. Seriously, when we first sat down with Ms. Mullins I was afraid she was going to call the police. I really was. But then things started changing. You know, how when the Lord draws really close and everything feels different?"

Katie reluctantly answered, "Well, yeah."

"OK, well, that happened. I mean right there in the DFACS office. Ms. Mullins changed her whole demeanor. She really is such a kind old lady. She said she has been doing this for a long time. And, she looks it, actually. I mean, that tired look in her eyes. Like she has seen enough pain and she is just over it. You know?"

"But, Tina, I don't know for sure but I think you could get in serious trouble here."

"I know. But this is even crazier. When she started talking about becoming a Foster Parent, I started freaking out a little bit. And then everything inside started to calm down and I just knew this was what I am supposed to do. Even crazier was when she ushered us out of the office, the peace inside was so strong, I was not even concerned about breaking the law. You should have seen us. Barry carrying the boy and me the baby. Both of us lugging diapers, formula, all kinds of necessities. If it wasn't so serious, it would have been comical. Things went from crazy to crazier. And now, here we are at home with two children we don't even know. And the incredible thing is, I am actually OK with all of this."

"Girl, you have lost it for sure this time. I cannot wait to get home and see what is really going on down there. And to meet this Barry guy. I swear, Tina, this is too weird. However, I know that you can hear from God and if you say you have this incredible peace, then I am just going with you on that. Have you told your mom the full story yet?"

Tina laughed a little in spite of herself. "What do you think?"

"Well, that is probably best for now. No use in making your parents a part of this. I just hope the next call I get from you is not from Fulton County Jail. If it is, I am not accepting the charges!"

Tina chuckled, "Yes you will. I love you my friend. And don't worry about me. Just finish your trip and get back here."

Tina clicked out of the call just as Barry came back from his apartment. "Who was that?"

"Oh, my friend Katie. She is freaking out a bit. I am anxious for you to meet her."

"Well, she isn't the only one freaking out. That's for sure."

CHAPTER FOUR

Reality

The days passed slowly and quickly, all at the same time. It had been two weeks since the explosion had interrupted Tina's life and changed her routine and her priorities. The explosion and the investigation of the cause faded from the news. Tina's priority now was finding the parents, but today was at hand and as usual, there was much to do taking care of two little ones. Baby Girl had learned to pull up on the furniture and that alone kept Tina busy.

Her apartment was slowly being transformed into a child friendly environment. The crib she found at Goodwill fit snugly in the corner of her bedroom. Several moms in the apartment complex donated sheets, toys, and various items she never knew she needed. Thank the Lord, the South was still the South. Folks take care of each other. Ms. Mullins was a gem for sure. Her home visits were unexpectedly cheerful and helpful. Tina knew there were things she overlooked for the sake of the children. She suspected that at this point in her career, helping the children was more important than keeping protocol. I mean, what were they going to do? Fire her? They obviously knew how valuable she was, besides, that would most likely be a relief at her age.

The little boy started speaking a bit and told her his name was Justin and that he was two years old. This information did not help in the search for his parents, but it made life easier for Tina. Justin was struggling to adjust to his new, temporary life in the tiny apartment. He slept on Tina's sofa, but nightmares often kept him up much of the night. It was almost always the same lament. "I want daddy, I want daddy. Daddy, where you go?" The cries tore at her heart and she found herself laying awake and waiting, hoping against hope he would get through the night without a bad dream.

Last night was particularly difficult and Tina spent a long time sitting on the couch, holding Justin and trying her best to comfort him. She was beginning to understand that he was not actually Baby Girl's brother, a fact that surprised Barry and her since the lady led them both out of the fire. It was also strange that he never asked for his mommy, but always daddy.

"Oh no you don't, missy!" Tina rescued the lamp from Baby Girl's reaching hands, and pulled her into her lap. She rested on the floor with her back against the wall. Holding Baby Girl close to her chest and stroking her silky hair was relaxing in a way Tina had never known. She sat quietly, breathing in the sweet smell of baby milk-breath while the hint of fruity shampoo tickled her nose.

Ahh, Lord, this is all so new to me. I certainly never envisioned spending my time in Atlanta holding someone else's child while my camera lay untouched on the shelf. Really, I am not complaining. It's just . . . Well, it's not something I expected and I'm not at all certain that I am up to the task.

Gradually, Tina quieted her questions before God and settled back with a deep sigh. Once again, her automatic "camera eye" began to work. Oftentimes, looking at life for her was like looking through an imaginary shutter. Everywhere she looked Tina saw potential photographs. Lighting, colors and composition all played around in her mind.

With a sudden burst of energy and a flash of light in her mind, she sat upright, shook her head and whispered to the atmosphere, "I need my camera."

Standing, she shifted Baby to her hip and hurried into the bedroom. Tina talked to the startled child as she reached up to the closet shelf to retrieve her camera. "Photos. Good photos of you my darling, and of Justin. We can post them at the DFACS office and perhaps the TV stations and the newspaper. Do you wanna be a star? Huh?" Baby looked back at Tina and mimicked her "ohhh" look, rubbed her sleepy eyes and nodded hesitantly. "Well, of course you do."

After snapping a few shots of Baby Girl, she settled down on the floor to review them. Right behind today's shots were the ones taken the day of the explosion. Although her plan that day had been to record the story of the explosion, she had only been able to snap a few before Baby Girl was thrust upon her. After that she was busy trying to calm her cries.

Reviewing the images brought back the terror of the day. Right behind the explosion shots were the photos from her shoot in Grant Park that same afternoon. She had promised the completed photos and story by the end of this month—only three days away.

With her entrance into this new world of parenthood, everything in her former life had silently slipped into the background. Once again, the doors opened in her mind and creativity raised its beautiful head. The images from her last shoot flew across her mind and storylines began to take shape. "Ahh . . . welcome back old life. How I have missed you!"

In the present though, Baby was crawling over to her favorite table and working to pull herself up to the forbidden lamp. Tina shot as many pics as possible before she had to abandon ship and grab the lamp. This was their new routine and Tina loved every minute of it. Smiling, she collapsed onto the floor once again with Baby in her lap. She sat leaning against the wall, stroking Baby's hair and pondering on their current situation. Baby slowly relaxed and before long she was dozing, snuggled against Tina's chest. The little power nap probably wouldn't last long, so Tina stayed put and allowed her mind to wander.

Lord, why is it that it seems to always take something hard for me to really pray? I know you are a good Father. I know you don't cause bad things to happen, but they just do sometimes. I am glad you are there for me when they do. Not that these kids are bad things. They are amazing. And I love them already. But, truthfully, I don't want to keep them forever. I mean, I would if you asked me to. But you would have to change my heart. Until then, can you tell me what to do and how to find the mother.

Silence.

Waiting.

More silence.

Tina leaned her head back against the wall and slipped into a light sleep. She dreamed she was running through the woods with her camera. Baby was on her back bouncing along as Tina ran faster and faster. Someone was chasing her! The trees slipped by in a blur and the sky overhead was becoming darker by the moment.

"Mommy!" Baby sat up abruptly, holding her chubby hands in the air and calling "Mommy." Tina woke and held her close reassuring her that all was well, but inside there was an unsettling feeling. Someone was looking for Baby Girl. Her Mommy? "Baby Girl, how on earth did you manage to invade my dream? This is too much drama for me," Tina whispered as she shifted baby to one hip and stood. "If that was my answer to prayer, it was surely an odd one."

Barry knocked on the door as he and Justin entered the apartment. As usual, Justin was quiet and stayed close to Barry. Justin was tall for two years old and Tina wondered if perhaps he was closer to three. His blonde hair and blue eyes were typical of a tow-head living in the South. Those eyes drew Tina in and melted her heart with their haunting sadness. He was much too young to have such depth of feelings but life had thrown him a blast that would not easily heal. Still, even with all he had experienced, Justin managed to maintain an upbeat attitude. Often that attitude put Tina to shame when she complained to God about her increased responsibilities.

And then there was Barry. Ah, yes, Barry. What a trooper he had turned out to be. Not only was the man, as mom would say, "too good looking for his own good," he was gentle and strong all at the same time. His way with the children was unexpected and compelling and he could make them smile at most any time. In some ways he seemed to connect with them more than she did.

She did, however, connect with Barry in a most delicious way. His six-foot- three frame was well outlined and that shock of curly brown hair gave him a little boy look. Normally, she fell for blue eyes, but Barry's soft brown eyes pierced her soul with their intensity. At times he unknowingly tossed her the adorable little boy look that blew her away. Other times he gave the impression he was so strong he could handle anything that came his way. He was a hero around her apartment. Funny how their relationship grew stronger with every hurdle they faced while trying to solve this mystery.

The latest hurdle involved a go around with Children's Services. Ms. Mullins was on a leave of absence due to medical issues. This left Tina in the hands of a young, energetic play-by-the-rules girl. Even though Tina had been approved as a Foster Parent, the girl was pushing to place the children in a "more suitable" environment. In addition to that, every attempt to get help finding the parents was blocked with red tape and vague promises. Each time, they returned home with nothing but the standard diapers, food, etc. Fortunately, though, the new agent had not yet surprised them with a home visit.

The longer she had Justin and Baby in her care, the more she realized she would not let them go to just anyone. Their presence had awakened places and feelings in her heart she only suspected existed. After three months, Justin rarely cried for his daddy and the nightmares were less frequent. At times he questioned when Daddy would come but seemed to understand that he was safe and loved where he was. Both children called her mommy. She realized it was a generic "mommy" since she filled that role at present, but still, it was enough to cause her to hold them a little closer and protect them a bit more.

Tina, Barry and her friend Katie joined forces and arranged their schedules so one of them was always available to care for the children. Mondays became Tina's day to handle client calls, marketing and follow up chats. She did her best to schedule photography shoots on Wednesday and Friday. That left Tuesday and Thursday to edit the photos and work on the story line to accompany them. Working at home for the editing and writing part was simple since both Baby Girl and Justin took long naps.

Barry worked from home on Fridays and kept them in Tina's apartment. Katie worked as a receptionist for a family doctor. Their offices closed at noon on Wednesday and her boss had graciously agreed to give her the full day off to babysit. Of course that meant a slight dock in her pay, but Katie never complained. She loved helping and she loved the children.

CHAPTER FIVE

Christmas in the Country

Tina's parents visited for a week and helped with the children, but the rest of the Brogans were anxious to meet them. Permission was granted by DFACS and arrangements were made for a Christmas trip back to Chickpea. Early on Friday morning, Barry was loading his Lexus 330 with two car seats, luggage, snacks, Christmas presents and all the paraphernalia needed for even a short visit with a toddler and a baby. Justin was watching carefully, eyeing each item as it was situated in the trunk.

Suddenly, without warning, Justin started running across the parking lot yelling, "Daddy! Daddy!" One car honked its horn while another slammed on brakes. Barry sprinted after him, yelling for him to stop. Justin reached the man he was chasing and threw himself around his legs. Startled, the guy looked down and picked up Justin, just as Barry arrived. There was an awkward silence while Justin stroked the man's face, tears running down his flushed cheeks.

"I'm sorry, the guy said, but I don't know this little fella."

Barry tenderly explained the situation. "I'm so sorry, sir. This is Justin and his daddy has been missing since the day of the hotel explosion. Apparently, you reminded him of his daddy."

The guy hugged Justin close and pulled his little head over on his chest. "I'm so, so sorry, little man. I would love to be your daddy, but I do not have any little ones. I am sure wherever your daddy is, he is looking for you."

He handed Justin back to Barry and clamped Barry on the shoulder. "Good luck to you. I hope you find him." The man walked away with a bit of a slump to his shoulders, shaking his head in sadness.

After reassuring Justin the man was not his daddy, Barry walked back to the car and sat down in the front seat. He held Justin close while they both cried and Justin stammered about his daddy. Barry did his best to comfort the little boy. "I'm so sorry, son, but that is not your daddy. Oh, buddy, I am so sorry. I wish it was your daddy. I really do. I understand. I know it hurts, I know."

"Daddy misses me. I want him."

After a time, the tears dried and Justin understood the man really was not his daddy. The sadness in those little eyes broke Barry's heart. All he could do was promise once again that he would do his very best to find Daddy. In his heart he wondered if that would ever be possible. Chances were the man died in the explosion.

Tina and Baby Girl joined them a few minutes later. Barry gave her a *"You're not gonna believe this"* look and shook his head slowly. What in the world? Once they were all packed and on the road, Justin and Baby Girl fell asleep and Barry had a chance to explain to Tina what had happened. In a shaky voice, she reminded him that at least now they had a general description of what Daddy looked like. Tall and slim. Brown hair. Probably dressed often in a suit. It wasn't much, but it was something.

The remainder of the drive was somber until they exited off I-75 about noon. The children woke up as Barry slowed and then turned onto a paved two-lane road that took them through the countryside surrounding Chickpea. Justin was in awe of the cows and horses. Baby picked up on his excitement and jabbered right along like she knew what was happening. Apparently, Justin had seen cows up close at some point. He reminded Baby not to touch the ones with horns which caused Baby to create an original three word song for their entertainment. Tina and Barry laughed like real parents and then laughed because they laughed like real parents.

They traveled twenty miles to their first turn onto Baxter Road, another paved two-lane. Barry mentioned that he had expected more country than this and Tina laughed and said, "Just hold on. It's coming."

Justin began kicking his feet and yelling, "Barry! Stop the car! Hurry."

Barry spun his head around at Justin and then back at Tina. "Don't look at me," she responded. "I have no idea, but it sounds important."

He pulled the car over to the side of the road, got out, walked around and opened Justin's door. "What's wrong, Justin?"

"Pee Pee." Barry looked back at Tina with raised hands and a shocked expression on his face.

"This one's on you," she smiled. "Come on, he's a little boy. It's no big deal."

Barry was obviously taken aback by the child's request in the middle of nowhere, but reluctantly unbuckled him and sat him down on the ground. Justin marched over to the first fence post and looked up at Barry, "You too."

By now, Tina was losing it in the front seat. She promised to turn her head, but not before she assured Barry it was OK, he should go ahead too. To which he responded with such a look of disdain, she laughed out loud.

Justin finished his business, and walked back to the car. Barry picked him up and buckled him back in. As he pulled back onto the road, Justin's voice was a little shaky from the back seat. "Daddy showed me that."

Four miles down Baxter Rd, they passed the first dirt road. There was no street sign, but Tina explained that it was Baxter Lane. Two miles more another dirt road—Baxter Drive. Finally, around a small curve, the third dirt road came into view. Again, no street sign. "Let me guess, Barry said, Baxter Circle?"

Tina giggled "No, this would be Brogan Lane! Yep. We have a family street!" Brogan Lane took them three more miles into the countryside before they turned left onto the mile-long driveway that led to Brogan Manor. The gravel drive was lined with Bradford pear trees. Scattered in the field beyond was the pecan orchard.

"So, I think those may be pecan trees?" Barry asked.

"WOW! Listen to you, city boy. How'd you know that?"

Barry shrugged his shoulders and looked out at the trees. "Just a little something I picked up."

"Yeah, where'd you pick that info up? Doesn't sound like a typical conversation you would have."

Barry finally lost it and started laughing. "From you, of course. You talk about picking up pecans and shelling them and all the ways your mom uses them."

"I knew that."

"Sure you did."

After a minute he shook his head in disbelief. "OK You win. This is country!"

Mom and Dad had outdone themselves with the decorations. The house looked beautiful with lights up the walkway, on the railings of the wide, covered porch, and the rooftop. Tina smiled seeing everything lit for the children even though it was mid-day and the sun was shining. Her parents lived in the house alone now, but Christmas was for everyone who visited—especially for family. Mom had celebrated her sixty-fourth birthday a few months back and she was still as energetic as ever. Her reddish-blonde hair always looked beautiful with, of course, a little help from her beautician. For as long as Tina could remember, her mom had walked almost every day. The exercise combined with healthy eating habits had rewarded her with a nice size ten figure.

Daddy, on the other hand, could use some lessons from his wife on the exercise front. He still maintained the yards and most Saturdays he could be found puttering around the out buildings, doing what only he understood to do. His refusal to hire anyone to help with repairs actually worked to his favor in two ways. He saved money of course, but he was also forced to stay a little active. His frugalness kept him and his wallet somewhat in shape. That was a good thing, since he did like his Southern fried foods.

Once inside the house, everyone began talking at once, but Justin stole the show when he saw the nine foot Christmas tree with presents galore piled underneath. His face lit up as pretty and bright as the tree itself and he began talking rapidly in little boy sentences about his mommy. He said green was her favorite color and Christmas was her favorite time of the year. Then, turning to Tina with a confused expression on his face, he asked, "Where my Mommy?" All the other chatter slowly came to a stop as the adults listened with tears in every eye. This little boy captured their hearts in an instant.

Before now, he had not talked about his mommy, only daddy.

Tina wondered what the story was and where his mommy could possibly be. Perhaps she was alive somewhere. Perhaps she was looking for her little boy. Struggling to speak over the lump in her throat, Tina suggested they not let Mom's lunch get cold. Her dad picked Justin up and held him close while they all made their way to the table. Tina, for one, had suddenly lost her appetite.

Justin had shown them early on that he did not know Baby Girl. But still, he had never talked about his mom. *Was this a divorce situation? How many parents are we looking for here?*

It was wonderful having her Mom and sister close to help with the children. Neither Tina nor Barry realized how consumed their lives had become with the children. On Saturday afternoon Grandma and Granddaddy took Justin and Baby to visit Santa. Tina and Barry took the opportunity for an excursion into the backwoods and possibly a chance to get some good shots of the countryside. Winding country roads with fence lined pastures were some of her favorite shots and she had missed the lazy afternoons rambling down deserted roads.

Chickpea's picturesque town square was approximately five miles south. Tina suggested they go around the square and out the other side to view a few horse farms that were in that part of the county. Tina acted as tour guide while Barry drove. Hamilton's Antique shop was on the corner. "I have spent many hours wandering through there," Tina mentioned.

"I never understood why people wanted to buy old furniture when they could buy new and better, for less money."

Tina looked at him like he was speaking a foreign language. Which, to her, he was.

Now he was laughing. "What? I mean it. It all smells musty and it's old and used. I don't get it."

Tina tucked that little bit of info back in her mind to think on later. Personally, she loved antiques. Anything that had a history and a story always caught her attention.

Most of the square was taken up with sandwich shops, book stores, gift shops and of course Alexander's Hardware. Alexanders had been there since her mom was young. It held everything you could think of along with a lot you did not want to think of.

Older homes lined the back side of the town square. Some had been renovated; others were in various stages of disrepair. It was a glimpse into a time that had passed by in most places, but not here.

After a ride around the park located in the middle of town, they turned the car southward and headed out of town.

The landscape here was prettier with more openness and fence lined pastures. They drove in silence for a time, enjoying the peace of each other's company. After a while they abandoned the car and started out on foot, relishing the feel of the cool air and the crispness of the day. The barren trees and brown underbrush reminded Tina of her dream. But this time, she wasn't running and in the place of Baby Girl was Barry, strong and capable. Still, a vague sensation of someone chasing her encroached onto the perimeters of her mind.

Off to the left side of the road was a clearing lined on three sides by trees. A broken fence lay at the top of a hill so they could not see what lay between the fence and the trees lining the back of the property. One look at Barry's face and Tina was off in a run up the hill. Barry overtook her before she reached the top and grabbed her arm so he could pass her. In the scramble, Tina lost her balance and fell headlong into the brown grass, pulling Barry with her as she went down.

Tina's first thought was for her camera. She spotted it a few feet away lying safely in a mound of grass, but as she started crawling to it, Barry grabbed her ankle and pulled her back. Laughing, they rolled over to their backs and lay side by side in the cool grass. The sky overhead was clear and blue without a cloud in sight. It felt good to be silly and laugh at nothing. Tina had become uncharacteristically serious since the explosion. Today was good for both Barry and her. There had not been a lot of romance between them, but there was something even deeper. A mutual respect for all they had come through together and, at least for Tina, a dream of much more to come. She expected Barry to kiss her lying there in the winter sun on Christmas Eve, but all he did was reach over and take her hand. They lay like that for a time before they stood up and brushed themselves off, gathered her camera, and headed back to his car.

Tina stole a glance at Barry's face and wondered if she was reading too much into their relationship. Afterall, they had been together every day for weeks now and during all that time there had been no romance from him. *Maybe it's all in my head. Perhaps he is just not interested in me.*

Christmas morning began early in the Brogan household. Justin and Baby were showered with presents from their new grandparents. Justin was so engrossed in his Leapster, he completely skipped breakfast. Tina had to allow him to leave his toy on the table beside him just to get a few bites down mid-morning. No one was excited about leaving the toys for church, but Grandma insisted.

The afternoon brought another round of presents from cousins, aunts and uncles, as the family gathered for a traditional Christmas meal. It was an early bedtime for two sleepy babies after a long day of celebrating. Monday morning, after an early breakfast for the adults and a sleep in for the little ones, it was time to head back to Atlanta. The drive back was peaceful and quiet, giving Tina time to mull over the afternoon lying in the sun. Something was not quite right about all that.

Tina decided to test the waters, "I think it went really well with the kids and my family. I hope you had a good time too?"

"I did have a good time. Your family is awesome. And that food. How in the world did you manage to stay so slim with those desserts around all the time? Your mom is a wonderful cook!"

"Well, that food wasn't always around. Mom cooks big for special occasions but the rest of the time it's lighter and healthier. Except for when my dad insists on fried chicken with biscuits and gravy."

Barry gave that deep chuckle that made Tina laugh just to hear him. "You are very fortunate to have a big family. Even more fortunate to have one that actually enjoys being together. My childhood was very different. I am an only child and Christmas dinners were much more formal."

"Chickpea is a nice place to raise a family. I love the open countryside and the slow motion lifestyle. I guess that would be weird for you, huh?"

"No, not so much. I assume most of the younger people drive into the city for work?"

Then before Tina could answer, he continued with a smile, "I really enjoyed our afternoon in the grass."

Well, at least she had that. She could live with that for a while.

CHAPTER SIX

Closed Doors

Back in Atlanta, Tina and Barry resumed their new life and hectic schedules with a bit more contentment. Being reminded there were people praying and loving both of them made their struggles just a little easier. As winter faded slowly into springtime, the jonquils outside her apartment began to bloom and tiny green leaves appeared on the trees in the parking lot.

Often on Saturdays Tina and Barry packed everything into his Lexus and drove to Piedmont Park for a picnic. Several hours strolling Baby while Justin played in the sun made for a fun and relaxing day. More and more Tina enjoyed spending time with Barry. They had never even kissed and yet she felt a closeness with him that she had never experienced before. Could this be just a glimmer into what it meant to parent children with a man she loved? If so, she was more ready than she had imagined.

On one such Saturday afternoon, Baby fell asleep in the stroller and Justin found a friend with a set of small cars. He was playing happily driving the cars over twigs and rocks. She and Barry sat in the swing watching contentedly. Slowly, quietly, Barry reached over and took her hand. "Have you ever wondered what it would be like to have a family of your own? I mean, this afternoon takes my heart places I had not planned to go for a long time."

"I know. I was actually thinking the same thing. It's crazy how we met and all this is even wilder, but today it feels so right."

Then the kiss—sweet and deep and from her heart. She prayed he felt the same and from the look in his eyes as their lips parted, Tina thought something had just happened to both of them. They sat with their foreheads together enjoying the moment. With a deep sigh of contentment, Tina squeezed his arm and smiled before turning to check on the children.

Baby Girl was still dozing in her stroller. Damp, frizzy curls were plastered to her sweaty brow, but the breeze kept her content. And Justin . . . Justin!!! Justin was not there. His little friend was still playing with his cars, but alone. Her heart dropped and she stood and called his name. Where was he?

"Barry, where is Justin?"

"Oh, he probably wandered off a bit. I'll go look for him. I'm sure he's fine. You stay here with Baby."

Tina anxiously moved the stroller back and forth while she stood and looked in every direction for any sign of Justin. How far could a little boy go in so short a time? It had only been a couple of minutes since he was playing right close to them. It seemed like forever before Barry came rushing back up with a frown on his face. He shook his head and reached into his pocket for his phone.

"What are you doing?"

"Tina, he isn't anywhere. We have to get help. And quick!"

Tina's heart stopped and all air left her lungs. Sitting down slowly on the edge of the swing, she closed her eyes and tried to think. He has to be OK. He must be. Flashes of the time he ran across the parking lot to a complete stranger ran through her mind. Oh, noooo. Surely he would not go off with a stranger. Surely not.

Barry was calling the police on his phone. He

could wait for help if he wanted to, but she was going to find her son. "You stay with Baby. I will find him!"

Several people close by heard what was happening and stepped up to help. In a shaky voice, Tina described the tan shorts, brown and black striped tee shirt and sneakers that he was wearing. Everyone around was encouraging, assuring her that he was probably fine, but she could tell by the look in their eyes that this was getting more serious every minute he was gone.

While Barry explained the situation to the police, Tina and the others spread out and began searching the park, all the while calling out his name.

It's my fault, God. What was I thinking? I know not to take my eyes off these kids. Not even for a minute when we are in public. How could I? Please, let him be OK Please. Help me.

Over and over they called his name, with no response. More people joined in the search. Tina's heart was pounding out of her chest. She spied the little boy that Justin had been playing with. His mom was holding him tightly while she called for Justin. The lady walked over and put her arm around Tina's shoulder.

"I'm sure he's fine. I know you are terrified right now, but we will find him."

"Thank you. I cannot imagine how he got away so quickly!"

Where was Barry? And the police? We need help. *Oh, God, we need help.*

Tina heard it first. It seemed like it was coming from way over a slight rise. Yes, that was it! That was Justin's voice!

"Mommy . . . Barry!"

Tina ran pell mell towards the sound. Just as she reached the top of the rise, she saw him walking excitedly, tugging an older lady by her shirttail. In his arms he carried a wiggly puppy, which matched the two puppies carried by the lady. Tina reached him and slid down on her knees with open arms. She grabbed him and hugged so hard he ouched and tried to wiggle free.

"Justin, where were you? We were terrified. Barry called the police and everything. Oh, honey, dear sweet boy, do not ever do that again."

Tina realized the lady was still standing and holding the two baby pups. When she finally let go of Justin, he sat down and snuggled his puppy close to his heart with a big smile.

"Where did you find him?"

The lady reached out her hand, "I am Birdie. Birdie Longshire. Are you his Momma?"

Tina stood and took the lady's hand. Shaking it

carefully, she sized up the woman standing before her. Was she on the up and up? Or had she been caught and was trying to slither out of it. "Yes. I am his mom." At least for now, she thought.

Birdie nodded to a bench. "Could we sit for a minute please?"

"Of course, but first let me tell everyone that Justin has been found." She waved and motioned to those who had not seen the reunion. Just at that moment, Barry, pushing the stroller and talking with an officer, walked up a path coming from the opposite direction. "Barry! We found him!"

Barry's reaction was much the same as Tina's. He held the boy for a long time before he took him over to the bench. Placing Justin on his lap, he explained to the officer that all was well. The officer spoke into the mic on his lapel and after being assured all was truly well, he said goodbye and moved back down the path.

Barry looked at Birdie and Tina with raised eyebrows. "Where did you find him?" he asked.

Tina looked at Birdie. "I am wondering that myself." She wanted to be kind to this elderly lady, but she still was not sure what was going on.

Birdie settled the two pups on her lap and smiled. "First, let me say, this little guy is fast! It was all I could do to keep up with him pulling on my shirttail.

I had no idea he had followed me until we were way over yonder from here."

Tina was not understanding. "Are you saying he followed you?"

"Well," Birdie began, "I walked by where he and another little guy were playing with their cars. Just about that time, one of my puppies jumped right out of my arms and down to where they were playing. I picked him up as quickly as I could. I know how little boys can get hold of a puppy and not want to let go. I didn't pay much attention, but walked on. It was getting hot and I was tired.

After a bit I heard your little guy talking to himself. I turned around and low and behold, he had followed me way over the little hill and around a curve. Well, as you can imagine, I had no idea what to do. I had already walked too far for me. So, I sat down on a bench to rest a minute and see if he needed help.

All he wanted to do was play with the puppy, but when I looked around, I didn't see any adults that were with him. I didn't mean to take so long, but I had to get my breath a bit before I started back to where I saw him playing. I must tell you, I was really glad to hear you answering his calls. I was just about done in."

"She says I can have a puppy too, if you say it's OK. Is it OK, pleassseeee?"

Tina looked over at Justin still holding the puppy. After all he had gone through to follow that puppy, how could she say no? Looking at Birdie, she held up a finger to Justin. "Just a minute, honey, let me talk to Miss Birdie."

Birdie assured her that the puppy would be ready for adoption soon. She also explained that a puppy is a lot of responsibility, especially in a small apartment. Not the least would be housebreaking her, and teaching the Baby Girl and Justin how to be gentle with the pup.

Tina listened carefully to everything Birdie had to say. This was definitely not in her plan. She tried to get Barry's attention to talk this over. Although he did not live in her apartment, he was a big part of their lives. He would need to help out at times with the dog. Tina tried to get some sort of commitment from him for just that. It was useless. Barry nodded absently and agreed to anything she asked him. All he wanted to do right then was play with Justin and the pup.

Finally, she somewhat reluctantly agreed to the puppy. Justin was beside himself with excitement; running in circles while the puppy chased him. The squeals from Baby Girl and Justin melted together with yapping from the puppy. She had to admit, even with the new responsibilities, having a puppy in the house would be fun for all of them.

The little ball of fur was barely old enough to be separated from its mother when they picked her up a couple of weeks later. Justin decided he would name the puppy Pepsi. Tina looked at him intently for a few seconds before she asked very gently, "Why Pepsi? I mean it's a nice name, but Pepsi is a drink, you know."

"Yep, It's a drink. And it's a puppy. A puppy named Pepsi."

There was apparently no reasoning with an approximately four year old boy. Pepsi it was. The puppy was brown with white spots and an adorable wet, brown nose. She wiggled her way into all their hearts. She also wiggled her way into just about every place in Tina's apartment.

Patience. Patience. Tina repeated the word softly about a thousand times that first month, but finally Pepsi could be trusted to use the puppy pads and sleep in her crate at night without crying. Mostly. The chewing was another story, but from her research, Tina expected that to end before long. The upside was the photos—a little boy and a baby girl with a wiggly puppy. She took about a million shots of the three of them.

Each one was adorable to her, but also to her followers on Instagram. After a while, the kids and pepsi drew more attention than she did. Actually, she picked up a few photo shoots from people following the kids. She hoped the parents or a family member would notice the pics and contact her, but so far that had not happened.

The trips to Piedmont Park became more frequent and lasted longer as the temperatures reached into the 60's and then the 70's. The dogwood tree popped white and shone in the sunlight. Atlanta in the springtime is a beautiful place to be and it became even more beautiful as she and Barry grew more and more intimate, pouring out their hopes and dreams to one another.

Tina learned that Barry was not only a loving, kind person, he was also quite wealthy, which caused her to wonder why he lived in the small apartment complex. His father owned a large construction business. Of course, like most fathers, he had hoped Barry would one day take over the reins. Barry had other ideas. As he related his conversation with his dad to Tina, she heard the intensity in his voice.

"I explained to dad that working with my hands, or overseeing people who did, was not something I excelled at. I love working with people, teaching, selling, or anything that has to do with helping people better understand a concept. I needed him to see me, to see who I am and what I am good at. I wanted him to approve of me as I am, not as who he wants me to be.

"Finally, dad agreed and I attended the University of Georgia. I graduated with a degree in Communications. When Dad passed away, I sold the company to a longtime family friend and formed my own consulting firm. I am not getting rich, but I love what I am doing. And, I have my inheritance money to carry me until business improves."

Barry was more than generous in his financial help with the children. In fact, Tina could never have made it without his monthly gifts. "I have no desire to live like the affluent," he stated one day in the park. "I grew up that way and it isn't something I enjoy or need. It makes me feel alive when I can help someone else. That is more important to me."

The days sped by with no information on the parents' whereabouts. Even though she loved the kids, learning to care for two small children was challenging to say the least. Runny noses, tummy aches and skinned knees however, were simple compared to balancing her dreams with Justin and Baby's future. As life on the surface became more comfortable, even predictable, Tina could not ignore the undercurrent of uncertainty surrounding them all. The children's lives were, at least for the moment, in her hands and she felt the responsibility down to her toes.

Even so, in spite of everything going on inside her heart, Tina accepted her new responsibilities without too much complaining. Even Pepsi, the puppy, found her place in the midst of what had become Tina's life. The chewing did not stop, but got worse and somehow the cute little puppy grew into a large, energetic puppy-dog. If she kept growing, it would be impossible to keep her contained in the apartment, much less in her crate. Justin adored Pepsi and insisted she sleep as close to him as possible. Some days Tina wanted to put the animal outside and hope some kind soul would take her in. But, then the silly dog would cock her head and look up with those beautiful eyes that melted her heart. Tina knew it was a losing battle when Justin announced, "Pepsi is family now, right mom?"

She smiled and replied, "Yep, Pepsi is family now."

Space was tight and alone time was rare, but she had Barry and Katie to help. Barry was her pillar. He took the kids when things got too rough or she had a deadline. He helped financially and even cooked occasionally or treated them to McDonalds or Chick-fil-A. The real help, however, came through his presence. Just his smile and encouragement built her up and helped her keep moving forward.

Another Christmas had come and gone with Barry, Katie and Tina still taking complete responsibility for the children. Together they decided it was time to take the initiative themselves and find the missing parents or make more permanent arrangements. The Monday after Christmas started with a bang, literally. Construction crews were on site early cleaning up the remains of the old building and making way for a new hotel.

Workers with rescue dogs, insurance companies, law enforcement officials and investors had swarmed the property for months ensuring all the victims had been recovered. They verified it was actually a faulty furnace that caused the explosion. Apparently there was a main gas line that ran underground close to the hotel. The investigation had taken almost two years, and the eye-sore that had once been a prominent hotel was finally being cleared. The new building would soon stand on the same ground.

Tina was up early making the day's schedule before Justin and Baby woke. Katie would be babysitting today while Barry joined Tina in rechecking every possible lead to locate the parents. As usual when she thought seriously about locating the birth parents, her heart was divided between hopeful expectation and dread.

Katie picked up her morning coffee and headed downstairs to Tina's apartment. "Good morning," she said as she poked her head in the door. "Looks like they are finally getting serious about cleaning up the hotel site."

Tina welcomed her friend with a hug. "Yep, they were busy early, weren't they? So much for sleeping in. Not that I have been able to do that in forEVER."

Barry knocked as he opened the door and joined them with his own coffee. "What's so funny in here?"

Tina smiled and received her morning hug from him. "We were just talking about how long it's been since I could actually sleep in!"

"Well, my daddy always said sleep was overrated."

Tina and Katie shared a look. "That's because your daddy was a man."

Over a breakfast of scrambled eggs and toast, the three friends put together a plan for the day. Afterward, Tina dressed the children and Katie settled down to feed them breakfast. Baby Girl was happy in her donated high chair and Justin was busy slurping up the last of his cereal when Tina and Barry headed out the door.

The first stop was Grady Hospital. Walking into

the administration offices and taking a number made Tina's legs go weak. More and more she was wondering how she would react when, and if, they found the parents. Barry, ever the charismatic salesman, took the lead in talking with the clerk and managed to get them through to a supervisor. Sitting in the supervisor's office, Tina reached over and held Barry's arm. "I'm not sure I can do this. What if we actually find the parents? What would we do? These are our children now. You know?"

As soon as the word *our* was out of her mouth, she wanted to take it back. Too late. It hung in the air. Barry did not refute the statement, but neither did he confirm it.

The supervisor was very helpful, even going beyond what they expected. Tina noticed the smile the lady continually threw Barry's way, but ignored it. After all, they needed all the help they could get.

Public files from the day of the accident recorded three Jane Doe's that were brought in by ambulance the day of the explosion. One had passed away. One recovered and was discharged a week later. The third had been unconscious and remained in a coma for several weeks before being transferred to a mental institute for treatment of amnesia. Grady personnel had no information on her diagnosis, nor where she might be at present. The supervisor explained that even if they did have the information, privacy laws would not allow her to share it.

There were six John Doe's. Four had died and two had been identified and released. Neither of the identified John Doe's had mentioned a young son or a baby girl on their family list.

Next on the list was Children's Services where Tina did most of the talking. Their new rep took the photos which Tina had taken of the children a few days after the explosion and posted them along with the available information on a large bulletin board in the waiting room. As they left DFACS, Tina looked at the board and could not find the photos among all the others posted there. "Why do we waste our time? Everything we try brings us to another dead end. Maybe the Lord wants me to keep the children. Maybe I am supposed to adopt them. What do you think, Barry?"

Barry put his arm gently around her waist and smiled. "I think you are tired and hungry. Let's take advantage of our babysitter and grab lunch. What do you say? Katie will not mind, I promise. How about it?"

Before returning to the apartment they double-checked with the Social Security offices, the hotel's temporary administration offices, the DMV, St

Joseph's and Piedmont Hospitals. They also talked with the day supervisor at Strathmore, the hospital where Jane Doe number three had been sent. It would take cutting through major red tape to get any information out of them, and then it could all be another dead end.

Home was warm and inviting as Justin came running and threw himself into Barry's arms while Tina picked up Baby from her pallet on the floor. "So, don't you think it's time to give this sweet girl a name?"

"Probably. I mean, we can't just call her Baby forever. In fact, she isn't a baby anymore. More of a wide open, nothing held back toddler. DFACS identifies her as Jane Doe Number Something-or-other, but that's a little insulting."

Tina chucked. "I agree. But right now I know you have work and I am tired. Let's think about it later, OK? Dinner here at about 7:00?"

"Sure. Works for me. See you then." With a quick hug, Barry was out the door and over to his apartment to catch up on work.

Tina needed to remember, he did have a job after all! Dropping onto the couch, she brought Katie up to date on the day's lack of progress.

"I have no idea what to do anymore. My apartment is so small and I am seriously over my head in caring for them. No one seems to be interested in helping us. Everywhere I turn it's a closed door. I am trying not to get discouraged, Katie, but it's just so frustrating."

Katie reached over and hugged her friend. "I know, I know. I cannot imagine these two growing up without knowing their parents. Or who they are or where they came from. It's so sad. But, on the other hand, they are fortunate to have you. Tina, stop selling yourself short. You are doing a great job. Better than most people would. This cannot last forever. Sooner or later something has to give."

Tina laid her head back on the couch and held Baby close to her chest, singing softly and breathing in the fragrance of her soft skin. Justin was busy with his Leapster. Katie gathered up her computer gear and with a wave whispered, "I love you, hang in there," before she disappeared out the door. Justin waved goodbye without looking up from his game. Tina relaxed into her own world and dozed lightly, with one ear open to Justin.

"Help me!" Tina turned to see who was calling for help. The woods were quiet and empty all around her. "Help me!" Again she heard the call and again she looked but all was still. Tina felt a shiver go up her spine and began to walk faster. Baby was riding comfortably on Tina's back while she took photos of the trees. It was a dreary winter day with little or no color, but the outline of the barren trees made for a unique ambience in her photos. But now she felt uncomfortable. The peace had evaporated. "Help me!" Tina started to run, holding her camera with one hand and reaching around to balance Baby's sling seat with the other. She heard the footsteps getting closer and closer. Baby's breath was hot on her neck and her own breath came in spurts. "Mommy!" Tina sat straight up and shook her head to clear her mind. The dream. Again. The running, the fear, someone chasing Baby and her.

"Mommy." Baby stroked Tina's cheek and smiled that sweet smile that melted Tina's heart. It was only a dream, but once again she knew. Deep inside, Tina knew. Baby's mommy was alive. How would they ever manage to locate her? And what kind of woman was she? Was she a good mother? Just because she may be Baby's biological mother, didn't mean she was the right one to raise her? Did it? And where has she been all this time?

CHAPTER SEVEN

Goodbye?

Three months later the new hotel was coming along nicely but the search for the parents was at a standstill. Life was anything but routine for Tina as she balanced career and motherhood. Not to even mention balancing her funds to cover all their expenses. Thankfully, Barry's presence brought fun and excitement into her life and she often daydreamed of making a life with him.

The one and only kiss way back in the park still confused Tina. Theirs was a strange relationship for sure. No romance, but a deep love and friendship. She wanted much more, but having him close on a daily basis would have to do for now. Perhaps it was because of the children. After all, they barely knew each other when they were thrown together by fate with the very real responsibility of raising two children.

One afternoon, Barry returned early from work and knocked on her door. Tina smiled as she opened to let him in. Hopefully, this meant a night out with the kids, maybe she would not have to cook. "I have some news we need to discuss. Can we go into the kitchen and talk for a few minutes?"

Tina sat quietly while Barry laid out a new plan, one she never dreamed would happen. The longer he talked, the more difficult it was to hold her tongue. What in the world was going on? Her head spun and her stomach lurched. Finally, she could no longer stand it.

"Let me get this straight. You are leaving? Leaving me and the children? Not only leaving the apartments here, but you are actually moving out of state. For good!"

Anger came uninvited and with it a hurt deep inside that grew by the minute. Surely this was not happening. Barry had promised to help her. He had promised to stay close and help with the children. And now he was leaving? Her world began to collapse around her. Yes, she understood everything he was saying. Yes, she knew that she had no right to order his life around. Of course she knew all that.

And yet, still, he had promised. And if she were to admit the truth, she was in love with him.

Barry patiently explained again, "Tina, I am so sorry, but this is an opportunity I just cannot pass up. This New York based firm is actually interested in my little company. Can't you see the potential here? I mean, this has been my dream and hope. Frankly, I didn't really think it would ever happen, but if it did, I was thinking several years down the road, after I had built my clientele up more. Come on, Tina, you are the one always telling me how God directs our steps. I certainly did not go after this. They came to me!"

"Oh, so now you are throwing God back at me. Great. Thank you, Barry. Thanks a lot."

She watched as he took a very deep breath and looked up at the ceiling for a minute and blew it slowly out. Finally, he spoke with a controlled gentleness. "Tina. Please."

She knew her attitude was out of line. She tried to control it, but at this point all she could think about was the fact that he was leaving her. Nothing he could say would make it any better. And then the other shoe dropped and the anger nearly exploded out of her mouth. He very quietly said, "Can't you just be happy for me?"

Now it was her turn to look at the ceiling and

take a deep breath. "Happy for you? Well, yes, I am happy for you. You are going off to a new adventure, a new city, new apartment. And I am staying here in this tiny apartment, without you to help me two days a week. Without you to help with errands and all that comes with taking care of two children. Children, by the way, that you talked me into keeping. So, yeah, Barry, I am thrilled for you."

"I will still be a part of their lives. I will still send the monthly check and travel back to Atlanta as often as possible. I love those kids. The last thing I want to do is hurt them, but this is something I have to do. Please, Tina, try to understand and see it from my point of view."

Somewhere in the distance she heard his voice explaining how he did not want to leave her, and that he had thought he would be in Atlanta for a long time. But now, he had this amazing offer. He could not pass it up. He just could not. She heard sadness mixed with excitement in his voice and it sickened her. But, what she did not hear was any mention of his love for her.

After he left for his apartment, Tina lay across her bed and tried to get herself together. Her emotions were running amuck and she couldn't have that right now. She needed to think. And yet, she did not want to even consider how her life was about to change. Slowly, she opened her heart to the only One who could always help.

"It's too much, God. I cannot do this. You have pushed me too far and I cannot do this." Even as the words crashed in her heart, she knew better. She knew from somewhere deep in her spirit that her Heavenly Father would never push her too far. If this was His plan for her, then He would make a way. Dang it. He always made a way, but this time she was most certain it would not be the way she wanted.

Early the next Friday, Katie, the children and Tina waved goodbye and watched Barry drive out of the parking lot. So, that was that. She and Barry had parted ways and she was left alone with two small children. Oh, he had apologized and begged her to understand. She had said all the right things in order to keep the relationship intact. For the children if nothing else, but her heart knew it was over.

Katie slipped her arm around Tina's slim waist and gently turned her around and back towards the apartment. She had been holding Baby Girl and now she laid her in the crib and sat down on the couch beside Tina. Justin stood at the window and both women could feel the rejection and sadness emanating from his little body. He could not comprehend the depth of what was happening, but he could see the tears, he knew something was not right. Poor kid.

He did not deserve all that life had dealt him at such a young age. Did God even think about the children when He allowed tragedy on the earth? Tina immediately asked the Lord to forgive her for the thought. Of course He thought about the children. Of course He did. Tina and Katie talked for a while and then Katie suggested McDonald's, but Tina could not bring herself to move. Baby Girl had fallen asleep in her crib, so Katie took Justin and promised to keep him until she heard from Tina.

The pain in Tina's heart was so strong she could barely catch a breath. It wasn't just that Barry was leaving, it was the fact that her entire life was once again crumbling before her eyes. Her career, her apartment that was too small for a family of three plus a bigger-than-expected dog, her time, her social life, and now the strength of Barry was gone as well. She wished the tears would come but they stopped somewhere in her chest where there was no outlet. Confusion, along with frustration, heartbreak and anger stormed through her heart. Tina clutched the couch pillow and slowly laid over, her mind reeling in disbelief. Finally, the tears flowed, not cleansing and healing, but tears of devastation, anger and despair. Even in the darkness, she heard His voice, "I will never leave you." She didn't believe that nor did she care, at least not right now. Right now, she let the tears come until her mind and body finally calmed and she drifted into a light sleep.

Baby was crying, it seemed from somewhere far away. Tina slowly came awake and sat up. Then she remembered. Barry had left. Oh, he had said all the right things, but he left. And now she was alone in this bizarre life that had evolved over the past two years. Katie was close but she could never fill the void Barry had left. She understood the career choice and the challenge but what about their relationship? What about the kiss? The talks? Their dreams? Was she imagining the connection between them? Baby cried louder, and Tina knew she was hungry. Reality won.

Barry drove slowly out of the parking lot and onto I-85 North. Leaving Tina and the children was not an easy thing to do. He was a man of his word, always had been, and he had given his word to Tina. And now, he had broken that promise. But, how was he to know an opportunity like this would come along so soon? Sure, this was his goal but by his thinking it was at least five years down the road. By then, the children would be settled with another family and he would have fulfilled his self-imposed obligation.

Barry's heart ached, he could easily have cried, but his mind overruled that emotion and continued with the logic of his actions. The move was wrought with anxiety. On the one hand, he was pumped and ready for a new challenge, but on the other hand, there was Tina . . . and the children.

He had to be honest with himself. At one time he thought perhaps he and Tina might have a future, but somewhere along the way, the relationship stagnated. The children, of course, took up most of their time, but it was more than that. His disengagement from Tina had nothing to do with the kids. He loved them. He loved Tina too, but not in a romantic way. She was a wonderful, beautiful woman with a heart as big as Texas, but there just wasn't any chemistry.

Over the months he had pondered that fact and the answer was always the same: it just wasn't there. She was exciting and fun to be with but if a woman doesn't turn your key, then she doesn't turn your key. For that reason alone, it was better to put distance between them before she became more attached. He would never want to hurt her, she did not deserve that. Yes, he had made the right decision all around. It was time for the next phase of his life and unfortunately, it did not include Tina. With a heavy heart, he switched over into the left lane and set his thoughts towards New York City. It was going to be a long drive with plenty of thinking time. For now, he just needed to clear his mind and concentrate on driving. His mind agreed but his heart still hurt for the pain he had caused in the heart of his friend.

CHAPTER EIGHT

A Bigger Hurdle

For Tina, the next weeks crept slowly by, with little interest outside of the daily challenges of children, housework and photography. She had a few good shoots, mostly for a law firm that had a prominent presence in the Atlanta area. Her photos were used on billboards, magazine and newspaper ads and even on a few television commercials. It was a good opportunity and proved to be more lucrative than she had originally thought it would be. One of the lawyers, a widower, approached Tina about dinner after work one afternoon but she declined without explaining her reasons. Jerry took that as a no forever and left her alone after that. Tina did not think much about it. She was not in the mood for a relationship, even if she had the time, which she didn't. Still, he seemed like a kind man. Under different circumstances she would have probably accepted the invite.

Late one evening, Tina was relaxing in front of the T.V. after Justin and Baby were asleep. There was nothing of interest on any channel and after flipping through several times, Tina pressed the "off" button and dropped the remote on the table beside her. The tiny apartment seemed even smaller as she sat there in the stillness. It was bedtime; tomorrow would be a long day with two photo shoots and two interviews scheduled. The interviews always took much longer than expected. People tended to get distracted down rabbit trails when talking about themselves. Thank goodness for Katie's help with babysitting. She willed herself to get up but inertia had taken over and she sat staring at nothing.

At times, thoughts of tomorrow and the next day, and next month or next year threatened to consume her. Tonight, it seemed that fear lurked at every turn intimidating her to stop mid-stream and take the kids to DFACS. She could easily rebuild her normal, safe life. The thoughts of safe and comfortable were enticing, but then she would envision Justin and Baby being carried out of the apartment by someone from DFACS. No, that was not going to happen.

She had chosen this path when she chose to keep the children. No matter that Barry had left; she could do this, and alone if necessary. Once again, apprehension over the future was temporarily pushed back to the perimeters of her thoughts. Taking a deep breath, Tina spoke softly into the stillness, "If you will help me, Lord, just help me, then together we can do this. I will not give up if you won't."

Tina slipped into her bedroom and crawled under the covers. She fell asleep quickly before she lost her new found strength and determination, hoping it would still be there in the morning. It was around 4:00 A.M. when she slowly woke from a deep sleep. Her heart was strangely peaceful and still. Then, ever so slowly, the realization that she was safe washed over her. Safe. She really was safe beyond anything she had ever imagined. No matter who came or who left, Tina was safe. Warmth and security wrapped her in their arms and held her close. There was no need to fear; Love covered her soul. Lying there on her bed nothing else mattered. The pillow, so soft and warm, slowly became her Lord's chest as He held her. Tina drifted back to sleep.

Morning sunshine always brings reality as thoughts of the day ahead push themselves into the mind. For Tina, it was like a wrestling match with each responsibility vying for her attention. She sat at the small dinette in her green P.J.'s, with her coffee close at hand and began to write out the day's plan. For months now, Katie had been diligently attempting to teach her to use a daily schedule. Tina was giving it her best shot, but some days it just was not worth the effort. Sitting there with her long red hair pulled into a messy ponytail and no makeup to hide the freckles, she could easily pass for a teenager. But inside, Tina did not feel in any way like a teenager. As the normal burden of facing the day tried to swoop over her, she realized something was different this morning. Tina put her pen down and leaned back on the chair. The memory of last night flooded over her. She was safe and she could do this.

The realization that neither Barry, nor Katie, nor her parents were her strength surprised her. They were her safety net, but nets could break. Sometimes the weight was too much for them to bear, but she now understood in a way she never had before that Jesus was not her safety net, He *was* her safety. "Lord, I have no idea how you managed to bring me to this point, but I know it had to be you last night. No one else could do that—only you."

As long as she could remember, Tina had been afraid on some level. When she was a very young child, back before her parents had given their lives to God, there was a lot of fighting and arguing in her home. Her memory was vague but the feeling of being terrified during the night was very real. Daddy was a drinker back then and when he drank, he got very ugly. She could not remember the things he said but she remembered the way it made her feel—she felt afraid. And now, today, she felt safe. Only God can reach down to the depths of a soul and pluck out hurts and heal wounds. "Daddy, I wonder what happened to you to make you that way in the first place? What happened in your childhood that you never told me? Whatever it was, I am so glad you and the Lord got it all straightened out."

Tina rarely listened to the local news, it was too depressing. But today she had an inkling to see what was happening around Atlanta, so she turned on the television. The top story was about a young girl in foster care that had died. She had somehow dropped through the cracks in the overworked office and went unnoticed for two years. During that time her foster daddy continually abused her. Now he had killed her. Tina's heart broke at the sordid details of the little girl's plight. Only seven years old and so much pain.

Justin had earbuds in while he played his 3DS, and Tina instinctively put her hands over Baby's ears, held her close and rocked her ever so gently. How could a person do such horrible things to a little child? To anyone? Her mama-bear protection over Justin and Baby grew a little bigger that day and she determined in her heart to fight for these kids, no matter what it took.

Early the next morning, the phone rang. Social Services, DFACS, was on a hunt to ensure nothing like that ever happened on their watch again. In their determination to clear their name, some of the Case Workers were becoming unreasonable in their expectations. Tina braced herself for the scheduled visit.

The doorbell rang thirty minutes before the case worker was expected the next morning. Of course. Why wouldn't she show up early? Sneaky like she wanted to catch Tina in some way. "Good morning . . ." Tina's voice trailed off when she realized this was not the lady she was expecting.

"Good morning, are you Tina Broga?"

"Yes, may I ask who you are?"

The lady standing before her was definitely not the young, energetic social worker that had been covering for Ms. Mullins. In a no nonsense, very impersonal tone, she introduced herself as Ms. McGowen. She handed Tina her card.

"May I come in, please?"

"Yes Ma'am. Please, come in."

Elizabeth McGowen was a slight lady with short graying hair and stern features. Her navy blue business suit and practical shoes summed up her personality perfectly. No nonsense. Tina's first impression was that Ms. McGowen was an annoying person. Still, there were rules and regulations that had been put in place for the children's protection. Tina determined to be polite and professional.

Ms. McGowen's tight smile as she told Tina the requirements no one had taken time to outline before, made Tina's stomach churn. She found herself imagining how she could wipe that smirk right off her face. The woman had no idea what she was asking. Basically, Tina's apartment was too small to house three people. Each child was expected to have their own bedroom. Tina's heart dropped as she listened to each new demand and the fourteen day deadline to have everything in place. DFACS had taken the children's fingerprints on one of the earlier visits and attempted without success to match them in their database. Ms. McGowen wanted that repeated. And last, but certainly not the least, was Justin's school. Since he was only five, Tina, Barry and Katie had taken turns homeschooling him. Though HomeSchool was legal in GA, it was very clear that DFACS preferred public schools. That would throw a serious wrench in her home based business.

Justin and Baby had been issued a social security number under the names John Doe and Jane Doe. The numbers were used to keep track of them through the system but after a year, the Agency thought it necessary to properly name them. The Agency would take all necessary legal steps to declare the children foundlings. This act would throw them into the system as children up for adoption with no parental authority other than the Agency.

For a few moments, the two women sat in a quiet staring match. Finally, Ms. McGowen marched to the door, laid her hand on the knob, and then hesitated. Turning and looking Tina directly in the eye, she said, "Look. You are young. You have been wonderful to care for these two children. But, now it is time to release them back into our hands and let us take proper care of them. We can place each child in a home that will more perfectly meet their individual needs." With one more tight smile, she was gone.

Tina smiled politely as well, but in her mind the thoughts were racing. "Release them?? Proper care?? Excuse me? They are not something to be released. They are my children and I will continue to care for them." Tina started to slam the door but realized Katie was standing there with a strange look on her face.

"We need to talk."

Tina and Katie sat in McDonald's and talked while Justin ran in circles around the playground. His socks were hanging on the end of his toes and his food was barely touched, but he was smiling. His occasional belly laughs as he caught his new friend were more important than a cheeseburger. Justin could eat anytime, but this freedom from the sorrow of missing Barry was much needed. Baby sat in a high chair and played with her Happy Meal toy.

The question on the table was how to afford a three bedroom apartment. Tina's career as a photojournalist had suffered over the past two years and some months. At this point, making the rent even on her small apartment was a stretch. Barry promised to send money each month to help with the children and Katie helped with babysitting so Tina could work. However, even with the three pulling together, it was not possible to continue like this. Changes must be made. Tina was considering looking for full time employment but that would mean full time child care or placing the children in a state run day care. Neither option was agreeable to Tina. They sat watching the playground. Neither of them had answers.

Katie broke the silence. "Maybe we could find a four bedroom apartment and split the rent and the child care."

Tina thought her heart would melt right out of her chest. "You would do that?" The next half hour was spent discussing possible locations, financial arrangements and schedules. They could do this.

Tina returned home with new energy. It was possible; it very well could work. When Barry Face Timed to talk with Justin and her that night, she explained everything that had happened and asked his advice on moving forward. His phone calls were a highlight of her week but she realized the connection between them was fading. It was sad to let go but once again, reality had to be faced. Barry was slowly backing out of their lives. Out of *her* life. They talked for a bit and Barry promised to help in any way he could from New York, but just as he was hanging up, Tina caught sight of the tall, slim, blonde lady entering the room behind him.

And then she cried.

Somehow, facing the fact that Barry would not be returning threatened to end more than just her feelings for him. Deep in her heart, Tina tried to let go of a dream. After months of struggling to follow her heart, her mind told her it was time to surrender. Putting the burden on Katie to help her with a bigger apartment was not fair. She needed to face the truth. Keeping the children was impossible. It was more than she could handle, even with Katie's help.

Bedtime routine was automatic at this point, but tonight, knowing it could all end soon, she relished each tiny incident. She let the giggles over the funny soap beard and the pointy shampoo horn seep into tiny places in her memory. Her love for Justin and Baby had grown to epic proportions and the thought of putting them in the hands of strangers was unthinkable. Foundlings. That was how Ms. McGowan referred to them. Foundlings. It was a term DFACS used to distinguish between orphans and children who were abandoned. Well, she had *found* them and they had *found* her, now what was she to do? They had not been abandoned.

After the second reading of *The Cat in the Hat*, Justin begged for just one of *Are You My Mother?* He was asleep before she got to the big bulldozer. Baby was fast asleep in her crib, Pepsi was sleeping close to the couch and Justin was snuggled down under his favorite Spiderman comforter. Tina headed for her own bed with a heavy heart.

She stretched out under the covers, turned off the light and lay staring at the ceiling. In the background was the ever present hum of traffic on I-85. Funny, when she first moved here from Chickpea it seemed a lot louder. Now she only noticed it at times like this, times when the silence in her soul was too much to bear. Death comes in many forms. It could be the death of a relationship, the death of a dream, the death of a career or the death of a home. Even if everyone knew all along it was a temporary home. "Death is painful, Lord."

And again Tina cried—deep, aching, sobs that could not be explained. After a while, the crying ceased and the sadness increased. And then once again, like months before, she heard His voice. "I will make a way in the wilderness." But this time, she cared. She cared very much. And she believed. The voice was strong and beautiful and went through her emotions and down to her very core. Peace. Nothing had changed, but she knew beyond a doubt that He was here. No matter how things turned out, He would make her OK. He had a plan. She just knew it!

Surprisingly, both Justin and Baby slept late the next morning. Tina sat in the oversized chair enjoying a rare second cup of coffee, watching Justin sleep the sound sleep of innocence as she mulled over last night's happenings. Her heart and mind were unusually calm but still she suspected change was coming quickly. She had turned her phone off last night and now the soft vibrating sound took a while to get her attention. Stepping into the stairwell, Tina answered.

It never ceased to amaze Tina how her parents knew what was going on in her life without her telling them. That was often a two-sided coin, but today it was a good thing. They all knew that her mom was the sensitive one in the marriage. They also knew that dad respected that and listened to her. It was rare indeed for him to go against his wife's wishes. Today, Tina could tell something was up by the sound of her mom's voice. First of all, she was talking a bit in circles. Finally, Tina said, "Mom, please, just say it. What's going on?"

With a little chuckle, Mom suggested perhaps Tina had her own dose of intuition. In a soft voice filled with concern, mom laid out a plan. The bombshell was a direct hit.

"Would you consider bringing the children and moving back home with dad and me? We could help with Justin and Baby. There's plenty of room in the house. Each child could have their own room. In addition, you would have child care free of charge. That would free you up to have more time to develop your business."

It was genius. It was tempting. It was devastating. Tina could resume her life and still have the children close, yes. But her dream of living in Atlanta and creating a name for herself as a photojournalist would be over. Chickpea was too far from Atlanta to allow a commute on a regular basis. Opportunities in the small country town were slim to none. It could very well be a deathblow to her business. And yet, if she was going to keep her promise to help the children, it may be the only way. One more step towards giving up on the life she had planned. One more step back into the life she had outgrown. At the same time, it would be a step towards a better life for Justin and Baby.

Since Chickpea was in GA, DFACS should have no objections to the move. The children would love living with their surrogate grandparents. It all sounded really good on paper, but in Tina's heart it sounded like failure. For days she struggled with what to do. Finally, after looking at the calendar for the 100th time, she had to admit the deadline was quickly approaching and no other solution seemed feasible.

Tina plopped down on the couch. *So, is this it then? Is my dream really over? God, can you give me something here? Some assurance that my life as a photographer is not over before it really gets started?* The silence only irritated her. Finally, through gritted teeth, she surrendered. *Fine, God. I will do it your way. I will move back. There, it's all yours.*

After explaining everything, Tina could see that Katie was a bit relieved. Turns out, her new boyfriend was reluctant to become involved with raising two children. Next step was a consultation with Children's Services. Fortunately, they agreed to the move as long as a caseworker in Chickpea did a home visit and approved the dwelling and the environment. Of course there had to be background checks run on everyone who lived there, but since everyone knew everyone in Chickpea that would not be a problem. Her parents were well known and respected.

It was final. Tina's short lived adventure into Atlanta was coming to an end. Her dream of becoming a famous Photojournalist was unraveling. This was a turn she never expected; a U Turn from her plans. There was sadness in her heart but she could not turn back now. The smile on Justin's face when she told him Pepsi could run outside and still sleep next to his bed at night brought a smile to her own face. She loved this child and she loved Baby. Life had failed her in some ways but had given her precious, unexpected gifts all at the same time. To say it was bittersweet was a major understatement.

Her mom answered after only one ring. "Were you waiting for my call?"

"Well, as a matter of fact, I was. It's been a few days and I was trying not to call you. I do not want to press you, honey. Really, I don't. It's just that things seem so difficult for you right now and we are sitting here with all this room, and . . ."

"Mom. Stop! Give me time to talk."

"OK, honey, I'm sorry, it's just that . . ."

Tina couldn't help but laugh. "You are wasting your breath, mom."

"Oh, so, you don't think our offer would work for you? I understand, really I do . . ."

"I'm coming home, Mom. I want to take you up on your offer and move back home."

Mom whispered to her husband that Tina was coming home which made Tina laugh all over again. "I can hear you, Mom."

After mapping out strategy for the move, Tina hung up the phone and sat staring. She felt numb, but relieved.

Somewhere in the back of her mind, Tina remembered hearing a teaching about choices. As a teenager in Sunday School, she understood it was not what life brought to you, but how you reacted that made the difference. Funny, sitting in class with her friends and half listening, it seemed like a simple, logical theory. In truth, it was far more complicated. Her choice to agree to keep Justin and Baby for a short time had resulted in a lifestyle change and ultimately a completely new direction. Dreams birthed in her heart as a young teen had been sifted, rearranged and finally discarded, all because of that one choice. But, Tina knew that given another opportunity, her reaction would be the same. She was who she was, a product of her family upbringing, her genetic makeup, and her walk with God, though it was at times distant. Yes, she would do it all over again.

Tina's lease on the apartment ended the same day as the ultimatum issued by Ms. McGowen. The timing was perfect to make the move back to Chickpea. Baby was likely over two years old now, depending on her actual age at the time of the explosion. She was happy and well adjusted. Her little-girl curls, bright blue eyes and dimpled smile captured the heart of anyone who spent even a little time with her. Justin was excited at the prospect of going to a "real" school. He had lost that sadness in his eyes and was content with his life. She had not failed. Deep inside she knew that. Still, the ending of their time in Atlanta was disruptive on many levels.

While Tina packed the last few items, Baby Girl teased Justin by running in circles around the living room coffee table. Her *running* left a little to be desired, since she got so excited she fell more than she actually ran. The squeals and giggles were annoyingly beautiful in a way only a mom could appreciate. Running and laughing were two of her favorite things. Her chubby little legs just did not move as quickly as the rest of her. At this point Justin was merely walking in circles so as not to meet her coming around the coffee table. Pepsi was lying in the sun in front of the window, watching intently with her head cocked to one side. It was almost as if the dog was smiling. It seemed only a short time since Baby Girl was struggling to pull up using the same coffee table as a help. The two years had flown by in a blur and yet every detail was etched on Tina's heart.

The apartment was packed and Tina was ready to leave early on Saturday morning. Her dad and mom arrived around 10:00 with their Ford Explorer pulling a small trailer. Mom's mouth dropped open when she walked into the apartment. "Goodness! Where did all this STUFF come from?"

Before Tina could come up with an answer, Daddy stepped up with a big smile and a hug. "We are thrilled to have our girl back home. You have no idea how quiet the place has been. Having you back and the children along with you has made me happier than I have been in a long time. Thank you, honey, thank you for coming back home. I understand, it may only be for a little while, but let's just take one day at a time and see what happens, OK?"

Tina laid her head over on his chest and remembered how safe she had always felt there. "Oh, Daddy. This is such a big move for me. I appreciate all you guys are doing to help me. Please don't think I am not grateful. I am so, so grateful. It's just such a huge turn in my life. Do you understand that? Is it

OK. that I feel this way? Am I being tremendously selfish?"

In his patient way, her dad just held her close like she was a little girl. After a bit, he pulled away and looked deep into her eyes. "Honey, there is not a selfish bone in your body. If there was, we would not be doing this today. Not many people, much less young girls just kick starting their life, would be willing to do what you have done. No, honey, you are definitely not being selfish. You are putting these kids ahead of your own desires and doing the responsible thing. I am so very proud of you. I have no idea where you got your gumption, probably from your mom, but you certainly have a truck load of it."

"Thank you, Daddy. You always make me feel so loved. I can almost believe it when you say those things."

"Almost? Get outta here girl. You know it's true. It's all true."

Wiping a few tears of her own, Mom asked, "Are we gonna do this or what?"

By early afternoon, the trailer was loaded, the keys turned in and the five of them were ready to head south to Chickpea. Saying goodbye to Katie was heart rending. They promised to keep in touch, to travel back and forth, but really, who does that? Tina's heart was heavy with the thoughts of all she was leaving. But, it wasn't about her. Not this time. Her daddy was right about that part.

Her mom insisted on the children riding with them. That was fine with Tina. She made sure they were safely buckled in and ready to go. Justin talked incessantly about his new life while Pepsi barked and Baby squealed. Dad pulled out of the parking lot and she followed. The quietness in her car matched that of her heart—like the calm before the storm.

Father,
My heart is heavy today and I'm sorry for that. I know you are working and helping me and all I seem to do is complain about me and my needs. I am sorry. I know that you will work all things together for my good and in the end it will be good, but right now, I need help believing that.

CHAPTER NINE

The Big Break

Tina sat rocking and daydreaming on Mom's long front porch. It had been months since she returned to Chickpea. She missed her Atlanta apartment and the life she had only scratched the surface of before everything changed. And now here she is in Chickpea . . . again. Back to the familiar faces and places of her childhood. Back in the same church, although she had changed pews and now sat close to the back in case the nursery sign lit up with Baby Girl's number. Everything was the same and yet everything was different. How quickly she had adjusted to living on her own. How quickly it had all fallen apart.

On some days Tina relished the fun of raising two

children and being surrounded by family but at other times she longed for—even grieved for—her life in Atlanta where she was surrounded by people of a similar mindset. Most of her friends in Atlanta were recent college grads ready to conquer their futures and make a difference in the world. She rested her face on her hands and tried not to cry.

Oh, God. I am sorry, but I hate it here. Not hate. No, that's too strong No, I don't hate it. But maybe I do hate it a little. What I hate is not having a life. I hate sitting and watching life pass me by. And I hate that I hate it. I hate that I cannot just relax and be content. I want to be the person you are asking me to be, but you gotta help me here. You have to change my heart if I'm gonna survive this.

Tina sat for a few minutes, just pondering where she was in life. Finally, she wiped her eyes, sat back and picked up her coffee mug. As she sipped the now cold coffee, her mind drifted to Katie. What was she doing today? How are things going with her new boyfriend? The idea of Katie and her boyfriend brought back thoughts of Barry. He still called occasionally, but they both knew it wasn't the same and Tina suspected the time was soon coming when he would completely fade from her life. So much had changed. *I don't recognize my own life. I am not even sure I recognize you right now, God.* After a few minutes, she stood and took a deep breath. *OK, I am not going down this dark hole. I know better than this.*

She walked over to the porch rail. A hummingbird hovered around the pink blooms of a flower sitting on the porch rail. Tiny and delicate, its little wings moved so rapidly they blurred with the action. Two squirrels scampered around the lawn, up and down a nearby pine tree while Pepsi lay with her ears perked, daring them to come closer. There was no denying the beauty and peace of this place, but at this particular moment in time, Tina wanted more than beauty and peace. She wanted action and adventure and challenge. Over the past few weeks, she had traveled and photographed desolate country roads and streams and lakes. When possible she had one or both of the children in tow, trying to recapture the enjoyment this had brought her in earlier years. Although it was fun and she enjoyed being with the children, there was something missing. The sugar was gone from the candy bar. It felt like walking in a season that had finished. Time had moved on and yet here she was back in the past.

As word spread that she was back in Chickpea, Tina picked up a few photo shoots with the county newspaper and some with local institutions. It was enough to keep her juices flowing and bring a little money into the household, but not enough to keep her business or her dream alive. She absently wondered if it may be time to make a trip back to the city and stir the pot. She needed to be seen and to see some of her former clients, to assure them she was still very much in the photojournalism business. It was a thought. Perhaps, just perhaps she could pull it off. If Mom was in agreement, it might just be possible.

The soft vibrating of her cell phone caught her attention. She did not recognize the number on the screen and hoped that meant it was a professional call.

"Hello."

"Miss Brogan?"

"Yes."

"Tina?"

"Yes."

"This is Jerry Williams from Saunders & Johnson Law Firm. You may not remember me, but we met a while back when you were doing a photo spread for our firm here in Atlanta."

Tina's ears perked up much like Pepsi's. Of course she remembered Jerry. He was the nice looking widower who had asked her out. That had been flattering, but she was hoping this call was a professional matter rather than a personal one. Jerry went on to explain that he was calling to inquire if she was still doing photo shoots in Atlanta. *Well, yeah! At least she would be if anyone hired her.* Keeping her tone even and hoping he could not hear her pounding heart, she explained her move and that she would be happy to travel to Atlanta. He did not have time to go into the details of his proposal but asked if she could drive in and meet with him on Tuesday.

Tina managed to remain calm until they finished their call. Atlanta! Photo shoot! Thank you Jesus! Oh yeah, I am definitely interested and then some.

Her next call was to Katie. If she was going to meet with Jerry at 8:30 A.M. on Tuesday, she would like to stay Monday night at Katie's apartment. A paying job AND a night with Katie. It was amazing how quickly things could change. Life was looking better all of a sudden.

Katie assured her she was thrilled and would love to have her stay over. Once that arrangement was settled, Tina went inside to check with her mom. She took extra care not to take her parents for granted just because they were close and open to babysitting at any time. The children were still her responsibility and her first priority.

After explaining everything to her mom, Tina stood waiting for an answer regarding the babysitting. Her mom smiled and reached over to give her a quick hug, "Oh honey, that is wonderful. Of course we will keep the children. Go, get back to your life for a few days. Stay as long as you like. It will be good for you! Seriously."

Tina hit the stairs like a teenager before she realized she actually had three days to pack an overnight bag.

Monday afternoon she hugged the babies, went over their schedules with her mom again, placed her overnight bag in the backseat of her car and slipped in behind the wheel, and sat. The tears that stung her eyes were not what she had expected. It took a couple of minutes to assure her heart that all was well with the children and she would see them late tomorrow. Her mom stood on the porch with Baby Girl on one hip. Justin was happily playing with his action figures on the steps, oblivious to anything else. Smiling, Tina wiped her eyes, waved and pulled out of the drive.

It was invigorating to be heading back to the city and to Katie. They had much catching up to do. Tonight was their night—no boyfriend. Dinner out was a rarity these days and even then, the choices in Chickpea were not all that great. On that thought, Tina opened her phone and selected her favorite playlist, while she drove much too fast up I-75. The sun was shining, her heart was free and she sang as loud as she wanted to.

Katie was just as excited as Tina and dinner at The Cheesecake Factory was complete with the obligatory slice of cheesecake. Just because. Tina was anxious to hear all about the latest Mr. Wonderful, but Katie was vague and changed the subject. That was strange, normally she would rave on and on about her current beau. There must be trouble in paradise these days. She let the subject go and moved on to bring Katie up to date on the children.

"Justin is getting so tall! It makes me think back to the day he chased that guy across the parking lot. Maybe his daddy was tall and he is going to take after him. And Baby girl, OMG! She's Something else. She is jabbering. Of course we only catch every few words, but she knows exactly what she is saying. And what she wants. There's no fooling that girl."

Katie was soaking up every word with a happy smile on her face. "I so need to see them in person. FaceTiming is great but I need some cuddle time. Do you think they remember me at all?"

Tina looked at her friend in mocked shock, "Of course they remember you. You are Auntie Katie. That will never change."

It was peaceful and freeing to have an entire

evening to just sit and catch up with each other. They talked too long into the night but the early morning sleepy eyes were worth it.

Tina pulled into the parking lot at Saunders & Johnson a little after 8:00 A.M., did a quick check-over in the mirror, collected her gear and used her foot to push open the door of her S.U.V. She pressed her navy blue skirt with her hands, straightened the blazer, patted her pearls and glanced down at the matching blue pumps. Goodness, she looked like she was going to church in Chickpea, or worse yet, a young Ms. McGowen. Tina shuddered. A wardrobe update was definitely in order. Perhaps she could stay one more night and do a little shopping at the Mall of GA before returning home. She would call Mom and check. She felt certain Katie would be fine with her staying over tonight.

With one last look down at her outfit, she turned and walked toward the door. *OK, Lord, here we go. Help me please. You know I really need this job.*

The foyer was large and open, decorated Southern style with fresh flowers, soft cushiony sofas and wing back chairs. There were mirrors strategically placed on the walls between paintings of colonial estates from years gone by, along with one beautiful photo of the green at the Masters in Augusta. The colors were perfect and Tina knew the photographer had probably taken many shots to get the perfect one. His persistence had paid off for him. The entire effect of the room put Tina at ease immediately. It created a peaceful ambience for a law office where most people came during times of stress and difficulty.

Tina walked over to the receptionist. "Good morning, my name is Tina Brogan. I have an 8:30 appointment with Jerry Williams."

"Good morning, Ms. Brogan. Jerry is in a meeting but should be finished shortly. Would you care for something to drink while you wait? We have coffee or water."

"No, I'm fine, but thank you."

Tina pulled out her cell phone and texted her mom to ask if it would be possible to extend her stay another night. The reply came quickly that it would be fine. The babies were doing well and Grandma was more than happy to keep them another day. Tina smiled reading the text. She loved her mom so very much and in spite of their differences on some issues, they had a great relationship. Next she tried calling Katie but did not get an answer. Just as she started to text her, Jerry came strolling across the foyer, hand extended and a welcoming smile on his tan face. She had forgotten how appealing he was. "Good morning, Ms. Brogan. It's good to see you again."

"Good morning. And, please, call me Tina."

Jerry smiled and extended his hand towards the second door on the right. Tina stepped into the office and was immediately impressed with the size as well as the decor. This guy either had good taste or a good decorator. She accepted the chair he offered and was somewhat surprised when he took the seat next to her instead of behind his desk. Turning his chair to face her better, he asked about the children.

"Well, they are growing and changing every day. As we talked on the phone, we still have no word on their parents. They have, however, settled into their new surroundings and are normal, active children. DFACS approved me as a Foster Parent, which takes away some of the stress. We are not overly concerned with them being moved at this point."

Jerry nodded, "Well that is good news. I know it means a lot to have some semblance of permanence."

Tina waited for him to continue. She mused in her mind how interesting it was that he should even bring up the children. When they had talked briefly about the explosion back when she did the other shoot for his office, he had seemed disinterested almost to the point of being rude. And now, he was making a point to show his interest. Maybe it was a sales tactic. She wasn't sure what to expect.

After a brief pause, Jerry leaned forward with his forearms on his knees, allowing his hands to dangle between his legs. He took a deep sigh that was almost a groan, and looked Tina in the eye.

"I never told you that day we talked, but I was in the explosion. My son was also with me that day. He was killed in the fire. I was knocked unconscious and suffered a head injury. When I woke up from the coma several weeks later, I was in the hospital and my son was nowhere to be found."

Sitting up straight again, he looked at Tina out of tormented eyes. The silence between them was heavy with pain and memories. Neither of them were able to speak. Jerry sat quietly for a few minutes before he regained his composure and continued.

"I am certain you are wondering why I am telling you all of this now."

Tina nodded slowly, not wanting to be rude or uncaring, but she was wondering why he was telling her these personal details. She sat quietly waiting.

Jerry ran his hands through his hair and nodded with understanding. "The job I am offering you has to do with the explosion. You will be working closely with me and with many of the victims' families. I want you to know that I am not just a bystander. This is very personal to me as well."

Tina unconsciously bit her top lip to stop the quivering. She had not expected this assignment to have anything to do with the explosion. Immediately, her thoughts went to the children and how this could affect them.

Jerry continued. "It was several days after the explosion before the rescue workers uncovered my son's . . . body. . . . He was under the debris in the foyer area where he had been standing with me."

Tears streamed down Jerry's face as he struggled to get the words out. "He was burned beyond recognition but because of his size and bone structure and also the location of his . . . his . . . body, they assured me it was Billy. My wife, Marcy, had died six months earlier from cancer. We buried him next to her. In the space of a few months my entire life was ripped from me and everything I loved was gone.

I don't talk about it often, the pain is still too much, but I want you to know that I am not indifferent to how this project could affect you and possibly even your children. I am right there with you. Just in a different way."

After a few moments Tina was able to whisper, "I'm so very sorry." After more heavy silence, she reached for his hand and held it briefly before he pulled away and apologized for putting all this on her.

"I just felt it was important for me to be completely honest with you. If we are to work together on this project, there may be times when my reactions would seem strange unless you knew the background. It is only fair that you know where I am coming from. Especially since you have been so open with me about your experiences."

Both of them were shaken and Jerry suggested they take a short break, get a cup of coffee at the Starbucks in the front café and regroup. They walked slowly through the foyer, not speaking.

As they walked, Tina thought over exactly what he had said. It made sense in some ways, but there were some holes here and there. For one, why didn't he ask for a DNA test to be 100% sure it was his son? And why did he fail to mention it last time but be so open about it now? Was he on the level or could he be so crass as to use this as a ploy to get close to her? That made no sense. But, still, it was all a little strange.

Tina sat at a small table while Jerry placed their order at the counter. With a quiet determination, she pushed her tumbling emotions back and did her best to listen when Jerry walked over and sat beside her.

"After three years, the hotel is opening their new facility in a few months. While this is good news to the employees who have either taken lower paying jobs or been left without work for the past three years, it is frustrating to the families who are still waiting for settlements on lawsuits filed against the hotel. They feel their settlements should take priority over money spent on opening a new hotel. This latest timeframe has them in somewhat of an uproar.

Research has revealed that the hotel management was aware of the need to replace the faulty furnace. Your job would be to create human interest articles for the plaintiffs with photos and background stories of the clients. I remember that you took a few photos that day. More importantly, your work for us last time was very impressive. All of us here agree that you are the one for the job."

Tina tried to remain professional as he quoted their price range for the project. The bitter sweetness of the offer was staggering. She could quite possibly be helping to represent the very parents she and Barry had searched for. If that was the case, she could meet them and never realize it. Then again, this could be the time Justin and Baby Girl's parents showed up to take back their babies. Tina's heart was split once again between hope and dread.

If she agreed to the contract, her service would include photos, behind the scenes stories, and a comprehensive presentation for the defendants' lawyers. In addition, her photos would most likely be purchased for use in television commercials and newspaper ads. The ads were geared at creating public awareness of the hotel's reluctance to help the families who had lost loved ones as well as three years of lost wages for others. Jerry apologized for the late notice, but needed the background stories and photos ready in approximately forty-five days.

Tina was barely able to comprehend all Jerry was saying. Her mind was already working out the details of such an undertaking. She would need to hire assistants, do hours of research, spend time on site in Atlanta, and perhaps add new equipment. Still, with the price the firm was willing to pay, plus a percentage once the case was settled, she would come out way ahead. Of course she wanted this contract, but first she had to talk to her parents since this would require their help with the children. And Katie—would she be open to letting Tina stay at her place when necessary?

It was close to noon when Jerry and Tina shook hands and agreed to make the final arrangements by week's end. Tina walked out with ideas flying rapid fire through her brain. It would be quite a challenge to capture the emotions and struggles of the victims in photos with only a brief article for each one. The interview process would be crucial of course. Each family would have its own dynamics and ways of coping with their grief, making it imperative for her to handle each situation fittingly.

The car was hot from sitting in the sun so Tina

started the engine and leaned against the outside of the door for a few minutes. In the middle of one of the random brain swirls, she remembered her decision to shop for a new wardrobe. After hearing the details of the job, it was even more appealing and necessary. A quick text to Katie asked if she could stay over another night. She would wait until she was back at the apartment to call her mom. This was something that needed her full attention and right now her thoughts were running all over creation. Instead of heading south to the apartment complex, she turned onto I-85 North towards the Mall of Georgia.

The adrenaline rush was making her hungry. Her first stop was the foot court. By the time she finished her Chick Fil A sandwich and fruit cup, her heart was starting to calm. First she wandered through Nordstroms. After a few walks down wishing lane, she checked over the sale racks and finally left and made her way to The Loft.

Next was The Limited, followed by Charming Charlie's for an outfit to feed her latent hippy self. And last, but certainly not least, a visit to the Coach Store. It was 4:00 by the time she made her way back to the car and loaded her treasures into the back. Feeling quite satisfied with her day, Tina pulled onto the highway and headed south towards Katie's apartment.

Now that her brain swirls had subsided and coherent thinking returned, Tina began to seriously ponder the pros and cons of the contract. It would take a lot of preparation to pull this off. She was definitely up to the task, but had to remember there were people in her life that depended on her, namely Baby Girl and Justin as well as her parents.

She pulled into the familiar parking lot and was pleased to find a space close to Katie's apartment. Actually, this was the same space she had sat in three years earlier on the day of the explosion, the day her life changed forever. And now, here she was again, with another life changing opportunity before her. She made a mental note to do something special for this little space. Maybe flowers surrounding it, or a chalk super star in the middle.

As before, Tina pushed open the driver's door with her foot then stood and turned to reach into the back seat for her packages. Her arms were overloaded but then so was her credit card, so best to just thank the Lord and move forward. Turning, she saw Katie standing on her deck talking with someone. OMG! Could that be Barry??? Tina's heart did the customary flip as she recognized his profile. But then, before she could move, Barry leaned over and gave Katie a full on the mouth kiss followed by a bear hug that could only mean one thing.

Tina's mouth dropped open, the packages fell to the ground, and all she could do was to stare. At that moment Katie looked over Barry's shoulder, straight into Tina's eyes. Shock filled her eyes and she pushed Barry away and started running down the stairs with Barry right behind her.

Tears flowed freely down Tina's cheeks as she bent to retrieve her packages. Shaking and grabbing bags and throwing them in the car, she was trying desperately to escape before they made it down the three flights of stairs. She managed to start the engine just as they reached the car. Katie was crying and Barry was obviously flustered. Before they could say anything, Tina backed out of the space and gunned the engine out of the parking lot.

What had just happened????

Tina drove straight down I-85 and onto I-75S. She wanted to go home. She needed to be home. She needed to hold Baby Girl. The pain was too great to utter a sound, only an occasional sucking in of her breath. Her mind refused to even try to understand. She drove. Rapidly. Not thinking. Just driving. After almost an hour, rational thinking began to return and Tina realized it would bring more pain to everyone involved to go home like this. Her mom would know immediately that something was wrong. No, she could not go home just yet, even though that was the one place she wanted to be right now.

The next exit offered the normal fare of fast food restaurants but all she wanted was a Coke and a clean bathroom. That being accomplished, she returned to I-75 and instead of continuing home, headed north, back towards Atlanta. Tina remembered her belongings were at Katie's. No matter, she definitely had new outfits and it would be easy enough to pick up toiletries. She drove slowly now in the right hand lane, looking for an exit with a reasonable hotel. Sleep. That's what she needed: sleep. After checking in at the Holiday Inn Express close to Downtown Atlanta, Tina made a quick trip over to CVS and purchased a toothbrush, toothpaste, shampoo and deodorant. Apparently, that last minute dash into Victoria's Secret this afternoon had been providential.

After a hot shower Tina collapsed on the queen sized bed in her new P.J.'s and stared at the ceiling. There were still no words to put this all together. The pain in her heart was too deep to explain in mere words. There were tons of messages and calls from Katie and Barry, but she ignored them all. *At some point I will have to face this, but not tonight, Lord, not any time soon.*

The awful thoughts of betrayal began to creep unwanted into her mind. It was impossible to keep a calm heart or mind at this point as she stared at the ceiling and talked to the atmosphere. "Katie, how could you do this? How could you? You are my best friend in all the world. And Barry. I know we are no longer a couple—perhaps we never were. But, you had to know I loved you. Granted we never spoke of those things, but we talked about our dreams, our goals, and our lives. I just assumed we had a future together. For weeks after you left for New York I expected you to return. To call me and say you made a mistake. Well, obviously not! You did call, but not me, you called Katie. Obviously, I am the fool here."

On and on her words tumbled into the stillness. This betrayal was more than she could even imagine, much less accept. *Lord, this is too much. Who does this to a friend? I feel so stupid, humiliated! To think I have been longing for a relationship with Barry and all the while he is longing for Katie. My friend. How could I be so blind? When I talked to Katie, was she ashamed? Why didn't she just tell me? How pathetic can I be?* She continued to beat herself up until a numbness settled over her heart. She literally felt the shell forming. This was not going to be an easy fix.

Finally, Tina lay quietly. Her emotions were spent. There were not enough tears to wash away the hurt. No explanation that satisfied her soul. Nothing except emptiness. The gentle voice deep inside came softly, *"don't beat yourself up. It's not what you think."*

Yeah, right! I saw what I saw, God.

Her vibrating phone brought her out of the darkness she had fallen into. It had to be one of them. . . . Again. Why couldn't they just leave her alone? She had turned it off but the vibrating hum kept reminding her. She could just put it on silent, but what if Mom needed her? The screen lit up again but this time it wasn't Katie or Barry, it was Jerry's office. Groaning to herself, Tina tapped the green receiver and mumbled hello.

"Tina? This is Jerry. Did I catch you at a bad time?"

"Jerry." Summoning all her strength and putting on a false front, she sat up in bed. "No, of course not," Tina fibbed. "What's up?"

"I know this is last minute notice, but you mentioned possibly staying in town to do some shopping so I thought I would take a chance. For the past couple of years, I have been attending a support group for people affected by the hotel explosion. We meet tonight at 8:00 at St. Paul's Church. Would you consider joining us? It would give you an opportunity to meet some of the people who were on the front lines that day. All of them lost someone in the explosion and are still healing and learning to deal with their loss. Of course, we must be very sensitive, but perhaps meeting some of the people will give you more of an insight to the ongoing pain they deal with everyday."

Tina groaned to herself and sat up on the edge of the bed. She assured him that of course she would go. Hanging up the phone, she shook her head in disbelief. *God, why can't you just leave me alone and let me lay here?* She breathed a deep sigh, rubbed her eyes and headed to the bathroom. Even though her world was falling apart, she had a job to do and this was part of it. Jerry suggested they meet at the church in an hour. Fortunately, it was only a few blocks from her hotel.

The church basement was sectioned into several smaller meeting rooms using sliding partitions. Jerry directed her to one in the far corner where fifteen or so folks sat talking quietly. The folding chairs were arranged in the traditional semi-circle. Across the back was the folding table with a few snacks, coffee maker and bottled water. The atmosphere in the room was subdued but not overly sad. It seemed to be respectful of men and women dealing with extended pain, the kind of atmosphere where the occasional laughter was a welcome relief to all.

Tina slipped quietly into the seat next to an attractive older lady. Jerry took a seat next to her just as a middle-aged man in a suit stood and moved to the front of the little room. The group appeared to be between their early thirties and mid- sixties. It was sobering to realize the one common denominator in this room was grief. Tina wasn't sure she would be able to endure this for very long. She felt a bit ashamed as her own pain dimmed in the light of what these people were dealing with.

The leader was talking but Tina's mind was wandering, thinking some of these people could easily be Justin or Baby Girl's parents. Her stomach knotted up and the familiar shaking deep inside started. Mentally she dove head-long down the rabbit hole of imagining what would happen when and if their parents were identified. Jerry was gently poking her arm. The room was silent; all were watching her face, waiting for an answer. To what?

"Your name, whispered Jerry. He asked for your name and your relation to the explosion."

"I'm so sorry, Tina replied. I was overtaken for a moment with the reality of what you are all dealing with. Please forgive me. My name is Tina Brogan. I was not involved in the explosion, but at the time I lived right across the street and was one of the first on the scene."

Glancing sideways at Jerry, she decided to leave it at that for now. Jerry nodded his approval and the leader moved on around the group. One and another told of their loss, their healing, emphasizing the truth that a measure of healing does come, but slowly. The lady next to her began to talk.

"As most of you know, I lost my husband in the explosion. John worked in the maintenance department at the hotel. He had been there for over ten years and loved his job. He enjoyed seeing all the people in and out of the hotel. He liked being able to help people. I know it's been several years, but that day . . . the day of the explosion, gets me every year. Each year I am hoping and praying I can get through the day without a breakdown but so far I haven't made it through a single time. It just all comes barreling down on me. People tell me it's normal. I suppose it is, but sometimes it's just hard to handle."

Tina wanted to hug her and tell her about Jesus and that she would see her husband again, but she thought the lady probably knew that. Her pain was in the present tense. As the evening progressed, one after another related how they were doing. They told what their main need or hurt was. Several asked for prayer. *Dear God, if there is any way, no matter how small, that I can help some of these people, please let me. Please help me to help them.*

Around 9:30, Jerry walked her out to her car and opened the door for her. Tina's heart was heavy from so many things, but this meeting had put a lot of issues into the proper perspective. Her troubles with Barry and Katie, although still painful, seemed less important. The big change was in her attitude towards Justin and Baby Girl. What if somewhere, in a group much like this, there was a mom and dad grieving over two little children, children who were not dead, but very much alive and very happy in their new lives. What if?

Back at the hotel, Tina put on her new pajamas and crawled back under the covers. Would this day full of emotional roller coasters never end? Her phone showed more texts and missed calls from Barry and Katie. Just looking at the numbers caused her heart to constrict. It was difficult to put a name to her feelings, but the closest was betrayal. Betrayal by two people she loved and respected. And no, it did not compare to the pain she had witnessed tonight but still, it was her pain and it went deep inside her soul. It would one day be only a scar from a wound that had healed, but right now it was a gaping hole.

Sleep did not come easily as she tossed and

turned, going over and over different scenarios in her mind. What she would say, what she would do, how she would explain herself, how she would make them feel the same sadness that threatened to engulf her. Such were her thoughts as she slipped further into her private cave and closed the door.

Tina's last thought as she slipped into a restless sleep was a quote from a devotional she had read a few days back: "Self-pity is an ugly animal that blinds us to the reality of God's eternal purposes in our lives." She did not like or agree with that statement.

Sometime in the early morning, before the sun came up, she woke up with a start. Was someone knocking on her door? Surely not! She sat frozen in the middle of the queen sized bed, holding the covers close to her chest until she heard the would-be intruder move to the next door where he was met by a somewhat irate sounding female.

Great. Now she was awake and a million thoughts were waiting for her. Reluctantly, she tossed the comforter aside and stumbled into the bathroom. Her plan was to go back to sleep as quickly as possible, but by the time she returned to the bed, her eyes were wide open and her mind was racing with all that had happened.

"It's too early, Lord, and too soon to think about forgiving. My heart hurts and my head hurts and I just want to sleep." Tina curled up on her side, closed her eyes and did her very best to stay hidden in her own world. Inside her personal cave, she was aware of all that was going on outside, around her, but none of it reached in to bother her. She was safe and protected and no one knew what she was thinking, therefore she did not have to make excuses or give explanations. But sleep would not come. Finally, as the sun tried to peek in through the heavy curtains on the hotel window, Tina surrendered and got up. "Now what?"

The tiny coffee pot on the dresser was just big enough for two cups. A few minutes later, she was propped up in the bed with a hot cup of fresh coffee, a notepad and her favorite pen. As was her new custom, she planned to write out her list to organize all that the job would require and all that needed to happen in the next few weeks. There she sat, pen poised above the paper, but the only thing that came to her mind was Barry . . . and Katie . . . and their betrayal.

Finally the dam broke, again, and the tears rushed from her heart up to her eyes and down her face. The coffee sat cold on the nightstand and the notepad and pen were on the floor before she mumbled her way back to God and began the long, painful journey of forgiveness. It was 9:00 A.M. before she was able to pick up her phone and send a quick text to Katie. It read simply, "I am sorry. I love you and will call you later." Of course Katie's replies began immediately but Tina ignored them and headed for the shower.

Check out was at 11:00 but then what? Face the music. That's what her dad would say. "Tina, face the music." Though it would be more painful than anything in her life, she would give it a try. Even in this dark place, she realized the danger of bitterness. More importantly than that, she realized how very much she wanted to keep her friendship with Katie. There had to be an explanation, a way to fix this.

As she went about getting dressed and gathering up her few things, she wavered back and forth. Should she go or should she call? Could she really do either? Again and again, she decided to just go home and leave it. Every time those thoughts came, she realized the gaping hole that would leave in her heart. Each time, her resolve strengthened and she was determined to get to the bottom of this.

After a short text to Katie asking to come over, Tina went into the lobby. She managed to eat a small breakfast of toast and fruit along with a cup of coffee before making the short trip to Katie's apartment. Katie was so upset over hurting Tina she had taken the morning off from her job at the doctor's office. Thankfully, Barry had returned to New York and would not be in Atlanta again for a couple of weeks. The familiar parking space was open but Tina refused to use it. Instead, she parked at the far end of the lot and walked to the stairwell. With a heavy heart, she climbed the three flights and knocked on the door.

Katie's tear stained face and red rimmed eyes were all it took for Tina's heart to break anew. The next few minutes were a jumble of tears, sniffling, hugs, apologies and forgiveness—all between two friends who loved each other and treasured their friendship. After a while, the crying subsided and they sat looking at each other in silence. The next step would be more difficult, explaining what had happened. Why had they kept this new found love between Barry and Katie a secret from Tina? Katie fingered the waded tissue in her hand and sat staring at Tina out of puffy eyes. With something between a sniffle and a sob, she took Tina's hand and began.

"It all started very innocently. When you moved back to Chickpea, communication grew less and less until we rarely talked. It was during that time that Barry began the process of moving back to Atlanta. The partnership in New York was not what he had expected. The new firm agreed to let him out of his contract with the understanding that he would not reopen his consulting business in New York.

He came to Atlanta to scope out office space and while he was here, called just to say hello and catch up. We had dinner and talked about our times with you and the children. The next night, Barry called again but this time our dinner talk was more about who we were currently. It was that night we both realized how much we had in common, but neither would admit that to the other. A few weeks passed and Barry came to Atlanta again, this time to look at apartments. He asked me to join him and offer advice on several possible locations. We spent the entire Saturday looking at apartments, having lunch and then dinner and by the time Barry took me home that night my heart was captivated. Neither of us wanted to hurt you, so Barry returned to New York with no mention of pursuing a romantic relationship.

With each subsequent visit, our hearts warmed until one night we were finally honest with each other about our feelings. The only problem was how to explain this to you. We both wanted to do it in person. So, when you called to say you were coming to Atlanta, Barry made plans to be here. Something came up at work and he was delayed a day but then you asked if you could stay another day, so it appeared to come together perfectly. That was, until we made the mistake of kissing outside my apartment door and you saw it all."

As Katie poured out her heart, explaining how it all came about, Tina tried her best to be happy for her friend. She knew Barry was not the man God had for her and understood in her heart that he and Katie had never meant to hurt her. Still, the pain was very fresh and very real. The heart wants what the heart wants and the mind does not always understand but in the end, she had to admit, this was a good thing.

Tina sat back against the couch and took what was her first really clean breath since she got here. "May I ask you a favor, please Katie?"

Katie looked at her with sad eyes. "As long as it isn't to stop being your friend."

Tina smiled and reached over to touch her friend's arm. "No, not that. No, Lord no, never that. I just would appreciate it if I didn't have to see or talk to Barry right now. I am going to be OK, really I am. I know he isn't the right one for me. But, honestly, I feel embarrassed and foolish for falling so hard when he was not reciprocating." She held up her hand to keep Katie from interrupting.

"Please, just hear me out. I will be OK after a bit, but facing him right now even to say everything is good between us, would be excruciatingly painful. Is that OK? I mean, can you just explain to him that I am fine. That I was just shocked. Please let him know that I have no romantic feelings for him. Just thinking about all that at this point is mortifying!"

Katie smiled through misty eyes. "I can definitely do that. Today. Honestly, he is pretty upset by all this. It will do him a world of good to know we can all be friends again at some point. But, we will not rush it. You can call the shots on that, OK?"

After a few minutes of silence, Katie suggested breakfast. "Man, that sounds good to me! I cannot even remember the last meal I had. Maybe the Cheesecake Factory!"

"Waffle House? And can you tell me all about your meeting at the lawyers?"

Over breakfast, Tina filled Katie in on the job offer. She was going to save the part about hoping to stay at her place for the last, but Katie interrupted her with an invite to do just that.

"I'm thrilled for you! It is SO time for you to get a break. And a possibility of finding the kids' parents. This could not be more perfect. And we get to be together more. Let me know when you will be back. Plan on staying as long as you like. And, no worries, I'll make sure Barry isn't here."

After gathering her things from Katie's apartment, Tina said her goodbyes, gave hugs and promises to call soon. This time the drive down I-75 was much more peaceful. The edge was still there when she let her mind go back to seeing them kiss, but she determined in her heart not to go there. Just don't go there!

Tina pulled into her parent's drive and jumped out of the car. She needed to see her kids! Now! The screen door banged shut behind Justin. He took the steps in record time and threw himself into her open arms. "Now, that's a welcome home!" Tina squeezed him tight and drank in the little boy scent of him.

He was all smiles, jabbering about everything he had done while she was in Atlanta. You would think it had been a month instead of two days. No matter, it was music to her ears. By the time she got inside the house, Baby Girl was running down the long hall to meet her. Ah, yes! It was good to be home.

"Hey Honey! Welcome home." Her mom was right behind Baby. "How'd it go? I kept waiting for more info, but I guess it's a lot to tell over the phone?"

"Oh, you have no idea. This is awesome. I need to talk to you and dad about possibly helping me with the kids. Let me get my things inside and we can talk if you have time?"

After hearing everything, her parents were on board and ready to go. It did not take much in the Brogan household to have reason for a celebration. The entire clan gathered on Sunday afternoon to hear all the details and offer any help they could.

"Well, now that you mention it," Tina began. Her brother spoke up and said, "Hang on to your hats and your wallets folks, here it comes."

After the laughter died down, she started again. "Actually, I do need some help. However, I do expect to pay, and pay nicely for your assistance. How 'bout that?"

Now she had their attention. "I need an assistant to accompany me on some of the photo shoots. I also need help with research. Nothing legal or too detailed, just background info on some of the families. You know, their economic profile, where they live, how many kids, stuff like that. Something to make a compelling story."

After dinner the men gathered in front of the television to watch baseball while the women sat on the front porch enjoying the fresh air and discussing more important things. Becca, her oldest sister, was not her usual talkative self but sat quietly rocking. Tina knew the look well; Becca was pondering something.

On the other hand, Lottie, now almost eighteen, was over the moon pumped about Tina's new job. Lottie was following in her aunt's footsteps and studying photography in high school. This was her senior year and plans were in the making for her to attend Valdosta State College in the fall. Tina knew where the conversation was heading but decided to let it play out at Lottie's pace. It was difficult to hide her amusement at the around-the-court way Lottie was approaching the subject.

"Aunt Tina, did I tell you that I am on the work-study program at school this semester?"

"Ah, yes I had heard that from your mom. How is that going for you?"

"I love it! My classes end at noon every day and I work at Target the rest of the day, just like you did. In fact, I suspect using you as a reference played a role in my getting the job. Several of my friends applied but were not hired. So, thank you for that."

"Glad I could help. Let me ask you something, would it be possible for you to miss a couple of days a week if you did your classwork and kept up to date?"

Lottie's eyes bugged out so far Tina was sure they would roll right out on the porch. The burst of laughter from the rest of the women caught her niece off guard. It seemed everyone knew what was in the works but all were waiting for Tina to make the offer. After much chatter and excitement, the plans were solidified and Lottie was officially her assistant. Tina was thrilled with the prospect of spending time with Lottie and getting the opportunity to help train her in photojournalism.

The plans were falling into place quickly. Katie's

apartment was open for the Atlanta headquarters several days a week, her mom and dad would babysit as much as necessary and Lottie would be her traveling assistant. The only position left open was a Researcher. Before leaving for home, Becca pulled her aside and quietly offered to do research from home for her. She did not expect a salary but Tina insisted. And now it was all in place.

Monday morning Tina called Jerry and officially accepted the contract. They made an appointment to meet in Jerry's office Tuesday morning at nine. The weekend had sped by with Tina making final arrangements and schedules with her parents, Becca and Lottie. By the time she left for Atlanta on Tuesday morning each person had an idea of what was expected of them. They also had an understanding that it could all change on a dime when she got deeper into the project.

CHAPTER TEN

Back in Atlanta

Driving up I-75, Tina had time to think over her life since the day of the explosion. She was a different person in more ways than even she understood. Her dream of being a recognized photojournalist was still alive, but now it was mixed with a little wisdom and a huge dose of reality. She smiled as she drove, thinking again of her Grandma and all the talks and dreams they had shared. *It's really happening, Grandma. I wish you were here to share it with me.*

She pulled into the parking lot at exactly 8:30. Her new outfit was much classier than her Ms. McGowan lookalike from last time. Inside, the receptionist ushered her into Jerry's office. Standing and extending his hand, he smiled and said good morning, then offered her a chair. As soon as she sat down in front of his desk, he pulled a file from a folder on his desk and carefully explained exactly what would be expected of her. He also confirmed the salary and the commission percentage she could expect if they won the case.

With all the particulars settled, he extended his hand and welcomed her aboard. "Now, I have prepared a list of possible clients for you to interview and photograph. Mr. Johnson is a senior partner in the firm. He and I have noted a tentative completion date at the end of each segment."

The time passed quickly as they went over each client. When Tina next looked at her watch it was 11:30. Jerry sat back in his chair and smiled. "It's been a good, productive morning. Would you care to join me for lunch?"

Tina's immediate acceptance surprised her. What was it about him that made her relaxed and comfortable and yet intensely aware of his presence all at the same time? His tall, lean build and sandy brown hair were appealing but not overly handsome, not like Barry. And he was older than her, probably by six or seven years. However, in his eyes she saw a glimpse of a depth that frightened and intrigued her all at the same time. She suspected he would become a very good friend.

They passed by the receptionist's desk where Jerry let Brenda know they were leaving for lunch. Tina ignored the smile that flitted around the corners of the Receptionist's mouth. She wanted to say, "It's just a business lunch, Brenda." She certainly was not interested in anything else.

Outside, Jerry asked if she had a preference. Tina politely suggested he should choose. "Well, he began, I am in the mood for something substantial. Do you care at all for the Cheesecake Factory?"

"Ummmm, who doesn't enjoy the Cheesecake Factory?"

The next few weeks were busy with preparation for the interviews. In the midst of it all, Tina helped her mom prepare for Easter with the Brogan clan. It was always a day of family fun with everyone dressed in their finery. Oh, the pics Tina took of the kids. She was as proud as any mommy alive. Grandma Joan had sewn Baby's lilac dress and even the little bonnet. Tina added the patent leather shoes and white socks with the little ruffles around the top. The dimpled darling thought she was something. And she was. Justin was just as charming in his three piece suit and black leather shoes topped off by an adorable "big guy" hat supplied by Granddaddy. Together they posed and smiled along with the rest of the Brogan grandchildren. The wonder of these two children being added to their family was not lost on any of them. Out of a terrible tragedy, the Lord had brought a new dimension into all their lives in the form of two beautiful children. Good food, fun, family, and celebrating Jesus made for the perfect day. When bedtime rolled around, not only the little ones were spent.

Early Monday morning, Tina, dressed in a new outfit that was fashionable and yet comfortable for a long day's work, kissed the still sleeping children and headed towards Atlanta for her first round of interviews. Since it was her first day of photographing, she decided to go it alone. Probably best to test the waters before bringing Lottie in on the job.

Jerry was arranging for five families to come in for a personal consultation. He had given her a quick background of each case from the police reports. It was not much to go on, but Tina hoped it would break the ice and get them to open up to her. She was counting on getting more from Becca's research.

The drive into Atlanta took longer than expected due to traffic problems and road work, but she passed the time thinking and planning. Her strategy was clean and simple; the problem was, the emotions connected to that day kept interfering. Tina walked a balance beam in her mind, she needed to be professional and at the same time empathetic. A good photojournalist must have a connection with her subject in order to relay the message needed. Over and over Tina mentally worded and reworded the questions printed out in an orderly fashion in the binder in her bag. Call her old school, but having a printed copy as backup just made her more comfortable. Too many times, a technical problem has caused a delay. Today, she would use her laptop but have the binder ready just in cse.

Lord, it's you and me now. I appreciate all the help others have given me, but ultimately, it's you and me. You can take a little and make it work, but if I can somehow give you a lot . . . then WOW. She couldn't help but chuckle at her own prayers. The Lord was probably laughing along with her. On a whim, she sent a quick text to Katie, "He who sits in the heavens laughs." followed by an emoji of a laughing face.

Katie's response was typical, "What???" Tina chuckled and turned her phone off so she could plan while driving.

It was almost 10:00 when she arrived at Saunders

& Johnson. A glance in the rear view mirror before she cut the engine and gathered her things, assured her that hair and makeup were still in good condition. Her new camera bag/purse was packed with everything she would need for the day. It was beautiful, soft brown leather that looked like a purse but inside had partitions and cushioning for her camera and lenses. There was an outside pocket perfect for the iPad or laptop and another which held her personal items. Pushing open the driver door with her foot, Tina remembered the day of the explosion. Hopefully, all the pain and trauma would come to some sort of closure through this. One could only hope.

Tina entered the foyer and stopped dead in her tracks. The entire waiting room was packed with people. All the couches were filled, extra chairs had been brought in and even more people were standing. Coffee cups had been emptied and magazines abandoned, indicating they had been waiting for some time. Surely these folks were not waiting to see her. Jerry had told her there would be four or five clients to meet with and photograph today.

Brenda, the receptionist motioned Tina over. "I'm sorry. I tried to call and warn you but didn't get an answer." Tina cringed, remembering she had turned her phone off so she could think while she drove. Before she could put words to her thoughts, Jerry appeared and ushered her to his office.

"I'm so sorry, Tina. Brenda only contacted four families but word got out and people just started showing up. This group is so close knit, it's difficult to keep anything quiet."

Jerry continued. "If it's OK with you, I have put together a sheet asking each family to write their story in as few words as possible. I was thinking perhaps this would keep them occupied while they wait their turn."

"That's a perfect idea. Thank you, Jerry. I am so sorry to be late. Traffic was horrible. I apologize, I should have called."

"It's fine. I understand completely."

Jerry motioned towards the door at the end of the hall. "We have a quiet place outside where the staff often sits for breaks and lunch. It is in the shade but has good light for most of the day. I was thinking that may work for the photos. Want to take a look before we start?"

"Yes, of course."

The place he suggested was actually very good for photos. The lighting was good and the seating would work well. Back inside, Jerry showed her to the conference room where she and the clients could talk privately before going outside for the photos.

The room was plush and comfortable with a beautiful mahogany table surrounded by straight chairs with leather seats and backs. On one side of the room was a row of windows with sunshine streaming in through the open blinds. "Thanks, Jerry. The light in here is uplifting. We will most likely need something to help dispel the heaviness your clients must be feeling."

Tina quickly positioned her IPad and set the camera to record. There were several legal pads on one end of the table along with a container of pens and a box of tissues. A pitcher of cold water sat in the middle of the table with several glasses beside it. A small bowl of mints completed the set up. Brenda had thought of everything. Tina would use her laptop to make notes as needed.

Sitting at the head of the table felt all too formal so Tina moved around to the side, pulled out two chairs and tried her best to look relaxed. Brenda had sent her a list of all the expected participants for the day. Of course, now that many others had appeared, Tina had no idea how many she would actually interview.

The first name on the list was Debra Calhoun. Mrs. Calhoun worked at the hotel and left her children at the day care center downstairs. She was not hurt that day, but one of her children, four year old Andrew, had been severely burned. Andrew was seven now and led a fairly normal life, but the past three years had been traumatic and painful for him with several surgeries, ongoing counseling, and months of physical therapy.

Jerry had been standing quietly watching Tina with a concerned look on his face. Now he smiled and asked if she was ready for her first interview.

"Yes, thank you. We should get started. They have waited long enough."

"Good." A few minutes later he ushered her first client into the room and introduced Mrs. Calhoun.

Tina stood and extended her hand. "Good morning, Mrs. Calhoun. My name is Tina Brogan and I have been retained by the law firm to put together a more in depth and personal recap of your loss than the official reports show. First, let me express my sincere regret for all you have endured. I was living directly across the street the day of the explosion and saw it firsthand. I cannot imagine the terror you experienced."

"Thank you," Mrs. Calhoun replied quietly. "These past years have surely been the worst of my life. I find the memories of the trauma seem to recur at will. Sometimes I feel I will never be truly at peace again. Of course I shouldn't really say that, since the Lord has been faithful to bring His peace again and again. It's just so hard to hold on to it."

"I understand."

They sat quietly for a moment, Mrs. Calhoun lost in thought and Tina trying to calm her nerves. *What was I thinking? This is way beyond my level of expertise.* Even in the thickness of the silence she felt the Lord's gentle presence. It was indeed out of her depth but never out of His.

Tina took a deep breath and began. "Mrs. Calhoun, I wonder if you would be able to give me a better understanding of your life since the explosion, especially concerning Andrew. We can either video you talking, record only your voice, or you can write it out."

"I believe it would be easier for me to talk it through, if that is OK with you. Can we try the video?"

Tina clicked on the video app on her IPad and motioned to Mrs. Calhoun to begin when she was ready. Outside the window a red Cardinal sat with its little head cocked and looked in the window, as if to ask what the problem was in there. The sunshine was muted as a white cloud passed overhead. The stillness in the room was palpable. Tina waited, hoping Mrs. Calhoun would be able to speak past the tears that were forming in her eyes and threatening to slip down her cheeks.

"Please give me a moment."

"Of course. Take your time."

Finally, after several minutes Mrs. Calhoun cleared her throat, dabbed at her eyes with a tissue and began to speak.

"As usual, I drove in to work about 8:00 that morning with my two children. Andy—we call him Andy—was in his car seat and Mary, my daughter, was buckled in her seat beside him. I parked my car, gathered the children and their bags and went inside. My first stop was at the DayCare Center located just off the lobby. Andy and Mary loved going there. Andy was in a class with three and four year olds. His teacher was Miss Rhonda. Mary was in a separate room with five year olds. Her teacher was Miss Susan. Mary was just beginning kindergarten at the Center and Andy was upset that he could not go in her class too. They gave me a hug goodbye and I went upstairs to the fourth floor break room and poured a cup of coffee. My day was scheduled to start at 8:30 but I liked to get there early and have coffee time before I clocked in. I had just walked into my cubicle and turned on my computer when I heard the explosion. The building literally shook.

I had no idea what it was but then I heard the

screams and my heart dropped. My first thoughts were for the children but before I could make it to the elevator, panic broke out on every side. I got to the stairwell and ran as fast as I could down to the lobby. Smoke was everywhere.

My heart was pounding and it seemed I was moving in slow motion, trying my best to get to the Center's door. Sirens sounded almost immediately. I could hear the children screaming but I could not move fast enough to get to them. Everything seemed to be happening in slow motion. Finally, I made it across the lobby but the center's door was locked. I still do not understand why that door was locked.

People were running from every direction trying to get out of the building while the firemen were trying to get inside. It was pandemonium. Ceiling tiles, sheetrock, all sorts of debris were falling from every direction. I only wanted to get inside the Center. Finally, after what seemed forever, a fireman broke open the door. The flames and smoke were everywhere but through the haze, I could see the children huddled together with their teacher. Mary came running to me out of the back room and I grabbed her arm and pushed her in the direction of the door, yelling at her to run and not stop. I will never forget the look of terror on her face. Thankfully, she obeyed and ran towards the door. I saw her safely reach the outside before turning my attention back to the room, looking for Andy. The firemen were now in the Center and I could see them fighting to reach the children huddled in one corner. It was then I saw Andy. He . . . he . . . was on fire. His shirt was in flames and he was screaming."

At this point, Mrs. Calhoun stopped and bowed her head. Watching the tears slide down her cheeks, Tina had to fight to maintain her own composure. So much pain was evident in this Mama's voice. After a sip of water and a few moments of silent tears, Mrs. Calhoun was able to continue.

"I lunged towards the door but a strong arm grabbed me and held me tight. My kicking and yelling that it was my son did no good. The fireman held me back until another one brought Andy out—still screaming, but thankfully, the fireman had extinguished the flames that had been burning on him. I wanted to hold him and calm his screams but there was nowhere on his body I could touch without hurting him.

Two EMT's took control. They tore off his clothes, put him on a gurney and I ran behind them as they pushed him through the lobby and out the door. The EMT's at the ambulance outside gave him oxygen and began checking his vital signs. Through the smoke, I spied Mary and yelled for her to come to me. Together we sat in the back of the ambulance and prayed while we were driving through Atlanta with sirens blaring and lights flashing. It was only a few minutes to the hospital but it seemed like forever. That ride was the most terrifying of my life. I never want to be in something like that again. Never."

Tina could see the emotional struggle going on inside of her client. Her voice was becoming weaker and weaker as she relived the horror of that day. "Perhaps we should take a short break. Do you need to check on Andy in the waiting room?"

Mrs. Calhoun appeared relieved to be able to get up and move about for a few minutes while Tina called Brenda and requested two coffees. Fifteen minutes later they were settled once again in front of the camera and ready to get back into the telling of that day.

"Once we arrived at the hospital, Andy was taken to the burn unit while Mary and I were instructed to remain in the waiting room. Mary was in shock. I was numb. I don't know, maybe I was in shock as well. I held her in my lap and we sat in the midst of others, not knowing what was going on behind the closed doors of the burn unit.

We were finally allowed to see Andy. My husband arrived and I filled him in on everything. I stayed with Andy and my husband took Mary home. That was the first of many long, agonizing nights. Over the next weeks, Andy underwent three surgeries. He was in unbelievable pain. The pain medicines the doctors gave him caused frightening nightmares. He had flashbacks and hallucinations.

The doctors removed skin from his thighs and grafted it onto his arms and hands. His face had sustained second degree burns. No grafts were necessary, but daily peeling and treating continued for several weeks. Once he was released from the hospital, Andy continued Physical Therapy for nine months. The daily ritual was painful and Andy cried every day for nine months while they worked and stretched his hands and arms, hoping to regain full range of motion.

This last year has been heaven compared to the first two. Andy can play outside again. He has full use of his arms and hands and amazingly his face has healed completely. However, the nightmares continue and his entire personality has changed from a happy, outgoing boy to a quiet and timid one. God has given us a miracle. We are very aware of how fortunate we are to still have him, but at the same time, it is heartbreaking to realize this could all have been avoided if only the hotel management had listened to their maintenance department. They played with people's lives for the sake of a few dollars. I am not normally one to sue but they should pay."

Tina reached over and turned off the camera. She was shaken by what she had just heard. Mrs. Calhoun sat staring out at the little bird while tears streamed down her face. Tina did not speak, but gave her client time to compose herself. After a few minutes, Mrs. Calhoun wiped her face, looked up and smiled.

"I'm sorry. It helps and hurts every time I talk about it."

"Do not apologize. I had no idea what to expect, but I commend you for being able to do this. Thank you."

Not wanting to be unfeeling, but realizing her camera would capture the emotion of the moment, Tina suggested they get Andy and walk outside and take a few photos. Mrs. Calhoun nodded and Tina asked Brenda to bring Andy in to them. Outside in the soft light, Tina was amazed at the tenderness she saw through the lens of her camera. This mother and son had experienced a tragedy and come through with an even deeper love for each other. They were survivors. The photos were going to be beautiful.

Tina wrestled with her own personal memories.

She very much wanted to ask Andy if he knew a little boy named Justin at the day care center, but something stopped her. Perhaps it would be too traumatic for him to talk about that day. After all, his mom had left him in the foyer with an aunt while she came in alone to retell their story. No, it was better to concentrate on her job at this point and leave other probing for a more appropriate time.

Tina said goodbye to Mrs. Calhoun with a promise to send her the pics as soon as possible. The next three client's stories were moving and their losses were just as great but as lunch time approached, the thoughts of little Andy were foremost in her mind. After her last client of the morning, Jerry knocked lightly on the conference room door and asked if she would please join him for lunch.

"I could use a break. I would love to join you for lunch. And this time we can eat lighter, OK?"

Over a quick lunch, Tina brought Jerry up to date on the morning's interviews. He too was moved deeply by little Andy's story, perhaps because of his own son's death that day. Tina had many questions about Billy and why Jerry never talked about him. Could she ask Jerry if he knew a little boy named Justin? Would it be too painful for him? "Excuse me?" Jerry had been talking and Tina had been thinking. He was asking if she was ready to head back. "Yes. I do not want to keep the people waiting any longer than necessary."

After lunch there were eight more interviews, each one heart wrenching. Jerry apologized to those who had not been seen but gathered their written stories and promised to get back with them as soon as another interview day could be arranged.

Tina was scheduled to stay at Katie's that night, but after the day's events, she really wanted to go home. She needed to see Justin and Baby Girl. She needed to hear their voices, their giggles and hold them tight. Just as she finished texting Katie to let her know she would not be coming over, Jerry came out of the building and walked over to where she stood beside her car.

"That was quite a day you had."

"Yes," Tina replied, "I thought I was prepared, but I wasn't. But then, what could prepare you for something like that? So much pain and heartache. Their lives were going along perfectly normal and in the blink of an eye everything changed. It's devastating to think about what they—what you all—have been through."

Jerry looked down at her fondly. "Your tender heart and open emotions are part of what makes you a great photojournalist. You have the ability to put yourself in another's place and relate to their feelings. It comes across in your photos and in your writing. That is one reason I knew you would be perfect for this job."

Tina was surprised at how candidly he complimented her. She saw the same traits in him, that openness and concern for others. It felt good to be in his company and know he understood what she was experiencing. "Thank you, Jerry. That is very kind of you."

"Would you have time to join me for dinner tonight?"

Tina glanced quickly at her watch and thought it would be good to relax a little and give the traffic time to clear before the long drive home. "Yes, that would be nice."

"How about Ruth's Crisp?" Jerry smiled at Tina's attempt to hide her surprise.

"Ruth's Crisp sounds wonderful. A little pricey, but I guess not for you lawyers. You guys travel with the big spenders, huh?"

"I wouldn't say that, but a good meal after a long day is worth paying for. Don't you agree?"

"Absolutely. Especially when I am not the one paying."

Jerry asked if she wanted to drive or ride with him. She decided to drive her own car since the restaurant was in the direction of home. At the restaurant, Jerry met her at her car, opened her door and dropped his arm casually around her waist as they walked inside. He had already called ahead and secured a reservation. The romantic inside her heart smiled while the practical side reminded her that she was not interested in a romantic relationship. Not at the present time. Who knew when she would ever be ready to open her heart again.

Following a delicious meal and a too-big dessert, Jerry suggested they take a walk around Centennial Park. After a few minutes they stopped and sat on a bench, close enough to hear each other but not really touching. "That was such a delicious meal. Thank you again, Jerry. And that dessert! Oh my, I do really need to walk now. Your eating habits could be dangerous for a girl."

"Ahh, you have no need for concern. Plus, I didn't notice you pushing back from any of it."

"Such a gentleman," she laughed and rolled her eyes.

After a time of chit-chat about the food, the people walking by and the weather, their conversation turned towards her work and the explosion. Tina had never spoken to him of her feelings regarding the day of the explosion, but somehow tonight seemed to warrant that.

"I was in a carefree time of my life, doing photo shoots, meeting new folks, making money, everything I had come to Atlanta to accomplish. The explosion changed everything in an instant. At first I was in shock and then I was angry about having the children literally dumped on me. Oh, don't get me wrong, my heart ached for them and how they were suffering. I would never *not* take them, but still, it was hard for me. After a few months my heart changed and I started praying they would stay with me forever. It was all very confusing."

Jerry nodded his understanding and waited for her to continue.

"You know, there was a guy who initially helped me. His name is Barry. He was absolutely wonderful with the kids. I fancied myself in love with him, but that did not work out. He moved to New York with his business. He is apparently in the process of moving back now. And . . . Tina gulped a bit . . . he is in a relationship with my best friend, Katie."

There, she had said it out loud. It hung in the air for a moment before Jerry responded. "Is that alright with you?"

"Yes, actually, it is. It was a surprise—a big surprise, but if I am to be honest, Barry and I never really had a romantic relationship, at least not in reality—only in my mind."

They sat quietly for a bit, each lost in their own thoughts. Jerry broke the silence.

"We have never really talked about it, but I get the feeling that you depend on God more than you say. Is it too personal for me to ask that?"

"No, it isn't too personal. I was raised in church and although my life is not always the example it should be, I do believe in God and I do depend on Him every day. Why do you ask?"

"Because I do too and it is comforting to talk with someone who feels the same. I suspected you were a Christian, not from what you say, but from the honest way you deal with life. Before my wife's death, I was never a religious person. My life was good and religion did not seem necessary, but during those dark months before she passed, prayers seemed to come up out of my heart without my bidding them to. It was like my heart talked in spite of my mind. Little by little the prayers became more important to me until one day I realized I was actually talking to God on a regular basis. That started me wondering if God ever really talked back to anyone. I knew something was happening deep inside me."

Jerry gave a wry half-smile and stared up at the sky for a minute before continuing. Tina sat very still, waiting. In her mind, she replayed how she had ended up in Centennial Park with a handsome lawyer who was broken beyond words. She knew it was important that he speak these things. Not especially to her, but to someone. And so she listened intently when he started to speak again.

"One day my wife was having a particularly difficult day with a lot of pain. I was beside myself as to what to do to help her. I had this weird idea of getting down on my knees beside her bed and praying out loud. She was in so much pain I am not sure she even realized at the moment what I was doing, but later we talked about it. She was a believer and had been since childhood, but I don't think she walked close, you know? We rarely went to church and after she got sick, it was too hard on her, but I would hear her talking to God during the night. After that day I started praying on my knees beside her bed on a daily basis. During one of her better times, she asked if we could talk about it. That is when she explained to me about asking the Lord to take over my life."

Jerry laughed a little and shifted on the bench before continuing. "I was appalled at the idea of turning the reins of my life over to anyone. That was not what my praying was all about. I was praying for God to heal my wife and help us in the life we were living. Turning over my life was never part of the deal.

It is funny to think about it now but I could not

grasp the concept of needing God in areas of my life other than our current situation. That did not deter Marcy. We talked long into the night. She would take a short power nap to regain strength enough to talk again and then she would start over patiently explaining how it all works. I knew the standard salvation talk but it had never penetrated my heart and become personal. That night it did. What finally got my attention was seeing that she was very close to dying and the most important thing she wanted to talk to me about was my relationship with Jesus Christ. When I realized that, I started listening, really listening. Sometime around daylight we prayed together and she cried with me as I sobbed my way to Christ and His forgiveness. It was a time I will never forget. Three days later she slipped peacefully into Heaven during the night.

There were dark days after she died, days when the only thing that kept me going was Billy. And then only a few months later, the explosion took him too. I was very angry with God. Remembering how she loved and trusted Him only made me angrier. My life since I gave it to him had been nothing but pain and, believe me, I told him that on a daily basis.

I am still not sure how or when the anger began to leave. It was a gradual process. Even though I was angry with Him, it was true that he was the only one who could help me. Slowly, I came to understand that He did not do these things to me. Oh, He could have stopped them, but He chose not to. Out of necessity, the verse about all things working together for my good has become my mantra."

On the drive home, Tina thought back on their long conversation, but all she could really remember was the gentleness she saw in his eyes. How strange that he had chosen to open his heart to her on such an intimate level. Jerry was a good man. A very good man.

Later that week, Jerry telephoned to bring her up to date on the case. The hotel lawyers were asking for mediation, explaining they wanted this settled before the grand opening of their new facility. This was exactly what Jerry had hoped for. He explained that mediation was different from an actual court trial. Both parties and their lawyers would meet at a neutral place with a Mediator. Each side would present their case and the Mediator would go between to try and bring an equitable solution for all concerned.

It would be less formal than a court trial, and allow the lawyers to submit extended personal information on their clients. In a class action suit, it was impossible for all the plaintiffs to attend the mediation, thus the need for Tina's presentation.

The next week was spent transcribing and editing the video interviews and photos. Arrangements were made for another interview day. This time Lottie accompanied Tina and helped with the photos. She also made notes while Tina asked questions. This expedited the process and Tina was able to see more clients in one day. Afterward, Lottie was exhausted but with a new insight on the importance of being able to capture emotions and attitudes with the lens of her camera.

Over dinner, Tina discussed the day with Lottie and answered her questions. "I was very proud of you today, you did a good job. I liked the way you interacted with each client. That's a really big part of being a good photographer."

"Oh, Aunt Tina, I was trying, but man, it was hard. I am so tired, I could go to sleep right here in this booth. I'm not even lying!"

Tina snickered. "I understand, I do. It's physically tiring, but on a shoot like today, it's also emotionally and mentally stressful. It takes everything we have to give it our all for such an extended day. But, seriously, you did great. And I will drive home while you sleep."

Jerry continued to spend time with Tina at lunch, dinner and any free time they had during the workday. Once the mediation date was confirmed, they upped the number of interviews for each week. It was exhausting, but necessary. Jerry's attentiveness and understanding of her feelings surprised and pleased her. Still, she was concerned he may be reading too much into their relationship. Barry was a thing of the past and Tina actually enjoyed spending time with him and Katie, however, she was not interested in forming a new and serious relationship. One afternoon after a long day working with the clients at the office, Tina walked to her car with the intention of spending the night with Katie. Barry was in town and the three of them were going out to dinner.

"Hey, what's your hurry?" Tina turned to see Jerry walking down the sidewalk towards her.

"Oh, hey Jerry. No hurry. Just heading over to Katie's and then to dinner."

Jerry's face showed his disappointment. "I had hoped we could have dinner together."

Tina thought for a second. "Why not join us? It's time you met Katie, I have certainly told you enough about her. And, Barry, too. I really think you will like him."

"Are you certain I would not be intruding?"

"Not at all. We would love to have you."

After introductions at Katie's apartment, they drove to their favorite place, The Cheesecake Factory, of course. Tina settled comfortably beside Jerry in the booth across from Katie and Barry. She knew this could get a bit dicey. Still, she was glad for her friends to meet Jerry. She certainly hoped they did not think they were a couple. Still, if she were honest, letting Barry think that would be a bit satisfying. Her snicker made the others look at her with raised eyebrows. "Oh, it's nothing. Just my mind wandering."

Katie was not going to let that go. "Oh?"

Tina gave her a look that silenced her, then another look that said "later."

They all sat quietly for a few minutes, perusing the menu like none of them had ever eaten here. Katie ordered her customary salad and Tina went for the spaghetti. After all orders were placed, the four of them sat staring at nothing. Finally, Barry broke the ice, "So, Jerry, I am glad to finally meet you. Tina has told us a lot about you and the project you guys are working on."

Jerry smiled. "She has told me a lot about you as well."

Tina cringed. This was awkward to say the least.
Barry seemed unfazed. "I hope it wasn't all bad."
Even more awkward.

Jerry chuckled. "No, not at all. In fact she was very complimentary."

Tina could not take it anymore. "OK, obviously there is a huge elephant in the room. And he is not leaving until we talk to him. So, here goes."

Katie let out a little nervous laugh, "Good grief, Tina, just put it all out there, why don't you?"

"Well, look. Jerry knows all about Barry and you. All about how I thought I was in love with Barry and then thought you had betrayed me. I explained that Barry is a great guy and you are my best friend. The two of you are perfect together and I have no animosity and no desire to go over all that again. So, let's just get on with our meal and be comfortable together. OK?"

The chuckles and mumbles around the table made it clear they were all in agreement.

Tina spoke up again. "So, can we bless the food before it gets here please? I'm starving."

Katie shrugged her shoulders, "Since you seem to have the floor. Why don't you pray?"

Tina shrugged back and bowed her head. "Lord, thank you for good friends who understand me and love me anyway. Please bless the food. Thank you Lord. Amen."

When they opened their eyes, the waitress was standing quietly beside their table holding a large tray loaded with food. "Oh, goodness, I am sorry," Tina said.

The waitress smiled and replied, "No problem."

Afterwards, back at Katie's apartment, they sat together in the living room and over a pot of coffee the conversation grew serious. Listening to him converse with her friends was pleasing, but also a bit concerning. Hearing him relate some of their experiences made her wonder if he had more than a friendship in mind. She certainly hoped not.

Tina's attention returned to the talk at hand when she realized they were discussing the day Justin and Baby Girl had been literally dropped in their laps. Tina was certain Jerry was not enjoying this turn in the conversation and yet he seemed perfectly content to listen to Barry and Katie as they described the turmoil it had caused. They explained how often the three of them had attempted to locate the missing parents. Tina's heart froze when she saw the sadness pass over Jerry's face. She recognized the "if only" expression and knew he was thinking of Billy.

Jerry sat quietly listening while Katie and Barry rambled on about their search for Justin and Baby Girl's parents. When the talk quieted down, Jerry mentioned that tomorrow was a work day and he needed to call it a night. He thanked them for the invite and stood to leave. Tina walked with him to the door and out onto the landing. Jerry stood for a moment with his hands in his pockets, looking out over where the new hotel was almost finished. Tina stood silently beside him, not wanting to invade his thoughts.

"Before my wife became ill, she worked at the hotel. Billy was just an infant then. The three of us drove in together when my schedule allowed. I would walk up the street to my office; she would take Billy into the day care and then go upstairs to the hotel offices where she worked. Since she passed, I had been taking Billy to the center every workday. He liked going there. There was another little boy named Billy there too. They were the same age and liked to pretend they were brothers because they had the same name. Isn't that funny? At three years old they thought the same name meant they were brothers. No matter if it was their first names that were the same. They were inseparable. The teacher allowed them to sit together as long as they were good during story time. And they were. He was a good boy.

The other Billy and his dad had just walked into the lobby. I remember Billy waving and wanting to go to him but I held his hand and would not let him. I needed my morning hug before I let him go. The explosion happened before I could get him to the daycare. I remember him holding my hand, pulling on it. Then he was gone. Just like that—he was gone. Three weeks later I came out of a drug induced coma and my life has never been the same. Miraculously, my burns were mostly second degree with only a small patch of third degree on my neck. My leg was broken and my ankle was crushed. I had bruises over most of my body. I still do not understand how the EMT's found me so quickly but it took several days to locate Billy. My memory of those last few minutes is foggy. According to my psychiatrist my mind has suppressed what is too painful to remember. Either way, I am not at all certain I want to remember."

They stood quietly in the dark for a few moments, and then, very gently, Jerry leaned down and placed a soft, quick kiss on her lips. Tina's heart fluttered unexpectedly and before she could respond in any way, he was off and down the steps without a word.

Oh, Jesus. What just happened? Her heart was a mixture of sorrow, excitement and a strange fluttering. Walking back inside, Tina could not hide the little smile that played around the corners of her mouth. Katie and Barry exchanged a knowing look as she passed through the living room and into her bedroom, closing the door behind her. Tina heard the laughter coming from the living room. No matter. Jerry had just stolen a tiny bit of her heart. Now what???

CHAPTER ELEVEN

DFACS

B ack home in Chickpea, Tina's parents were enjoying their time with the children. Justin was now in the first grade and Baby Girl was at least three. The DFACS worker was talking about giving them legal names and changing their status to make them available for adoption. Thus far, Tina had been able to postpone the change. The fact that everyone in Chickpea knew the situation, including the people at DFACS, helped make that possible. That was one more benefit of living in a small town. Still, they all knew the time was limited and one day they would need to face that decision.

As much as Grandma Joan enjoyed having the

children in her care, she had to admit it was taking a toll on her. Granddad helped, but the day-to-day care was left to her. She dared not say anything to Tina, for fear she would give up the job she was doing in Atlanta. She sighed and reminded herself there were only a few weeks left before the mediation. After that, Tina would be back in Chickpea and the heavy responsibility would be off Joan.

One sunny afternoon Grandma was working in the flowerbed while the kids ran around with Pepsi. It was hot and the bending and stooping was making it even hotter. Grandma raised up, looked at Justin and asked if he was ready for something cold to drink. He nodded and grinned as Baby ran up announcing that she was "thursty" too. A few minutes later they were settled in the porch swing with lemonade and a few cookies to hold off hunger until dinner time.

Pepsi came lumbering around the corner of the house and flopped down in the grass just at the edge of the porch steps. Something about the way she was walking caught Grandma's eye and a flicker of recognition hit her. "Pepsi, come here girl." The dog looked at her with tired eyes but clearly had no intention of moving. Grandma got up and sat on the steps beside her, rubbing the rather round belly. "O, my goodness, Pepsi girl. Have you gone and got yourself pregnant? How in the world did you manage that?" At this, the dog looked up, cocked her head, and stared at Grandma with a look of innocence.

Justin was off the swing and beside her in a flash. "Pregnant? Does that mean she is going to have puppies???"

Grandma wished she had bit her tongue before thinking out loud, but the damage was done. The secret was out. How in the world had this happened? Baby girl joined them giggling and rubbing Pepsi's head and repeating over and over, "puppies, we have puppies?" There were so many questions flying through the air, Grandma had no time to answer one before the next three came at her.

Thinking back, she realized Pepsi had been a bit sluggish lately, and had been gaining weight. She attributed it to the warm weather and being outside all day, but now she remembered the pretty German Shepard that had been in the yard several times a few weeks earlier. Tina was going to love this! Granddaddy too. Pepsi pregnant—and on her watch. O, goodness. Thanks to Pepsi, the household drama had just kicked up a level.

Well, perhaps this would give Justin something to take his mind off what he heard on a regular basis around the dinner table. Working with the families and survivors of the explosion kept the drama of it all in the forefront when Tina was at home. Justin had only a vague memory of that day, but it was impossible to keep from him that his mom and dad were missing. He was a bright six-year-old and well aware of his surroundings. Occasionally, he would ask questions like, "Will my daddy ever come and get me?" Joan was not sure if he wanted his daddy to come and get him or was concerned that he might. Tina had become his Mom and life in Chickpea was all he knew.

Becca jumped full on into her research for Tina. Because she was on Tina's payroll and had signed a confidentiality agreement, Jerry was able to procure a list for her of all the children who were in the DayCare on a regular basis. Joan had started helping Becca on the downlow. She was interested in delving into the information to look for anything she could find on Justin or Baby Girl. Surprisingly, there was no mention of a boy named Justin.

Trying to determine why no Justin was shown, she wondered if at two or three years old, the child had not spoken plainly and they had his name wrong. But, no names were listed that even sounded like Justin. She knew that in the years to come Justin would have questions concerning his parents and she desperately wanted to have answers for him.

Joan also looked for Jerry's son, Billy. There was a William Andrews and also a William Brownlee. Either or both of them could have been called Billy, but Jerry's last name was Williams. It was a mute point since neither of the boys had checked into the center on the morning of the explosion. How fortunate for them to miss school on that day. It appeared to be another dead end. She closed her laptop and pondered what could be the answer to Justin's name not being on the list.

Joan was relaxing later that afternoon while the children napped, when the doorbell rang. She stood, straightened her clothes, smoothed her hair and walked hesitantly down the long hallway to the front of the house. Through the glass window in the front door, Joan saw their DFACS representative standing on the porch. Oh no. And Tina was not home. Fortunately, Joan knew the Social Worker not only from her visits to the house, but the young lady had grown up in Chickpea.

"Hello Amanda, please come in."

"Thank you, Mrs. Brogan. I apologize for coming

without calling, but my new supervisor insisted it was time for an unannounced visit."

"Of course. I understand. You are welcome anytime. How is your mother, dear?"

"She's fine. Enjoying retirement and grandchildren you know. Actually, Mrs. Brogan, I was hoping to be able to talk with Tina."

"Well, she is in Atlanta today, working on a job there."

"Oh, is she thinking of moving back to the Atlanta area?"

"Oh, no. She commutes back and forth several times a week. This job is a temporary one. Can I help you with something?"

"I am sure you could, but my supervisor would not be happy with me if I did not talk to Tina directly on this issue. Can you tell me when she will be available?"

"She will be home late this evening but I am not sure about her plans for tomorrow. Perhaps she can call you and set up a time?"

"Hummm . . . I suppose that will have to do, although that eliminates the unannounced visit. OK, since I am here, perhaps you and I should at least talk about the children and how they are adjusting."

The next hour was spent going over the children's routine. After naptime was over, Amanda inspected their bedrooms and spent time talking with Justin to determine what he liked about living in Chickpea. Justin was accustomed to the drill by now and gave his normal answers assuring them that he was very happy. Baby Girl, at three, only played with Amanda and gave her answers in the sweetness that oozed from her little smile.

As soon as Amanda left, Joan was on the phone to Tina. Something was up, she could feel it in her bones. Their time was running out and Tina needed to get back here and do something. "Yes Ma'am, I will be home around nine tonight and will call Amanda first thing tomorrow and set up an appointment. I understand. Thanks, Mom."

Tina turned off her phone and sat pondering her mom's account of the afternoon. Yes, she agreed with her mom. Something was brewing. She sensed it as well. The drive home that evening allowed the quiet time she needed to evaluate all that was happening with DFACS. After a while of imagining the worst possible scenarios and working through each of them, she did her best to leave it with God and concentrate on something else.

Her mind wandered to Jerry. The kiss on the landing outside of Katie's apartment had confused her at the time. It was very different from the one she shared with Barry way back when. Still, after pondering on it for a bit, she decided it was just the surprise of the moment. In addition, with DFACS getting pushy, she definitely had no time for romance. That much she knew!

The mediation was only two weeks away and most of her work was finished. The final draft was due in three days, which would leave another week to make any tweaks and then have more copies printed for the mediation. Tina had not yet shown Jerry any of the photos. She had tried, but he always had a reason not to look at them. She knew it was because of his son and the horrible memories of his death.

Again, she wondered why he was even allowed to be involved in the legalities of the case when he was so very connected to it. In a few days she would be finished with her stint at the law office and she and Jerry would have no reason to keep in contact. Truthfully, she was relieved to put some space between them.

If only DFACS would hold off a few weeks before starting to apply pressure about making Justin and Baby Girl available for adoption. She was so close to having answers, so close. This mediation was going to bring things to light in several ways. Upon closer inspection, Tina found a blurred image of Justin in the background of one of her photos. It was taken as he came out of the burning building, but he was not with the lady who brought him to Tina.

She had also found another photo of the lady carrying Baby Girl. It only showed half of her face and that was blurred but still, someone could very well recognize her. So, perhaps Justin walked out alone. They all knew he wasn't Baby Girl's sister. So, why would the lady bring him with her to Tina and Barry? It was all very confusing. Both photos were included in the book she was putting together for the mediation. The photos along with family backgrounds and personal accounts from several of the victims were definitely going to play a part in the proceedings.

Amanda arrived at the Brogan house early the next morning. Apparently, she did not want to talk to Tina first, but wanted a surprise visit. This time she was accompanied by her supervisor, an older lady who had recently transferred from the Atlanta office. Tina walked down the hall and casually glanced out the window in the front door. Oh, no! The new supervisor was none other than Ms. McGowen. Tina's heart dropped. *Noooooo . . .*

Amanda was surprised to discover Tina and Ms. McGowen knew each other. After the pleasantries, Tina invited Ms. McGowen and Amanda to join

Joan and her in the living room. As they walked down the hallway, Amanda and Tina shared a knowing look. Obviously it had not taken Amanda very long to discern the type of office Ms. McGowen expected to run.

"I will not waste your time nor mine, Tina. It is past time for both children to be placed up for adoption. Now, either you will apply along with any other prospective parents that may wish to be considered, or we will remove them from your home and place them in another Foster Care until an adoption can be completed. The decision is yours. I understand you are currently not living here in Chickpea?"

Tina's reserve to be polite was wearing thin, but she managed a calm reply. "I think you have been misinformed, Ms. McGowen. I am currently living here and have been since my move from Atlanta over a year ago. My contract in Atlanta is a short term commitment. In fact, it will be completed in two weeks."

"I see. Well, you have exactly two weeks to give us your answer. At that time we will either begin the process of investigating you in regards to the adoption or the children will be removed."

"Ms. McGowen, what would happen if the birth parents were found after the adoption was final?"

"I seriously doubt that is going to happen. However, if such a thing were to occur, it would be placed in the court's hands to decide the fate of the children. Now, if that is all, I have other stops to make so I will say goodbye and wait to hear from you."

With one of her tight smiles, Ms. McGowen marched stiffly out of the living room with Amanda at her heels. At the door, Joan said a polite good-bye while Amanda and Tina exchanged looks of frustration. Well, at least Tina had an advocate in Amanda, which was something, but this ultimatum could not have come at a worse time.

CHAPTER TWELVE

I Couldn't Stop Myself

It was a sunny morning as Tina drove up I-75 towards Atlanta. How many times she had driven this route. Her little SUV could probably make the trip alone if necessary. Tina glanced over at her bag, holding the culmination of almost three months' work for Lottie, Becca and herself. Becca had been a great asset with the research. She weeded out anyone who would not present a favorable profile and added some who had been overlooked. Together they had narrowed it down to twenty-five examples to include in the mediation book.

Of course, the lawyers could not include each and every one of the plaintiffs in their presentation, so Tina's was meant to be more personal and tug on the heartstrings. Her photographs were some of the best she had ever taken. The emotions stirred by the interviews had come through clearly in her photos. Yes, she was pleased with the results of their efforts.

She still had not convinced Jerry to look at the photos; hopefully today he would be able to bring himself to do that. She wondered again why Jerry had not insisted on a DNA test from his son's body. It would seem a natural thing to ask. Of course he had been in a coma for three weeks and was overcome by grief and shock. By the time he regained consciousness, Billy's little body was long buried. He had faced the horrible death of his child, just a few months after his wife's death. She shuddered. How horrible. Sometimes she could feel such pain coming from him it was almost physical.

Will Jerry ever be truly happy again? Will he come to a place where he is not just existing, but actually living? Loving even? He seemed to open his heart to her, but then again, how would she know? She only knew what he chose to expose. How about his deep memories, his deep hurt? Would he ever be able to overcome that and be free to love? Really love. Or, was the magic of that deep love lost to him? Could he ever feel that again? And what did any of it matter to her? He was a good friend and she respected him. But that is where it stopped. At least for her. Questions ran through her heart like rolling thunder, starting out with a bang and then rumbling on and on until they faded into the distance.

She rolled into the parking lot of the law office right on time. The waiting room was calm and orderly with a few people on the comfy couches. Brenda greeted her with a smile and a slight wave. "Today's meeting will be held in Mr. Johnson's office."

The meeting started promptly at 9:00 A.M. Tina enjoyed working with Mr. Johnson and over the past weeks she had grown fond of the older gentleman with his stern manner. He was one of those people who earned respect easily with his confident and precise ways. And yet, Tina found him to be almost granddaddy gentle at times. It was easy to understand why his clients put their trust in his abilities.

Mr. Johnson looked over Tina's presentation without comment. She had spent weeks preparing the stories and photos in a pleasing layout and yet he took only a few minutes to inspect it. As he finished the last page and closed her book, Tina braced herself. She was not prepared for his smile of appreciation and glowing words of praise. Tina breathed deeply, not realizing until that moment she had been holding her breath.

Mr. Johnson did have one question. It was concerning one of the photos she had taken on the morning of the explosion. He turned the book around so she could see and pointed directly to the photograph of Baby Girl and the lady carrying her. His finger trembled ever so slightly as he pointed to the baby. "I remember seeing that baby. I was at the hotel that morning. Thankfully, I left before the explosion. The lady was holding her baby and standing at the desk when I left. She was asking if she could leave the baby for the day. I had completely forgotten that until I saw this photo. Do you have any information on what happened to the two of them?"

Tina sat with her mouth literally hanging open. How could she admit this was Baby Girl? How could she not? Mr. Johnson stared at her. She could not find her voice. Something in Mr. Johnson's calm and quiet demeanor triggered something deep inside her. After what seemed forever, Tina began to talk. Over three years of pain, confusion, fear and love poured out. She told him everything—how she had first wanted to find the parents, but as time passed and she became more attached to the children, her efforts lessened. She showed him the photograph of Justin that day. She explained her search and the uselessness of it all. Tina paused, blew her nose loudly and stared at him in disbelief. Had she actually just confided in the very man that was in charge of her job at the moment? *Please God, make me stop!*

But she could not stop. The door had opened and her emotions were too powerful to hold back. Tina explained the ultimatum DFACS had issued and her fear of locating the birth parents after finalizing the adoption. She managed to stop short of asking for his legal help, but just barely.

Mr. Johnson spoke gently. "You and Jerry have worked closely together on this case. Does he know all of this?"

She didn't expect that question. Why would he ask that? "He knows most of it. The latest meeting with Children's Services was yesterday and I have not talked with him about that yet. And he has not seen these photographs. I suppose the pain of looking over them is too much for him. He always has an excuse to avoid looking at them."

Mr. Johnson was quiet for a few moments. Tina sat in despair, struggling with her emotions and wondering why in the world she had gone to such lengths to explain her circumstances today of all times. And to her current boss at that! What if keeping this information from him compromised her position in some way? What if it compromised the firm's? Is that why he asked about Jerry knowing everything? Did she just get him in trouble too? Tina was working to calm her nerves and stop the shaking going on inside her, but without success. *Dear God, what was I thinking????*

"I knew, of course, that you were keeping two of the children from the explosion. Jerry filled me in before I agreed to hiring you." He paused and studied her for a moment before continuing. "I am certain these past years have been traumatic for you. I appreciate you telling me your story in your own words. I commend you for your determination to help these children. They are fortunate to have you."

Mr. Johnson looked at her evenly for several more minutes before standing and extending his hand. "You have surpassed my expectations. This book will be a great asset to our case. And knowing that you did this under the pressure of being intricately involved impresses me even more.

As for your personal situation, I would like to help you. Let me have a couple of days to gather more information and I will get back with you. And please, Tina, do not feel you have jeopardized your position here. If anything, you have gained my confidence in a greater way. The fact that you were willing to share your personal struggles so eloquently impresses me. I feel certain we will be able to use you in future cases. I will be in touch soon."

Tina walked out of Mr. Johnson's office and straight into Jerry. She quickly accepted his offer of a cup of Starbuck's and a time to recap her meeting. Walking down the shiny hardwood floors towards the lobby, the only sound was the soft clicking of her heels and the beating of her heart.

Tina ordered a vanilla bean latte and left Jerry to collect their orders while she found a clean table in a quiet corner. Laying everything out for Mr. Johnson had lifted a weight from her shoulders, but now she struggled wondering if she had put the case or Jerry in jeopardy. She still wanted to question Jerry on so many things that did not add up, first of all to ask him again to view the photos and then about the absence of a DNA test.

Jerry smiled from the counter while he waited on their names to be called. Just as he picked up the two cups and started her way, she heard his cell phone ring. Setting the cups on her table, he removed his phone from his coat pocket, tapped the screen and answered. His smile quickly faded, he nodded and mumbled something about being on his way and slipped the phone back in his coat pocket. "I'm sorry, Tina. I have to go. My Mom is in the hospital. I will call you as soon as I can."

Tina was stunned. Jerry had rarely mentioned his mother, only that she lived north of Atlanta on the outskirts of Chattanooga. Could today get any more bizarre? An hour later, Tina was in her car and driving down I-75 South. The thought of Chickpea and the children was most welcome, but as she drove, conversations with Jerry played out in her mind in rapid succession. She had needed to vent, explain, whine, to Jerry. And now this. Once again, Tina chided herself for being selfish. Of course his mother needed him. And of course he should go. He is a good son, a good man. And by her own confession, he is only a friend. Not really someone she should be pouring out her heart to. Or was he?

CHAPTER THIRTEEN

Becca's Research

Grandma Joan and Becca were sitting at the dining room table with their heads huddled over the laptop when she came in the door. The startled look on their faces told Tina there was something going on that she needed to know. "Hey guys, what's going on?"

Tina dropped her camera bag/purse on the table and her mom stood to give her a chair in front of the screen. This day was completely out of hand and Tina wasn't sure what to expect next. Becca opened up a list of the children who were actually enrolled in the day care center on a regular basis. Another list showed the ones who had already checked in the morning of the explosion. Her mom slipped into the kitchen and returned with a glass of iced tea for Tina.

She sipped the tea slowly and looked over the lists on the screen. "I'm sorry. It's been a crazy day already. I'm not sure what you are trying to show me here. I thought we were finished with all this. What am I missing?"

Becca looked over at Joan before she began, "Jerry's last name is Williams, right?"

"Yes."

"Well, there isn't a child with that last name showing on any list."

"Oh. Really?" Tina sighed. "I already knew that. Kinda. I admit it is strange, but confirms my suspicions that he was actually Billy's step-father. Why on earth would Jerry fabricate a story about a son he did not have? That is crazy reasoning. He never mentioned that he was Billy's step dad, but that would explain the name difference, and his failure to investigate back when he was first told of his son's death. Either way, I am sure there is a logical explanation. There must be. Jerry's grief is obviously very real."

And yet, there was that nagging question simmering just below the surface of her heart.

For the next hour, they went over records online from the day of the explosion. They dug into the law office's files from the hospital records, the EMT's reports, the records from the hotel and from DFACS but there was not a child named Williams. Finally, Tina stood and rubbed her neck. "I can't do this any longer. It's been a long day and I just need to relax my brain and spend some time with the children. Thank you, Becca, for allowing Lottie to watch them. She does a great job with them."

"Of course," Becca replied. "And you are right, it's enough for today. We can start again tomorrow, or whenever you feel up to it."

Grandma Joan stood as well, pushed her chair back and stood smiling. "Tina, there is one more small thing you should know."

Tina knew that look on her mom's face well. She probably was not going to like what came next. "OK, Mom. Let's have it."

"It seems Pepsi is going to give us some puppies in the not too distant future."

"Ummm . . . not too distant as in one day she can have pups, or not too distant as in, it is imminent?"

Grandma smiled that smile and Tina knew it was imminent. "How in the world did that happen?" Grandma Joan and Becca both laughed and Grandma said, "I asked Pepsi that same thing and I am telling you, the dog looked at me like I had two heads."

Tina laughed, imagining the look. "Do we know

how close the day is, and who is the responsible party?"

Joan explained about the German Shepherd and Pepsi's behavior change and suggested they make an appointment with the vet as soon as possible. She assured her that Justin and Baby already knew and were over the moon excited.

"Now, let's order pizza! No one wants to cook and I, for one, am starving."

Tina shrugged, knowing it was too late to close that door now. The puppies were coming, like it or not. At this point, she was not quite sure how she felt, but she thought it would be good for Justin and Baby.

Tina excused herself and headed upstairs to get the children for dinner "Mommy!" Justin met her at the top of the stairs and almost knocked her over when she squatted to catch his flying hug. Baby was right behind him with the biggest smile ever.

"Oh, guys. Y'all look so good to me! I need to hear all about your day."

"PUPPIES" both of them shouted at the same time while dancing up and down. Her mom was right, they were over the moon.

Lottie was busy picking up toys in the playroom and stuck her head out to give Tina a thumbs up. "It's happening."

After dinner, bath time and reading one too many books, the kids were settled for the night. Tina lay quietly thinking over her day. So much had happened, Mr. Johnson and her outburst, Jerry's mother, Pepsi, and the strange thing about Billy's name not being on the list. As she drifted off to sleep that night, she had a vague foreboding deep inside. Something was up. Something that may not be welcome in this family, and especially not to her friendship with Jerry.

Early the next morning, she was awakened by her chiming cell phone. Jerry's voice was calm and relaxed so she assumed his mom must be doing better. "It was a scare, but tests showed a treatable blockage. Mom had a stent inserted yesterday afternoon. They kept her overnight and will release her later today. My sister is staying with her and dad for a few days to make sure she obeys the doctor's orders."

"I am glad to hear that, Jerry. It is difficult when our parents reach that age where we realize they are not indestructible after all."

"Yeah. And I think that is exactly where I am coming to. But, on another note, do you have plans for today?"

"Ummmm . . . nothing I can't change. What's up?" Tina's mind was doing that thing again where instead of waiting for an answer, it ran in circles. Did she *want* to see Jerry today?

"What would you say to my driving straight down from TN and spending the afternoon with you? I would love to meet your children and your family. Perhaps we can take the kids on a short outing—maybe you can show me around the big town of Chickpea. And if possible, the mediation book?"

"Oh . . . Well, that would be nice, Jerry. I would enjoy it and so would the children. What time do you think you will be here?"

"Let's see, it is 7:30 now. Oh, I'm sorry . . . were you awake?"

"I am now," Tina laughed.

"Sorry, I was up early because I wanted to catch the doctor when he made his rounds. I am leaving the hospital in a few minutes and I should be in Chickpea about 1:00 if the traffic isn't too bad."

"That's perfect. We will be ready and waiting."

"We have much to discuss. See you in a few hours."

Tina lay staring at the ceiling and pondering over their conversation. Much to discuss? Whatever could he mean? This, combined with their findings last night, could make for an interesting day. Very interesting.

At 1:00 sharp, Jerry pulled into the drive in his Mustang convertible. The top was down, the sun was shining and Jerry was looking pretty good. Tina's heart did a tiny flip. Good grief! Where was this friendship going? Only God knew and He wasn't telling her anything!

Her mom and dad were anxious to meet Jerry. In order to not so subtly have their inquisition with Jerry, Mom had cooked a delicious lunch of homemade chicken pot pie and a tossed salad. The aroma of baking pastry over bubbling chicken filled the house. No one—ever—would not think it was a warm and homey place. Grandma Joan was an expert at putting folks at ease.

The children were down for their nap when Jerry came into the house. Tina had planned it that way for two reasons. One, they needed to be rested before their afternoon out and two, she wanted time with Jerry and her parents before introducing Justin and Baby into the mix.

Mom was warm and hospitable and Dad was kind and quiet. He normally reserved his corny jokes until he had a chance to interrogate the newbie. Mom inquired about Jerry's mother and then they sat and talked for a while about nothing specific. Weather. Sports. The area.

The timer dinged and Mom excused herself to

put lunch on the table. Right on cue, Baby started crying upstairs. Tina laughed and headed up the stairs to get her. By the time she had Baby changed and ready, Justin was awake and in the bathroom. Soon, all three were ready to descend the steps and meet Jerry.

Entering the living room from behind Jerry and her Dad, Tina was talking and laughing with the children when Jerry stood and turned around. His face went white, his mouth fell open and right before her eyes, he began to tremble. Justin quickly hid behind her and Baby wrapped her arms tighter around her neck. What in the world?

Grandma Joan came to the rescue, grabbing Justin and Baby and making a quick exit to the front porch. Dad stood and moved over to stand beside Jerry with his hand on Jerry's shoulder. Tina was stunned. How could he react like that in front of her children? Her anger was thinly veiled as she walked over and laid her hand on his arm.

Jerry sat down weakly, and looked at Tina with tear filled eyes. "I am so sorry, Tina. It's Justin. He looks so much like Billy. I often imagine what he would look like now and Justin is so close. I never expected him to look so much like Billy. There is no doubt that Billy is dead. The coroner assured me it was his body they found. There was even evidence of a broken finger. Billy had a broken finger when he was a year old. It was him. I know that. I probably scared Justin half to death. Please, let me get it together here and maybe I can talk to him."

"It's OK, Jerry. I understand. You look like you have seen a ghost." Actually, she wasn't sure it really was OK. Not at all.

A few minutes later, they joined Grandma and the children on the front porch. At first Justin was hesitant to come close to Jerry, but after a few minutes of Jerry explaining that he was not feeling well and apologizing for scaring him, Justin ventured close enough to shake hands like a big guy. Tina watched with a lump in her throat. She was so very proud of her son. *Her son.* At that moment, she knew what her decision would be. Justin was her heart son and she would adopt him. They had all lived in limbo long enough.

The lunch was lively with Justin impressing them with stories; most of them conjured up in his mind. Baby was a charmer as usual with her smiles and jabber. As soon as lunch was finished, they loaded the children into the back seat and were ready to drive away when Justin timidly asked if Pepsi could join them. Tina started to explain that it would be too crowded but before she could speak, Jerry answered.

"Of course. What's a good ride in the country

without your favorite dog?" Justin's smile quieted any objection she had and in a few minutes Pepsi was happily barking her way into the back seat. The oversized, pregnant, doggie sat prominently in between Justin and Baby Girl, as if she alone was responsible for their safety.

The first few minutes were filled with Justin's account of Pepsi's pending motherhood. Jerry smiled and nodded and looked questioningly at Tina while Justin rattled on. "She's gonna have fifteen puppies! And we're keeping 'em all. And Grandad and I are building pens and houses. You wanna help Mr. Jerry?"

Jerry chuckled and looked in the rear view mirror. "Well, now, I surely would like that. We'll talk to your granddad about it when we get home. How about that?"

Justin pumped his fists in the air, "Yes!"

Justin entertained them with prospective names of each of the 15 pups. Baby Girl chimed in with her selection of names, most of them exactly like Justin's. After taking the scenic tour around Chickpea they drove out into the country, stopping occasionally to explore a creek or a grassy meadow made for running. By now, the children were accustomed to her camera. Justin did not stop to wait for the shutter click, but Baby Girl made it a point to pose at every opportunity. Her favorite was a hand on hip stance with attitude oozing.

Tina thought back to when she and Barry had spent a Christmas Eve wandering through the countryside. She remembered the kiss that did not happen. And she remembered her confusion over that. It had taken a long time to understand their relationship, but now it was all clear. God had things in control all along, He just had not felt the need to enlighten her.

And what about now? What are you not telling me about today? Perhaps it was the sunshine or the children's excitement about riding in a convertible or maybe it was that Tina had learned to trust a bit more. Whatever it was, she was content to let God reveal His purposes in His time. Even her mind was abnormally calm and peaceful.

"It's so good to just wander through the woods today. These last few days have been a whirlwind. I don't normally get overwhelmed, but my goodness! It's been a mess! And I haven't even had time to tell you everything."

Jerry smiled and slipped his arm around her waist. "I have never seen you be overwhelmed at anything. You appear to always be in control."

"Well, trust me, appearances can be deceiving."

"So, what haven't you had time to tell me?"

They found a grassy spot and sat together while they watched the children run around. Pepsi was not interested in running today. Her time was close and all she wanted to do was lay and enjoy the sunshine. Tina laughed to herself. She was definitely not in the same condition as Pepsi, but she did enjoy sitting in the sunshine.

While she pulled out the sippy cup for Baby and the water bottles for the rest of them, Jerry leaned back on his elbows and waited. Tina kept one eye on the kids while she explained the ultimatum DFACS has lowered. "So, I am 95% ready to start adoption proceedings. I do want to try and hold off until after the mediation. It is possible we will find the parents. What do you think?"

"I think you have already decided exactly how you will proceed. Am I right?"

She could not help but laugh. This guy knew her too well already. "Maybe," was all she could say.

Both children fell asleep on the way home and Jerry stopped and put up the top so they could rest better. Even Pepsi surrendered to a quiet nap. When they arrived home, he carried Justin up the steps and into his room while Tina took Baby to her crib. Standing back and looking at the sleeping beauty, Tina was surprised to see how much she filled the crib. Time was passing quickly and soon even Baby would be ready for preschool. And a new bed. And a real name. Who was she kidding? Baby too, is hers now. Of course she would adopt her and do all in her power to give her a good life. And if by chance, the real mom appeared one day, they would work it out. Somehow. Tina wiped the tear from her cheek and turned to leave when she heard Baby mumble in her sleep. "Mommy." That was all and then the thumb went back in her little mouth and all was quiet.

Downstairs, Jerry was having a cup of coffee with her mom and dad. Later, they enjoyed her mom's dinner and talked about the day. After a bit, Jerry asked if they could sit on the porch for a while. Outside the air was cool and soft. Dusk settled gently over them. The sky was striped orange and blue as the sun began to slip slowly behind the trees. It was a perfect end to a delightful day.

Jerry stretched and spoke softly, "I suppose I had better start back. Atlanta is two hours away."

"Why not spend the night here?" Tina suggested. "We have an extra room. This house rambles on forever. When we were growing up it was full all the time. Anyway, I am sure Mom would not mind. You can leave early before traffic gets bad and be in Atlanta in time for work."

"Actually, that sounds wonderful. I am a little

tired to be honest and I have my bag from TN so I am covered on that end."

"Then it's a deal."

The sun dipped completely below the horizon and a peaceful darkness covered them. The tree frogs sang their songs, the wind rustled the trees and the rockers squeaked against the wooden floor. Tina smiled to herself. There were still many questions but for now, it was enough to relax with a good friend.

Jerry's voice broke through the silence. "Tina, I know I have been postponing looking at the photos in your book. I apologize for that, but you saw my reaction to seeing Justin today. I have been dreading looking at the photos you took that morning. Mr. Johnson has not yet announced who will accompany him at the actual mediation. In case he requests my attendance, I need to be aware not only of what is included in the book, but I must ensure that my own emotions are under control. With that in mind, I am wondering if we could go over the book in the morning before I leave for the office. This has been such a good day, I do not want to stir up those memories and have to deal with them tonight. Would you have time in the morning? It would need to be very early."

Tina breathed a long sigh of relief and thanked

God in her heart for this answer to prayer. "Of course, Jerry, that's a good idea. I really do not want to go into that tonight either. You are right; it has been a very good day. Let's leave it on a happy note and start over with the book in the morning."

After a couple of chocolate chip cookies and a glass of milk at the kitchen table with her mom and dad, she and Jerry each made their way up the stairs. After showing him to the spare room, Tina lay in her bed staring into the darkness with the biggest smile on her face. What a day! She could not remember when she had enjoyed herself quite so much. Walking along beside the creek holding hands with Jerry, listening to the kids giggle and Pepsi bark, the warm hug Jerry gave her when they parted on the porch, just the nearness of him, warmed her heart. With Jerry asleep a few doors down the hall, both children tucked away after a small dinner and a relaxing bath by their Grandma, all seemed right with the world. Uh oh, this was definitely not in her plan.

Thank you, God, for showing me the right direction to take. Thank you for bringing Justin and Baby Girl into my life. And now, Jerry. Oh, God, could it be that something will develop between us? My heart is holding back but little by little I can feel him inching his way in. And, thank you for giving me peace about the adoption. I know it is the right thing to do, I am certain of that now. Tina knew the Lord was listening, that He was close and that He understood. She drifted into a peaceful sleep.

The alarm on her phone seemed especially loud the next morning. Perhaps it was because her sleep had been sweet and uninterrupted. Tina stretched, rolled over to turn the alarm off and snuggled back down in her pillow. Just as she was dozing, she remembered. Jerry spent the night. Goodness, she had better get showered and dressed before he made his way downstairs. Her room had a private bath, but Jerry would need to step out into the hall to reach the guest bathroom to shower. Not a good idea to run into him before that happened. Nope, not a good thing at all.

Downstairs, Tina found her mom already busy in the kitchen. The coffee smelled delicious and bacon frying completed the perfect morning aromas. "Good morning, Mom. Thank you so much for letting Jerry stay the night and now, this! WOW. You must really like him." Grandma turned and looked at Tina. "I found this on the kitchen table this morning. It's from Jerry."

Tina stared at the piece of paper in her mom's hand. "Is he gone?"

"Yes, he was gone when I got up about 6:00 this morning."

"But, we had plans to go over the mediation notebook this morning."

Tina's heart fell and she reluctantly looked down at the piece of paper, obviously torn from the bottom of a page in a yellow legal pad. Her hand shook and she sat down at the kitchen table before she unfolded the paper and read.

> Tina, I am so very sorry to leave without talking to you, but I received a call about 4:00 A.M. My mom has had a stroke. The doctors believe she formed a blood clot after the stent. I must get to TN as quickly as possible. I have no idea what I will find but I will call or text as soon as I can. Please pray.
>
> Jerry

Tina read the note to her mom then sat holding the paper and staring out the kitchen window. "I know he needs to take care of his mother. I get that. I really do. I would not expect him to do anything else."

Joan turned from the sink and looked intently at her daughter. "I hear a 'but' in there."

With a shaky voice and misty eyes, Tina tried to

explain her dilemma. "I don't know, Mom. It's just that my whole life has been uprooted and everything I had expected to have is gone. To complain seems ungrateful when the Lord has been so good to me in many ways. But, you know, I have tried my best to accept this new life. I feel like I have given up everything to go with what He brought."

Her mom sat down gently beside her at the kitchen table. She laid her hand over Tina's and looked at her with an understanding smile and raised eyebrows. "But?"

"Well, but . . ." Tina could not help but smile a little at that. "*But,* I have prayed a lot over the past couple of years. More than my whole life probably. I guess I am maybe losing some of my confidence in God answering my prayers. Every time things start to come together something else happens. Now, just when Jerry was ready to open up about Billy, this happens and once again everything changes."

Joan was not surprised. She knew her daughter was going through the motions, but deep inside she was struggling spiritually. "Listen, first of all, we have every one of us been right where you are. It's nothing to be embarrassed about. The Lord already knows of course, but if you talk openly to him about it, he can walk you through the questions."

"I know. You're right, but at this point I am not

even sure I can hear his voice. The verse that talks about his sheep knowing his voice has become painful to me. Every time it crosses my mind I doubt myself all over again. So frustrating!"

"Well, you know why that is. The enemy likes to take God's word and use it against us. It's one of his favorite tricks."

Tina sat staring at her hands. Finally, she began again. "You know how people always say praying in Jesus' name has all this authority and power? Well, I have been paying, asking, declaring, even wishing in Jesus' name for two years now. All with no answer and no leads on the parents. And my love life, or the lack of one. Well, sometimes it just all makes me wonder why I even bother to pray."

"Oh, honey, I am so sorry. I know it has been a rough time for you. You know, don't you, that I have been so very proud of how you have handled it? I am not at all surprised you have questions at this point. Maybe I can help you, OK? In Biblical days we know that people were named to show their nature. Right?"

"Yeah, Mom, I know that. But I am not really in the mood for a Bible lesson right now."

Joan moved her hand from Tina's and leaned back in her chair with crossed her arms, and spoke softly to her daughter, "Of course you aren't, I get that. But just listen for a minute, OK?" At Tina's nod, she leaned forward again and started over.

"God gave Jesus his name, right? So, that means the name God gave Jesus describes his nature, right? Well, what was his nature? He said himself that he only did what he heard the Father say. He was always in agreement with the Father's will. Even in the Garden, he asked for the cup of suffering to be taken from him but then he said, 'nevertheless, not my will but thine be done.' His nature was always to surrender to his Father's will."

The light slowly began to dawn on Tina's heart. She was not sure she was going to like where this was going.

Joan continued. "So when we invoke the name of Jesus in our prayers, we are essentially saying that we pray in the *nature* of Jesus. And his nature is always to surrender to the Father's will.

Over these past few years you have prayed in Jesus' name, even declared in His name, right? Every time you prayed that, you agreed to surrender to the will of the Father. It is a powerful thing to align yourself with the Father's will. It does not always come easily. His will is always perfect but sometimes it looks anything but perfect to us."

Tina let the warm, salty tears slip down her cheeks. She nodded in agreement and understanding.

"So why even pray? What not just say, whatever you want God?"

"Oh, honey, how many times have I struggled with that very thought. But, the power comes in the agreement. We are co-laborers with God. We aren't name droppers, but we proclaim the name of Jesus over whatever circumstance we are praying about in order to come into agreement with God's will. The secret is in hearing and praying God's will and aligning our hearts with his."

Tina sighed deeply. "So, here we are back again at being able to hear God's will."

Joan smiled at her daughter, "Oh, he has his way of getting that across to us. We keep on keeping on and one day it all becomes clear. It isn't always a quick fix. Sometimes we just have to keep on walking in what we know until he shows us the next step. Tina, you can trust him. You know that, right?"

Joan reached over and hugged her girl close. "Let's not forget the flip side of that scenario. When we surrender and align ourselves with the Father's will, when we come into agreement with Him, our prayers are certain to be answered. There is no doubt that He will open his heart and pour out every blessing in order to bring his will to pass. And, ultimately, isn't that what we really want?"

Laying her head over on her mom's shoulder,

Tina sighed and let the full impact of her mom's advice settle down in her heart. "Thank you, mom. You have a way of making things seem so simple. How'd you get so smart, anyway?"

After a time, she prayed for Jerry's mother and for Jerry. "Oh, God, please let Mrs. Williams survive this stroke. Jerry loves her so very much and her family needs her. Let her body and her emotions recover fully with no damage. Use this time to encourage the family that you love them and are with them through this difficult time. It is scary, Lord, when our mom is sick. Moms are the strong ones in our lives. We need them. No matter how old we get, we need our moms. I pray this in *Jesus' name*!"

Joan listened to her daughter's prayer with tears in her eyes while she prayed along silently with her.

Tina's dad joined them and sat down quietly across the table. Unbeknownst to them, he had been standing just outside the kitchen doorway. He had listened to their talk with his own tears streaming. How he loved these women.

Over breakfast, Tina looked over at her dad and smiled. "You know guys, I probably have never told you, but praying with y'all has always been a big part of my walk with God. Even the short prayers over breakfast have been an integral part of my life. Praying with y'all early in the morning stays with me during the day. So, thanks for remembering to do that all those years. It means a lot."

She pushed her chair back and went around to give mom a hug and kiss her dad on the cheek. It was time to get the day started. The children should be awake soon. Baby Girl in the morning with curls springing in every direction and sweet smile, was a welcome beginning to her day. At almost four years old, the little girl was a spot of sunshine in all their lives.

As she climbed the stairs, Tina realized she had not told either of her parents of her decision to begin the adoption proceedings. She must do that today. It would impact their lives as well as hers, but she knew from their many discussions that her parents had her back in this. Like in everything else in her life. How she loved them.

Jerry called mid morning. "Hey Tina. You got a minute?"

Tina settled down on the edge of her bed, "Absolutely. I was hoping you would have time to call and let me know how things are going."

"Well, it looks pretty bad right now. The doctor doesn't think it is life threatening, but could well be life changing. There's some paralysis, but her mind seems OK. At least to me. I called the office. Johnson gave me a leave of absence."

A leave of absence meant he would be gone a

long time. "So, you think you guys are in for a long stretch, then?"

"Well, who knows, but I needed to let him know it could be a while. And Tina, I apologize for leaving so abruptly. I had to get on the road before morning traffic jammed me up."

"Oh, of course. Do not give it a thought. I would do the same thing."

"Thanks for understanding. I'd better get back in there. I will update you when I get a chance. And Tina, thanks for praying."

"You are so welcome and I will continue. Hang In there Jerry."

Sitting and going over the conversation in her mind, the book and the mediation seemed unimportant compared to all he was dealing with. However, the photos, the book, the mediation all could have been a turning point in his life. What if he knew the lady carrying Baby Girl? What if the photos helped him to open up about Billy and his life before the explosion? So many questions churned in Tina's heart. Well, they would have to wait.

Mr. Johnson called right after lunch and asked Tina if she could put together a slideshow presentation taken from her photos, videos and interviews. The book she had put together would be given to everyone involved in the suit but the slideshow would be shown at the mediation. She had actually been a bit disappointed that the only people who had seen the videos were the lawyers working on the case. It seemed a bit of a waste after all the work that went into them.

"Of course, I will start on it immediately."

A slideshow was the perfect solution. She should have offered that before. With all that was going on in her personal life lately, Tina's professional life had suffered a little. Visualization set to music could be profound. The mood she created with it could help set the tone of the mediation.

After putting the children down for their afternoon nap, Tina loaded Pepsi into the car and drove to the veterinarian's office. He assured her all was well and that delivery should be simple, but if he was needed she should call him. The due date was a couple of weeks after the mediation. At least she would be finished in Atlanta before the pups arrived. Dr. Logan also agreed to post a notice on his bulletin board regarding pet adoption in case anyone was interested.

Back at the house, Tina closed herself up in the home office she shared with her dad and asked for God's help in creating a meaningful video. The bonus this added to her pay was indicative of how important it was to Mr. Johnson.

As Tina worked through the afternoon, she listened again to the interviews. Some were complete with video images while others had only audio. Mr. Johnson was right about the impact it could make. It was impossible for each client to speak at the mediation. The video would give a cross section of the victims an opportunity to tell their story.

It took several days to complete the project, and on Monday morning before the mediation on Friday, Tina loaded up her car and headed north to Atlanta. She had plans to spend the night with Katie and catch up on her romance with Barry, plus get in an afternoon of shopping. She was also hoping to hear more news of Jerry's mom from someone at the law office. The last she heard from him, his mom was making progress, but slowly. She could speak a little and was going to Physical and Occupational Therapy every day. Jerry and his sister were taking turns helping with her care and their dad's emotions. Apparently, Jerry would not be attending the mediation.

As Tina drove, she pondered over what was taking place in her life right now. The two week deadline for an answer to DFACS was Friday, the same day as the mediation. Tina and her parents had talked at length and they were all on board with the decision for Tina to begin adoption proceedings. But, for some reason, Tina had yet to advise Ms. McGowen.

What was that niggling thing inside that held her back? Was it reluctance to accept the permanent responsibility? Although that was definitely a huge concern, she did not think it was the holdup. No, it was something else. Something she could not quite put her finger on, but Tina knew Ms. McGowen would hold her feet to the flame regarding the deadline. She was a *no excuses allowed* kind of woman.

Although Mr. Johnson took care to assure Tina she was welcome at the mediation, he also made it clear he understood her dilemma with the adoption decision. In the end, they both agreed that Tina would not attend the mediation overflow room but would stay in Chickpea and attend to her personal business there. It was disappointing after all the work she had poured into this project. Her biggest hope had been that she would meet someone who would recognize the photograph of Baby Girl when they looked at the book. She had to admit, however, that most everyone involved in the lawsuit had seen the book and the photographs at some point. No one had come forward to identify the baby. The photo of Baby Girl's mom showed only half her face, but still, it would be enough to recognize someone you knew. The blurred photo of Justin in the background of one of the shots had not brought anyone forth either.

CHAPTER FOURTEEN

Melinda

Melinda sat looking out the hotel window at the Atlanta skyline. Her mind was focused on what she had been told about her history with Atlanta, that unknown part of her life that called to her. According to hospital records, she had been brought to Grady Hospital via ambulance the day of a big explosion in a hotel on the outskirts of downtown. She was unconscious and had no identification.

They told me I was only unconscious for a little while. How can I have no memory of who I was before? That makes no sense. I still remember my time in the hospital clearly, but nothing before I arrived there. I remember feeling lost and a little terrified. I remember the doctor explaining that my amnesia was most likely temporary. That was four years ago. Four long empty years of trying to discover my identity.

Once again, as so many times before, Melinda retraced every step of those days. She was transferred to a mental hospital where more therapy and medication to recover her memory was futile. After weeks in the hospital and extensive therapy and medical tests, Melinda still suffered from acute amnesia. The hospital tried unsuccessfully to match her DNA with any that had been recovered from the explosion site. Apparently, she was at the hotel alone. Or, her family made it out without injury. Either way, there was no match with anyone found at the site, whether alive or deceased.

After the long battle, she checked herself out of the mental hospital and began the painful and involved process of establishing a new identity. Her new name, Melinda Simmons, was legalized by the courts after months of red tape, extensive research and medical examinations. The medical bills were staggering, but there had been help in unexpected ways. She was methodically working away at the balance. Thankfully, her case was handled pro-bono by a local law firm that works closely with the homeless in Atlanta. And now, almost four years later, she was still unsuccessful in finding any clues to her true identity.

Still, she knew there was a past life that lay just beyond her reach. At times in her dreams she saw a house and the face of a beautiful baby. Boy or girl? She had no idea. She also had no idea if that baby was hers and if so, what had happened to that baby.

If I was going to remember anything, it would surely be my child. A mother would know on a level that goes past her consciousness. Wouldn't I remember my own child even if I forget everything else?

Since her new name was not assigned when she left the hospital, she had not been advised of the lawsuit. Apparently, there had been notices in the Atlanta papers regarding the suit. How had she missed seeing them? Had it not been for an accidental encounter with someone who was also in the explosion, Melinda would not have known about that or the mediation set for Friday. A few weeks back, she had been in Atlanta for a business meeting and decided to drive by the site of the new hotel. Perhaps something would jog her memory. She had of course visited the site several times, even before the new building was up, but always she left the same way, dejected and more convinced of the uselessness of her search.

She was walking around the new structure taking a few snapshots when she saw another lady standing and staring, lost in thought. Melinda walked over to where the lady stood.

"Hello, I hate to bother you, but I saw you standing here and just wondered if you were somehow connected to the explosion that happened here a few years back. You just look so sad and a little lost standing here." Melinda knew she was clutching at straws but at this point, anything at all may be a clue that would help her.

"Yes, actually, my son and I were in the explosion that day. Why do you ask?"

Melinda swallowed the lump in her throat and tried to appear calm. "Apparently I was as well. Although I have no memory of that day."

To her surprise, the lady reached over and gave her a warm hug. "Oh, dear. I am so sorry. Is there anything I can do to help you?"

It took a minute for Melinda to be able to answer. Her chest tightened at the thought that this complete stranger was concerned for her. Amazingly, this lady immediately became a safe place. Her walls came tumbling down as she poured out her life over the past four years.

"After the hospital and then a mental hospital, I had to reestablish myself in every area. It's been an uphill battle that I have fought every day just to create an identity. No family, no friends, no home, nothing. The crazy thing was how I remembered everything going forward from the explosion and absolutely nothing from before.

"I was able to land a good job, rent an apartment and furnish it with the help of a local church. The people there were kind and helpful but they did not meet the desire for friends who understood me. Were there any? Were they looking for me? Where was my family? Wouldn't they have put ads in the paper asking about me? I searched the personals of several papers for months before finally surrendering and accepting that no one missed me."

The lady's name was Debra Calhoun. Her son, Andy, had been severely burned in the explosion. She and Melinda talked for an hour, standing in the newly paved parking lot while Debra described her memory of that day. Melinda listened intently, hoping against hope to gain some insight into her past. Unfortunately, Debra did not recognize Melinda and had no information that would help her. She did, however, tell her about the class action lawsuit.

Later that day, Melinda walked into Saunders & Johnson and asked to be included in the lawsuit. Mr. Johnson was skeptical at first since Melinda had no idea what her name was at the time of the explosion.

It was difficult for him to believe she could not be identified, even after so long a time. After extensive research, he relented and accepted her case. Since then, he had pelted her with a million questions. Still, there was no link to her and the hotel on that particular day other than the ambulance and hospital records. Her official name from that day was Jane Doe.

Melinda rested her head against the headboard and allowed her mind to wander once again to the dark corners of her psyche and the unexplained emptiness. She went over her time at the hospital and at the mental health care center. Thinking, pondering, wondering. Why had she been at the hotel? Was she an employee? If so, why was the HR department unable to identify her as one of the missing? Had she been alone? If she was a guest, why was she visiting Atlanta? Why wasn't someone looking for her? Were they? It was pointless to torture herself this way. That time was over and she had exhausted every avenue available. It was like she never existed. How could that be?

After her walk down memory-less lane, she resigned herself once again to being Melinda, shook off the fog and called to order room service. More and more, she hibernated in her room, her apartment, her own private world. Even the simplest of conversations often caused her confusion. Stress was always close at hand when someone made the slightest mention of her family, her youth, even where she lived. Living with the horror of not knowing who she was or where she came from was a constant in her new world.

Melinda had never been a praying person, but lately she was willing to try anything. As a last ditch effort, she prayed that somehow, through some means, someone at the mediation would recognize her. She was a person who had lived on this earth for at least thirty or so years, there had to be a place, a family who was missing her. Her life could not be wiped out and no one noticed. That was just not possible!

Friday morning finally arrived and Melinda was up and dressed long before time to leave for the mediation. Mr. Johnson's secretary had explained the mediation details in a letter to all the plaintiffs. Only the three plaintiffs chosen by the group would be allowed to sit in on the actual mediation, however, the remainder would view the proceedings from a large room set up on another floor of the building. It was equipped with a television so they could see everything that was happening. Melinda had no idea what to expect, but she wanted to be there early just in case.

The offices of the mediator were located in a beautiful restored home on Ponce de Leon Ave in Atlanta. What was once a parlor had become the reception area and was decorated with the same Southern charm as the law offices of Saunders & Johnson. Melinda was shaking inside as she walked up to the young receptionist and gave her name. After checking her identification against the list of approved attendees, the girl directed her to the elevator located in what was formerly the foyer.

"Are there perhaps stairs I can take instead?" Melinda needed to de-stress with a quick bit of exercise. The lady directed her to the back of the hall where she found the stairs. The beautiful, curved railings and shiny wooden floors made for an elegant entrance into the second floor rooms. *Even this house has a past. Even the stairs carry memories of those who climbed these steps in years past. Stop it, Melinda. Or whoever you are. Just stop it.*

Just to the left of the upstairs landing was an open door. Standing at the right of the open door was a sign: "Overflow Room." Several of the original rooms had been combined to create an open area filled with couches, wing back chairs, and small tables with two or four straight back chairs at each. Across the back was a long conference table surrounded by chairs. On the table were drinks, pastries and fruit along with tissues, notepads and pens. The large television screen was positioned on the wall at one end, making it easy to see from any seat in the room.

Melinda had expected to be one of the first ones to arrive, but to her surprise, there were already twenty or more people standing in small groups talking quietly. Slowly, deliberately, she searched each face, hoping for some flicker of recognition, but there was none. As she made her way through the crowd no one seemed to notice her or have any response to her face. The familiar feeling of despair and insecurity tried to overwhelm her. It was not that people were unkind, but to Melinda the lack of recognition was one more bullet hitting her squarely in the gut. Determined not to surrender to her emotions, she continued her perusal until, on one of the couches, she spotted Debra Calhoun and moved to take the seat next to her.

"Good morning, Debra."

"Melinda. It is good to see you again. I wondered if you managed to get in on the lawsuit. I assume you did?"

"Yes. Mr. Johnson took some convincing and they did quite a bit of research in a short time, but he finally agreed to take my case. Of course, you know I have ulterior motives for being here. The money isn't nearly as important to me as the possibility of discovering my identity."

Debra looked at Melinda with misty eyes. "This is such an emotional day for me; I cannot begin to imagine your pain. My husband and I have been praying for you since the day you and I talked in the parking lot. I know the Lord has your answers. In His time, I believe He will bring full restoration. Perhaps today will be a beginning to that end. I know we only met briefly but I feel a special connection with you."

Melinda was thankful for a kind word in the midst of her inner turmoil, even though she had little faith in the praying part. "Thank you, Debra. That means a lot."

"My husband and I did not want Andy to be here today. It would have been too much for him to understand but he had a child's understanding of what was happening and did not want to be without one of us. We decided my husband would stay with him, so I am here alone. I appreciate you sitting with me."

Melinda squeezed Debra's arm. "I have been trying to pray as well, but I'm afraid my faith is not what it should be. It seems I am talking into the air at times. I know you think He is listening. I just wish I had some tangible proof of that. But, I suppose that would eliminate the need for faith, huh?"

Debra's kind eyes reinforced her words. "The Lord knows our hearts and he knows our needs. I believe he hears the truth in our hearts, even if we cannot form the words. He is not upset with you for asking for a sign as long as you do not put that ahead of your need for Him."

Standing, Debra took Melinda's hand, and helped her up from the couch. "This may be a long day. Perhaps we should take advantage of the coffee and pastries."

After settling back on the couch with drinks and a small plate of goodies each, they spent the next half hour talking with a few of the other clients while they waited for the mediation to begin. About 8:45, Mr. Johnson and the Mediator walked into the room. The Mediator was a slight man in his late fifties. His cowboy boots extended out from beneath tan dress slacks and his outfit was topped off with a dark brown blazer sporting a western cut.

The mediator welcomed them and briefly outlined how mediation worked. "Good morning everyone. I trust you are all as comfortable as possible and have everything you need. I am sure Mr. Johnson has explained everything to you, but as a reminder, we have no way of knowing how long this mediation will take. Nor do we know if we will be able to reach an agreement today. Of course, this is not like a court trial, however, if an agreement can be reached, it will be legally binding and will eliminate the need for a trial. You will be able to see everything on the T.V. so I encourage you to take notes and pay close attention to the details as they unfold. Hopefully, we will all have good news by the end of the day. Thank you all for being here. I realize how important it is to each of you, and I promise you we will all do our best to come to a fair and equitable settlement as quickly as possible."

Mr. Johnson promised to meet with them in the room after today's talks. His assistant would keep them informed of any behind the scenes activities that were not seen on the closed circuit TV. As soon as the two men left, everyone started talking at once. Each person had their own ideas about how the proceedings should or would go.

From her spot on the couch, Melinda continued to survey the faces, hoping against all hope to recognize someone or for someone to recognize her. At 9:00 sharp, the lights blinked in the room and talk faded as the television screen came on. Mr. Johnson and another lawyer from the firm were seated on one side of a long table with the three representatives selected from the plaintiff's group.

On the other side were three lawyers from the hotel along with a lady who was introduced as the hotel's Chief Financial Officer, an older man who was head of Human Resources for the hotel and beside him, a representative from their insurance company. At the head of the table, the mediator stood, making the introductions. The mediator's assistant sat just behind him at a small table with her laptop. After all the niceties were completed, the mediator suggested they begin.

Debra cried softly through most of the first hour but Melinda was too intent on what was being said to have room for any emotion other than hope. The details of that day were described from a legal standpoint. Occasionally, someone in the room would utter their disagreement with the details, but as a whole, the room was quiet except for the sniffles and occasionally a sob. Hearing the pain and grief that began with the explosion presented in a cold, analytical way was difficult for all of them. Even as Melinda kept her eyes fixed on the screen, she was aware of the emotion in the room. Most of the people present were struggling to retain their composure.

The mediator continued to stand the entire time as he gave each side the opportunity to present their case. It was a long process and the atmosphere in the viewing room was heavy with frustration and anger mixed with apprehension. Mr. Johnson had told them earlier that this would be a difficult part since the hotel lawyers would attempt to minimize the effects of the explosion as much as possible. They attempted to place a percentage of the blame on the furnace manufacturer.

After a quick break, the mediator explained to the hotel side that he would now show a short video with interviews from several of the plaintiffs. The opposing lawyers knew this was coming and attempted to stop it, but the mediator denied their requests and motioned for his assistant to begin the slideshow.

The opening music flowed through the room with a foreboding tone that was at the same time rather soothing. The individuals who had been selected to appear in the slide show were seated close to the front of the overflow room. Most were holding hands and bracing themselves for hearing it all again. The video began and every eye was fixed on the screen as one after another recounted their memories and emotions of that tragic day.

Some cried as they told their personal story while others had a difficult time restraining their anger. The photographs taken immediately following each interview were heart rending. The expressions on faces and the look in the eyes showed their pain in an almost physical way. Melinda had no idea who had taken these photos and produced the slideshow but it was having a powerful effect on all of them.

By the time the last story was finished, almost everyone in the viewing room was crying. The screen went blank for just a moment before the scene from inside the mediation room returned. To Melinda's amazement, there were tears in that room as well. Even some of the lawyers were obviously struggling to maintain a straight face.

The next order of business hit Melinda like a ton of bricks. First, Mr. Johnson stood and asked to show a few special photographs. Debra grabbed her hand and squeezed as Melinda's own image appeared on the screen. Earlier that week, Mr. Johnson's secretary had taken a quick snapshot of Melinda for her file and now he was holding it up for all to see. "This lady's name is Melinda Simmons. She is with us today in the viewing room. Because she joined the case only a few days ago, most of you have not met her. Melinda was in the explosion that day, but due to extreme trauma she suffers from amnesia. She has searched for her true identity since awakening in the hospital afterward. If anyone in the viewing room remembers this lady or has any information concerning her identity, please get in touch with our office as soon as possible."

All eyes turned to Melinda. Her heart seemed to stop and breathing became difficult. Debra held her hand tightly as people in the room studied her face.

But, in the end, no one had a clue as to who she was. Melinda's heart fell and at that moment she would have gladly dropped into a giant hole. Mr. Johnson placed her photo back on the table, and thanked the opposing lawyers for allowing him to take a quick side trail to try and help Melinda. It was apparent that his reason for showing her photo was a two sided coin. It did, hopefully help Melinda. It also showed one more instance of the tragic results from the explosion.

At this point, the mediator talked for a while concerning how much money was available and the terms of any settlement they may agree to. He suggested they all break for lunch and explained that from this point forward, each side would be in a separate room and he would travel between the two. That would give each side the opportunity to discuss their options and requests privately.

Before they could all agree to lunch, Mr. Johnson stood again. "Excuse me, but, if I may, I would like to show a few more photographs from the day of the explosion. These photos were taken immediately following the explosion and give a small glimpse into the horror my clients faced."

The mediator looked towards the hotel lawyers and raised his eyebrows, questioning if they had objections. The lawyers looked at each other and then with a slight nod indicated they would allow the photos. Again, Melinda's heart stopped. There on the screen was a photograph of her holding a small baby. It was only half of her face but she knew, beyond a shadow of a doubt, she knew it was her. Debra gasped and sat up straighter. One by one, others in the room took notice and stared openly at Melinda. Mr. Johnson continued with several more photographs before placing them all on the table, thanking the group at the conference table, and with a slight glance at the CFO excused himself. His fellow lawyers and the Plaintiff Representatives followed him from the room.

For a moment, before the screen went blank, Melinda saw the expressions on the faces of the hotel lawyers as they were left sitting at the table. Mr. Johnson's timing to show the photographs was perfect. He had left the room with heart wrenching images and they knew it would be impossible to explain them away.

Many of the people in the viewing room approached Melinda with sad eyes full of compassion. Several of them offered their help to discover her identity. Her mind was numb and she really did not know what to do at this point. She had to get to Mr. Johnson and tell him she was in the photo. Who had taken it? She had to talk to them.

Debra slipped her arm around Melinda's waist. "It's a start, Melinda. It's a start." Over lunch, they brainstormed about ways to retrace Melinda's footsteps on the day of the explosion. By the time they returned for the afternoon proceedings, her heart had new hope.

For the next portion of the mediation, the viewing room could only see what was happening in the plaintiff's room. The afternoon dragged on with the mediator carrying messages back and forth between the two rooms. Melinda had difficulty keeping up with the proceedings. Her mind was elsewhere, thinking on ways to investigate that photograph. Again and again, she brought her mind back to the matter at hand. The money was very important to everyone in this room, she understood that and attempted to stay focused. But, she wanted even more to sit down face to face with the photographer. Someone had taken her picture. And she was carrying a baby. A little girl dressed in a pink sunsuit with white sandals. Could it be that the baby she saw in her dreams really lived? Did she still live? Where was she? Who had her baby?

The hours seemed like days and Melinda found it difficult to sit still. Her heart pounded, her breath came and went in spurts until she thought she would explode. Finally, Debra nudged her and motioned towards the screen. It appears they may actually reach an agreement today. Mr. Johnson had advised them earlier that it could take several days to come to a settlement that all found reasonable, but apparently the hotel management was anxious to put this behind them. Perhaps their reputation as an ethical and honest business family was justified.

By 6:00, both sides agreed to a settlement that surpassed almost everyone's expectations. Melinda was thrilled, Debra cried and shouts went up all over as Mr. Johnson walked into the viewing room. He was all smiles and accepted handshakes and thank you's with his customary warmth.

"We are well satisfied, as I hope you all are. Truthfully, I did not expect to be able to reach an agreement quite this quickly, especially such a pleasing one. First, let me thank you for your patience and your cooperation through this process. It has been a pleasure to be a part of bringing restitution and hopefully a sense of closure to each of you.

Now, I am sure you are all anxious to know how much this will play out for each of you. We should have an answer for you within a few days and a check in your hands within a few weeks. We will of course keep you all updated as to the timeline. It has been a long, emotionally draining day for all of us. My office will be in touch with you as soon as possible, but if you need to speak with me personally, please make an appointment. Again, thank you for putting your confidence in my office. I trust we have not disappointed you."

She was thankful for the large settlement, but all Melinda could think about was talking to Mr. Johnson and telling him about her photograph. She had to find the photographer. Perhaps they had more pictures from that day. As soon as he finished his explanations, a crowd gathered around him. Everyone was talking at once, asking questions and thanking him. Before she could make it to the front of the crowd, he slipped out the door and his assistant held up both hands to indicate no one should follow him. It had been a long day for him as well and they needed to respect his wishes to wait until Monday for their individual concerns.

CHAPTER FIFTEEN

The Adoption

Tina spent most of the day on Friday at DFACS, working on paperwork to begin the lengthy process of adopting what she already considered to be her children. It did not take long for her to realize once again that working with Ms. McGowen was difficult at best. It seemed the lady was doing everything she could to discourage the adoption. By the end of their first meeting, Tina was ready to load the children into her car and start driving . . . anywhere. She tried to remind herself that this process was necessary. She just needed to be an adult and do what was asked of her, no matter how far fetched it seemed.

Saturday morning Tina was surprised to receive

a call from Mr. Johnson. She had expected him to wait until at least Monday to give her an update. She could hear the smile in his voice before he told her the outcome. An agreement had been reached in one day. Although that was unusual, Mr. Johnson had indicated last week that it was possible. He thanked her for her input and said the slideshow was impressive and had helped to set the mood in the mediation room. After reminding her of his interest in helping her with the adoption process, he gave her an estimate of her commission. Tina hung up and sat staring for several minutes before she could speak that figure out loud. When Jerry had originally asked her to consider the job, he had explained there would be a salary but also a commission based on a small percentage of the settlement. She had not realized just how large the settlement could be. Her mind was a bit in shock.

"Mom!"

Her mom was in the kitchen cleaning up the breakfast dishes while Justin played outside with Pepsi. Baby Girl was doing her favorite thing, standing on a little safety ladder at the counter. She had her apron on over her clothes, just like Grandma, and was very busy pouring water from one bowl to another. It was how she "cooked." Tina scooped her up and kissed her face until she begged to be put down.

After explaining everything to a very surprised Joan, Tina instructed Siri to call Becca. She put her phone on speaker and tapped her foot waiting for Becca to answer.

Becca answered the phone very nonchalantly. "Hey Tina. What's up?"

"Well, your bank account for one thing, Becca. It's definitely up!!"

Her sister laughed. "Well, wouldn't that be nice? I assume you heard from Mr. Johnson?"

"I did. Are you sitting down?"

"Oh, goodness. No drama, please. Just tell me what happened."

"First, put the phone on speaker and summon Lottie. She needs to hear this too!"

By the time Tina explained everything that went down and finally got to the amount of the settlement, Becca's nonchalant attitude was out the window. When she quoted the actual amount of her commission and the amount of Becca and Lottie's bonus, her sis was squealing very uncharacteristically. Soon, all three were yelling, along with Joan in the background behind Tina. The uproar brought Dad, along with Pepsi and Justin, in to see what all the commotion was about. It was a heyday of epic proportions with everyone talking and laughing at once. Dad laughed watching Joan and Tina dance around the kitchen.

By noon all the women, including Baby Girl, were driving towards Macon, the closest town with a mall. As they rode, Tina brought everyone up to date on the adoption proceedings, the particulars of the mediation, and her plans for going forward with her career. Over lunch they planned a family dinner and celebration for Sunday evening. As the day progressed, she pulled Becca and Lottie aside and explained her plan to thank her parents for all their hard work by surprising them with a cruise. After learning about the cruise, each one tried her best to talk Grandma into a new swimsuit without explaining why. Tina laughed and thoroughly enjoyed watching it all go down. Her family was anything but subtle.

Much laughter and many hugs later, they arrived back at the house. Granddaddy and Justin had spent the day roaming around the countryside, practicing with the BB gun, then stopping for pizza on the way home. After a light dinner and a warm bath, Tina tucked the children in for the night and joined her parents on the couch for their Saturday night shows.

After only two sitcoms, her mom's eyes were

having difficulty staying open. "Aren't you tired, Tina?"

"Mom, honestly, I could run a marathon right now. Everything in my life is falling into place. Before long I will officially be a Mother. I can give Baby Girl a proper name. And she and Justin will be Brogans. And my bank account is very happy indeed. God has been so good to me. I cannot wait to get this adoption completed and see what the Lord has for us next! You know I will be building my own house for the kids and me. Close of course. Maybe even on your property?"

Grandma Joan smiled and patted her daughter's knee. "I am so happy for you dear. I really am. You've worked hard and you did a great job. It doesn't surprise me that you would want your own home. And we have a lot of acreage here. Don't think I'm not interested in your plans, but this older model is tired. Tonight, I am sleeping, tomorrow we will celebrate more. I love you, honey. See you in the morning."

On cue, Dad stood, took his wife's hand and suggested they "retire to their suite for the evening." Tina laughed and hugged them both. "Goodnight. Sleep tight."

After they left, Tina switched off the television and wandered out to the front porch. There in the stillness of the night, she opened her heart to thank the Lord for all His many blessings. The evening chorus of insects played around her and the wind caressed her face as she rocked and talked to God. After a while, she sat quietly, hoping to hear a whisper of love from the spirit realm. What she actually felt was a very slight, very soft warning of unexpected change coming. Almost like the fluttering of butterfly wings, it was so fragile she could barely perceive it. And yet it would not go away. Hoping that it was just a long day and all the emotion build up, she brushed it off and went back inside. After closing and locking the door, she turned out the lights and made her way upstairs.

Pausing in front of Baby Girl's bed, she laid her hand gently on Baby's chest and asked for God's divine direction and purposes to be fulfilled in her life. Then she went to Justin's room and did the same thing. The feelings that arose over such a simple prayer surprised and concerned her. What was going on that she did not know about? Did it concern the children? One of them, or both? An unexpected fear gripped her heart. What if Ms. McGowen found the parents? What if, at this point, she lost her children? They were hers. She was sure of that. At least in her heart.

Sunday mornings were always hectic. They had basically two moms in the house, plus a granddaddy, but getting two children and the three adults out the door for church on time was still an issue. Why was that? Maybe it was because she was determined that her two looked and acted as good as any child in the Sunday School. Ouch! That wasn't a good thought. Tina made a mental note to work on that one.

In the afternoon, the clan gathered for their dinner celebration. Baby Girl held up her arms to everyone who entered. She had apparently decided that her role was one of Family Greeter, and she was good at it. Justin, at seven, was enamored with his older cousins and followed along whenever they allowed. After a delicious meal, Tina stood, tapped her glass and asked for everyone's attention. It was all very formal even with the snickering going around the table.

"Mom, Dad on behalf of The Tina Brogan Photojournalist Company, and from one very grateful daughter for all the help and support you guys have given me, I would like to present you with an all-expense paid cruise to the Bahamas." Applause and shouts broke out all around as Grandma Joan laughed and clapped while Granddaddy stood and broke into his happy dance.

Remembering their shopping day, Joan put her hand against her cheek. "Oh, no, why didn't I give in and buy that new suit!"

Becca reached under her chair and pulled out a package. "Guess what this is?" More laughter as they made their way as a group into the living room.

Just as Granddaddy sat down at the piano, Tina's phone rang. "Hello, Jerry! How nice to hear from you." Tina raised her eyebrows at Becca and slipped out of the room to her favorite spot on the front porch.

"Hey yourself. I am hearing awesome things about you. Mr. Johnson talks like you are his long lost daughter. Apparently your presentation played a big role in the mediation. There's nothing like getting a hold on the ole heart strings to sway a decision. Congratulations are in order. You did yourself proud."

"Thank you, Jerry. I was sorry that I was not able to be at the mediation, but Mr. Johnson called me Saturday morning to fill me in. That must have been some day."

"Yes, I think so. Sorry I missed it too. But, on that note, my mom is improving very nicely. They have decided to give her time in a rehab center so my presence here isn't as necessary. My plan is to be back in the office on Wednesday of next week. Do you think you will be in Atlanta soon? I would love to see you and catch up. We never got to go over your photos and even though it's a mute point at this time, I still want to look them over. I could get them from the office, but would prefer having you show me. The mediation was going to be a sort of closure for me, but that didn't happen."

Tina smiled to herself. Yes, this could possibly answer some questions for her. "Of course, Jerry, I would love that. How about next Thursday?"

"Thursday is fine. Lunch or dinner?"

"Both. Let's make a day of it. We can meet in your office and have lunch then I can stay at Katie's and maybe the four of us can go to dinner. We can celebrate together."

"Great! See you then. And Tina, seriously, congratulations!"

Both? That was a bit brazen, as her mom would say. Tina could not believe she had said that. Her new found confidence might need just a slight adjustment. Her next phone call was to Katie who was happy to have her friend stay overnight. Tina walked back inside and joined in the family singalong. Life was good. So good.

Monday morning a worker from the local DFACS office appeared unannounced at Tina's front door. She had been dispatched by Ms. McGowen to inspect the home, assure the children's rooms were adequate and observe the interaction between Tina and the children. There was a special emphasis to be placed on the method of discipline being used. Tina resigned herself to the process and welcomed the young woman into the house. Ms. McGowen continued to do everything in her power to antagonize her, but Tina was determined to keep a calm demeanor and just get through the process.

On Tuesday, Ms. McGowen called very early to request that Tina join her in the DFACS office for more paperwork and an interview with a Child Psychologist. After that, it was an interview with DFACS lawyers. By Wednesday evening, Tina was convinced that she would need Mr. Johnson's aid after all. She would try to speak with him privately on Thursday when she drove in to meet with Jerry.

CHAPTER SIXTEEN

Where Is My Baby?

Melinda literally bounced in her chair as she sat with her legs crossed, one swinging up and down in rhythm to the background music playing in the waiting room. Even after the group meeting where Mr. Johnson had provided each of them with a letter explaining what would happen next and how long before they would receive payment, most of the plaintiffs requested a private meeting.

Melinda glanced over the letter for the hundredth time, folded it and stuck it back in her purse. No matter the money. She had a baby. She knew it. She had a history, a life. Her heart was bursting and her mind was racing too fast for her to understand the thoughts flying around inside. Finally, after what seemed a lifetime, the receptionist called Melinda's name and ushered her into Mr. Johnson's private office.

Sitting behind his massive desk, he was the epitome of professionalism in his three piece gray pin-striped suit, dark blue shirt and gray and blue tie. The ever present, but never used, hankie was peering perfectly out of the breast pocket of his coat. Something about him calmed Melinda. The shaking inside her began to subside and she gratefully dropped onto the offered chair.

"Good morning, Melinda. I assume you have read the instructions my secretary typed up for everyone."

Before he could continue, Melinda was on her feet again. The shocked expression on Mr. Johnson's face would have been comical if she were not so serious herself. "Mr. Johnson! Please, forgive me, but I cannot wait a minute longer to tell you. I saw a picture of myself in the photographs you showed last Friday!" Whew. There. She had said it. Finally! Dropping back into the chair, she blew out a ragged breath.

"Are you certain it was you in the photo? Surely you have seen the photo before. Would you not have recognized yourself then?"

"No, I have never seen the photo. I was told about a book of pictures but never had a chance to look at it. When you showed it on the screen I knew immediately it was me. Even though it only showed half of my face, I knew it. Debra Calhoun was sitting with me and she recognized me too. After that, several of the people in the viewing room said it looked a lot like me. Mr. Johnson, I was holding a baby girl!"

She saw the recognition hit his face. "Yes, I remember the baby. I saw her the morning of the explosion. I was focusing on the baby and did not look at your face in the photo. It was only partly shown and that was blurred. Here, I have the photos—let's look at them again."

As he pulled the photos out of a stack of files on the corner of his desk, Melinda stood and walked around to stand beside his chair. He glanced up but said nothing as she bent over literally cheek to cheek with him. "Here it is. Look very closely now, Melinda. I can see a resemblance, but this lady has blonde hair and is umm . . . a different size."

In spite of the seriousness of the situation, Melinda smiled at his obvious awkwardness in describing her likeness in the photo as compared to how she looked today. "I have gained a lot of weight over the past few years. Stress eating they call it. And as for the hair, it was colored at that time. When I woke up from the coma, my hair was half blonde and half dark. By the time I was released from the mental health hospital it was almost completely dark, so I decided to just go with it. Putting dark hair and more weight on that photo, can you see me?"

Mr. Johnson sat staring at the photo for a time before looking up at her again. Suddenly, Melinda was embarrassed by her behavior. She slowly raised up and walked back around to her chair, sat down and smoothed her skirt. "I apologize, sir. I have been so excited, I forgot about everything except finding the person who took this photo. I have waited for four years to get even the smallest break in finding out who I am. There are no words to express how it feels to have no idea of who you really are. Living in that void is so very dark and lonely. To lose my identity, to not know where I came from or who I belong to . . . well, it's more than you could ever imagine."

"No need to apologize, Melinda. I completely understand your eagerness. I am certain I would feel much the same way if I were in your shoes. As a matter of fact, I do know who took this photograph. But, I must tell you not to expect too much from her. The young woman who took this was not in the explosion. She lived nearby and was one of the first on the scene, but she has no connection with the hotel other than that. I met her when one of our lawyers suggested we use her as our photographer for the mediation photos. Her work is excellent, but again, I am doubtful she will be able to help you."

Melinda's heart fell to her toes. This was not what she had wanted to hear. Perhaps talking to the photographer was another waste of time. To the photographer, Melinda was just a face in the crowd. Not even a complete face at that. Why waste her time or the photographer's? No, she should go back home and forget all of it. Take her settlement money and use it to build a new life. She was Melinda Simmons now. Nothing was behind her except emptiness. She detested this emotional pit, but once again it pulled her down into a place of darkness and rejection.

Mr. Johnson was talking, but she was not focusing on what he was saying until she heard him say, "Would you like for me to set up a meeting with the photographer? You never know what she may have heard in the crowd that day. It's completely up to you, but why not cover all your bases?"

Melinda mumbled quietly, "Yes, thank you, sir. I would appreciate that."

The look of compassion on Mr. Johnson's face only made things worse. Pity. Rejection. She hated it all. She hated this lie she was living. She hated her life. Melinda walked out of his office with a heavy heart. Gone was the enthusiasm and excitement she had lived with since last Friday. Slowly, as she walked to her car, the familiar feelings of defeat surrounded her. "Why, God? Why?" Mumbling to herself she went through the familiar roller coaster emotions, as the loneliness and despair engulfed her once again.

Thursday morning came bright and sunny with just a nip of coolness in the air. It was a beautiful day for a drive to Atlanta and Tina was pumped to get on the road. She had a fat bank account waiting to be spent on a new wardrobe, maybe even a new camera. The adoption was going smoothly, despite Ms. McGowen's constant attempts to sabotage her. What was it with that woman anyway? Tina wondered again what had happened in the woman's life to bring about such bitterness. Shrugging off thoughts of her arch-enemy, Tina drove onto the ramp and proceeded up I-75 North.

The call from Mr. Johnson's secretary earlier in the week intrigued her. She said there was a lady that would like to meet with Tina. No details had been given other than the time of their meeting. First thing this morning she would meet with the mysterious lady and then have the rest of the day to enjoy Jerry's company. It was only his second day back at work, so his duties were still limited. He had marked the afternoon off just for the two of them. Yep, Jerry could be quite attentive at times. Again, she entertained thoughts of more than a friendship with him. No, she wasn't ready for all that right now. There was just too much going on in her world. Still . . .

Tina pulled into the familiar parking lot, cut the engine and took time to check her image in the mirror. Satisfied that all was well, she gathered her bag, pushed the left door open with her foot and stepped into the fresh air.

Inside, the receptionist welcomed her with a smile and congratulations on the case. It was as if she had actually played a part in helping these people. She never expected to be seen as a member of the team, but admittedly, it felt good. She was definitely at the top of her game and the only way she saw from here was up.

Mr. Johnson stood and welcomed her into his office. Again, she felt comfortable here in his presence. He could easily be a grandfather figure in her life. His mentoring during the case had been invaluable. And now, his offer to help with the adoption—well, he was a special man.

Tina shook hands and as she turned to sit, smiled at the lady sitting in the other chair.

"Tina, this is Melinda Simmons, Melinda, our photographer, Tina Brogan."

Our photographer? Hummm, she liked the sound of that—as long as he did not try to restrict her from other endeavors as well. Tina shook hands with Melinda Simmons, smiled and sat lightly on the edge of her chair. Her posture was impeccable. Thanks to her mom and Southern culture, Tina had been taught at an early age what is expected of a lady. Her hair was pulled up into a French twist and she wore dangling earrings. The rust-colored top was light and flowing, adding to the idea of softness and femininity she had created.

"Tina, Ms. Simmons and I would like to talk with you regarding one of your photographs. I have explained to Melinda that you may not be able to help her, but because of the urgency of the matter, I knew you would want to try."

While Mr. Johnson pulled out a file and opened it, Tina took time to really look at Melinda Simmons. Slowly, frighteningly, realization dawned on her. Oh, God, no. Please, no. Not now, God, not now. But, she knew, deep inside she knew. She could not deny the truth that she was looking into the face of the woman who had collapsed at her feet. She was looking at Baby Girl's mother. She looked different. Her hair was colored now, or it was then, and she was heavier and older. The trauma had definitely left its mark on her, but it was the same face. Tina groaned inwardly as tears threatened to expose her feelings. This was horrible. This just could not be happening. Tina stared at the photo Mr. Johnson handed her. Her hands shook and she fought the tears as she stared at Baby Girl and the lady carrying her.

Mr. Johnson stood and came over to her, placing his hand on her shoulder. "Tina, are you trying to tell us that you recognize Ms. Simmons?"

"No. I have no idea who she is. I only took the photo. I am so sorry, I cannot help."

At that moment, Melinda Simmons began to cry softly. "I had hoped and prayed you would have answers for me, Ms. Brogan. You see, I have amnesia. I do not remember anything about that day or my life before the explosion—not even my real name. I have seen a baby's face in my dreams, the baby I was carrying in your photo, but I have no idea who she is. Was that my baby? Where is my baby now? Who am I? The questions never stop. You were a glimmer of hope for me. Please, try and remember . . . anything at all could possibly help me find out who I am. Please, try again. Surely if you look closely you may remember something, anything."

Tina sat stoically in her chair. A cold, hard dread began to creep into her being. Mr. Johnson returned to his chair, leaned back and sat staring thoughtfully at the two women. The silence was deafening.

After a few moments, Tina heard the soft ticking of a wall clock. She had never noticed that in this office before. Then the chair creaked as Mr. Johnson leaned forward, still carefully studying her face. He knew, didn't he? He was a lawyer, for goodness sake. He knew when people were lying.

Lying, Tina was lying. How could she? Melinda Simmons was obviously desperate. But, then, so was Tina. She could never admit that this stranger was Baby Girl's mother. Never. She could never do that. God would not give her to Tina and then snatch her away. No. That would not happen. Tina sat staring silently at the floor. She was numb inside except for the lump of ice that had formed in her belly, and perhaps even around her heart.

Clearing his throat, Mr. Johnson pressed the button on his desk to summon his secretary. "Please ask Jerry to join us." Tina was shocked. Why Jerry? The reason was made clear very quickly, and Tina was crushed.

"Ms. Simmons, I think it would be a good idea for me to speak with Tina alone. Jerry Williams is one of our associates here. Actually, he was in the explosion as well. His own son was tragically killed that day. I believe he will be willing to go over the photo book with you. Between the two of you, perhaps something else will come to mind regarding your identity."

No. No. She had waited for months to have this moment with Jerry. After all, they were her photos. She should be the one with him when he first viewed the photos. "Mr. Johnson, I believe it may be difficult for Jerry to do this. He has yet to look at the photos."

"Tina, please trust me on this. It is time for Jerry to view the photos and Ms. Simmons is just the person to help him. They can help each other."

Although his voice was gentle, Tina heard the resolution in his tone. "Yes sir." And the ice around her heart intensified just a bit more. Everything was going down against her. Baby Girl, her day with Jerry, the respect of Mr. Johnson. Ice. Dread. Pain, incredible pain wrapped itself around her emotions and held her captive in the darkness of deceit.

Jerry knocked lightly before entering. After being introduced to Melinda Simmons and speaking a good morning to Tina, he was apprised of the situation and asked to help with the photos. He glanced slightly at Tina as he escorted Melinda out of the room. From the droop of his shoulders as he left, Tina knew he was as disappointed as she was.

Turning his attention to her, Mr. Johnson came

around and sat in the chair next to her. He pulled it closer and turned it just a little so he could look her directly in the face. He crossed his long legs, leaned back in the chair, and sat studying her face for a long minute.

"Tina, I believe you and I have come further as friends than this. We both know you are not being completely honest here."

She felt like a kid in the principal's office. But, seriously, after four years of looking for the parents, then finally deciding to go forward with the adoption, and now the mother shows up? After exhausting every avenue possible with no results, today, of all days?

This was to be a day of celebration. She was at the top of her game just a few minutes ago. And now, her entire world was collapsing around her. Everything she had hoped and planned for today just fell apart. What did she want anyway? To find the parents or to adopt the children? Apparently she didn't really know the answer to that. Her heart was split and hurting. That was all she really knew at the moment.

Sitting up straight and smoothing her skirt with nervous hands, Tina still found it difficult to look Mr. Johnson in the eye. Guilt does that. Like a father would do to his child, Mr. Johnson placed the tip of his finger under her chin and gently raised it so their eyes met.

"Please, Tina. Tell me what is going on."

Tina took a deep breath and looked out the window, hoping for the redbird to show up. It didn't. Turning back to Mr. Johnson's kind eyes was all it took for the ice to melt. "I know her. I don't know her name, but I know her." There, that was enough. End of story.

"And?"

"And . . . the baby she was carrying that day is Baby Girl. My Baby Girl." As the ice began to break, her emotions emerged full force and the dam broke. Tears streamed down her face in torrents of pain, fear, shame and guilt. And yet, deep inside, she still held on to her right to hide the truth about Baby Girl. Who was this woman? How did Tina even know she was really the mother? She had no proof, just her word. And Tina was not giving her baby girl up to anyone just because she happened to be carrying her. And what about Justin? The lady never mentioned him at all. Something was wrong with all of this. Still, she had to admit, the time had come. They would need to dig into Melinda Simmons' claim.

Mr. Johnson was stunned. Obviously he had not expected this. She watched him slowly stand and with his arms at his back, begin to pace thoughtfully between the desk and the window. Tina could only sit and wait while her world fell apart. Baby Girl. No, please God, no.

Mr. Johnson stopped pacing and lowered himself thoughtfully into his chair behind the desk. He flipped his pen on the desk for a few moments while he stared at Tina. "Let's not rush to any conclusions here. This may well be the lady you saw that day, or it could just be someone who resembles her. Obviously, she is convinced it is her, but she is broken in many ways and she is desperate. Her mind could be playing tricks on her."

Tina let out a long breath and slumped down in her chair. "Thank you, Mr. Johnson. Thank you so much!"

He stood again, came around and took her hand. "Come on, Tina, let's take a short walk and get a drink. We need to back up and think about what should be done."

As they walked down the hall towards the lobby, Tina was painfully aware of Jerry's closed door. She wanted so much to peek inside and see if he was alright. How was he reacting to the photos? Were they already plotting against her? Oh, God, I am so sorry. Why would I even think that? She shook her head to clear the thoughts and turned her attention to Mr. Johnson. "Should we check on Jerry?"

"No, I am certain he is fine. Let's concentrate on you right now."

It was strange to have someone in Mr. Johnson's position ordering a latte for her while she sat dejectedly at a small round table. Her soft, flowing outfit and the dangling earrings suddenly felt out of place. She would prefer to be in jeans, boots and a tee shirt. She knew that she appeared to be together and classy today, but inside she was afraid and her confidence had fallen into the well.

Easing down onto the small chair across from her, Mr. Johnson busied himself with pouring in the creamer and stirring his coffee. After a few moments he raised his eyes to hers and smiled. Tina relaxed a little and smiled back. "OK," he began, "I think it would be best to keep this information to ourselves until we have proof."

"Proof?"

"Yes, in the form of DNA evidence. When Melinda came to us and asked to be included in the class action suit, we did research to help determine her true identity. As a part of that, we asked her to agree to a DNA test. She did agree, and she also signed an affidavit giving us permission to use the results in any way necessary to discover her identity. I believe this falls under the scope of that statement. I need for you to take the child to her pediatrician to have a DNA test completed. Give me the doctor's name and number and I will have our office coordinate the testing so the results will be returned to me personally. Perhaps DFACS has already secured one, but I feel better getting my own. Is that agreeable with you?"

Tina felt a surge of hope. "Yes, of course. How long do you think it will take to get the results?"

"In most cases we have the answer within a week, but occasionally it is a little longer. Now, I have another client due any moment. If you will give my secretary the doctor's name and phone number we will take it from there. Please get the test completed as soon as possible. I will meet with Melinda again and help her understand the wisdom of moving slowly. And Tina, try to relax. This could be the answer we all need, or it could be a dead end street. Either way, it is something we absolutely must investigate. We should know soon enough."

Tina walked back into the waiting room. She was not quite sure how to proceed. Jerry was nowhere to be seen and Mr. Johnson had returned to his office. Tina needed to talk to her mom, but that should be done in person. Katie. Quickly she dialed Katie's number, but when she heard her friend's voice the lump in her throat made it impossible to speak.

"Tina? Is that you?"

Finally, Tina responded with a shaky, "Can I come over?"

She needed to leave Jerry a note to apologize for leaving without seeing him and ask him to call her later. As she stepped up to the receptionist desk she saw Jerry and Melinda out of the corner of her eye. They were coming out of the conference room together. Both of them had obviously been crying.

Jerry walked away from Melinda, came over to her and wrapped his arm around her shoulders. "Tina, are you OK? You have been crying! Can I do something?"

"No, Jerry. I just need to get out of here."

Tina looked deeply into his eyes. What she saw reflected there was painfully raw. She could feel his entire body shaking with emotion. "Jerry?" was all she could say.

"Tina, we need to talk privately. And now."

"I just talked to Katie and I am going over to her apartment. Would you feel comfortable talking there?"

"Yes, can we go immediately?"

Melinda stepped closer and with a sad expression said her good-byes. Jerry had her information and promised to call her as soon as possible. After Melinda walked away, Jerry turned to Tina. His face was serious. Frighteningly serious.

Outside, Tina murmured almost to herself, "It's crazy how half a woman's face and the baby she was carrying causes such a stir." Jerry looked at her quizzically, and she realized he did not yet know the entire story.

They agreed to take both cars since Tina had plans to stay overnight with Katie. As soon as she pulled out into traffic, Tina began to plead with God. There were no tears and no more ice lump, just a deep longing to be heard by her Heavenly Father.

Oh, God. I know you are here with me. Everything is going south so fast, I don't even know how to process it all. What does Jerry want to tell me? And is Melinda Baby Girl's mother? Will she take her away? Is she even capable of taking care of a child? Jesus, help us. Help us all.

CHAPTER SEVENTEEN

Jerry's Story

The drive to Katie's apartment was short and a few moments later, Katie ushered them into her living room. To Tina's surprise, Barry was there as well. Barry. After all they had been through together, it was only fitting that he should be present when she revealed the possibility of finding Baby Girl's mother. After giving Katie and Barry a hello hug, she and Jerry sat down on the couch. Before she could speak, Jerry took her hand and gently pulled her head over onto his shoulder. The gesture was unexpected but welcome. From her view on his shoulder, Tina eyed Katie with a questioning look.

She was fairly bursting to tell what was happening, and yet, Jerry seemed to be in a state of anxiety himself. After a few moments of silence, Jerry eased her upright and began.

"Tina, I care very much for you. You are an amazing woman. Your loving heart towards two children you had never met is remarkable."

Tina was confused. Why was Jerry talking like this now? Where was he going with this? Katie and Barry appeared to be as confused as she was. Turning to look at Jerry, she saw tears in his eyes.

He continued. "Today I looked at the photographs for the first time. You know that, right?"

Tina nodded slowly.

"Tina, I don't know how to say this. Remember when I met Justin? Remember how it hit me so hard?"

Tina drew her eyebrows together and nodded. She stared at him first and then Katie while she waited for him to continue.

"I have been avoiding looking at your pictures from the explosion because I was afraid it would take me back there and I might fall apart again. It took a long time to get to where I am now. Losing my wife, and then Billy only six months later almost did me in. As you know, I am still seeing a psychiatrist.

Working on the class action suit was Mr. Johnson's idea. He thought it would help me deal with my pain. In some ways it did, but in others it only made things raw again. And then, I met you and I started to believe I could have a life one day. I heard how the children were growing and loving and being loved after they had lost their parents that day. I saw how God intervened to give them a new mommy and an entire family. It gave me hope that I might find love again one day, perhaps even with you.

And then, mom had her stroke and my heart broke all over again. I could not bear the thought of losing her too. My family could have taken care of her without me, but I wanted, I needed, to be close to all of them. After a while, I realized I was slipping back into a victim mentality. Once again, Mr. Johnson backed me into a corner when he insisted I show Melinda Simmons the photos."

Katie and Barry exchanged looks and then at the same time asked, "Who is Melinda Simmons?"

Tina could not hold it in any longer. "Melinda Simmons could very well be the lady who fell at our feet that day. She may be Baby Girl's mother. I met her this morning at the law office."

All three started talking at once. She had no idea who was saying what, but she did see that Jerry had tears running down his face. Tina raised her hands and motioned for everyone to calm down. She explained the DNA plan and answered what questions she could. Finally, Jerry took a deep breath and asked if he could continue. The other three nodded.

"I do not know how to say this, other than to just speak it. I think Justin is Billy. I saw him in the photo book this morning. It was after the explosion and he was coming out of the building. So, you see, he IS alive!"

The bombshell exploded in the room and in Tina's heart. One look at Barry and Katie told her they were in shock as well. Suddenly, Tina was on her feet. "That makes no sense, Jerry. You are imagining things. Come on, you would have known your own son! Why are you saying these things? Perhaps you should just leave. I cannot even hear this. Dang it, Jerry! What is wrong with you??? And, besides, I know the picture you are talking about. It is so blurry you cannot possibly tell if it is really your son."

It made no sense. Justin was Justin and Billy was Billy. It was all too much and everything she had kept at bay came tumbling out. Her body literally shook with anger, fear and desperation. Katie stood, slipped her arm around Tina's waist and led her back to the couch. Barry sat stunned with his head in his hands. A solemn silence descended over the room. No one moved. No one spoke. Jerry didn't leave as Tina requested. Instead, he sat staring at nothing while tears streamed down his face.

Katie was the first to speak up. "Jerry, I know you would love to discover that Billy is alive. I know.

But, Justin never said his name was Billy. From the first day he said he was Justin."

Jerry took a shaky breath and looked directly at Tina, "Remember when you kept asking me why I did not have a DNA test done? Well, Billy is not my biological son. The test would be useless. I married Marcy, his mother, soon after Billy was born. Well, let me backup. Billy's father and I were childhood friends. We went through high school together, played football together, and double dated. I was Best Man at his wedding.

Right after they married he joined the Marines. He had always dreamed of being in the military but we all thought he had changed his mind when he married Marcy. However, true to form, he surprised us and enlisted. After basic training, he was deployed to Afghanistan for a twelve month tour. Marcy did not realize she was pregnant when he left. She wrote to him a month after he left, but we aren't sure if he got the message. He was killed after only five weeks.

Marcy and I spent a lot of time together after that. We bonded over our grief I guess, but after about six months or so, we started to see each other as people and not just partners in pain. I was very cautious not to let my feelings show. I mean, what kind of guy was I? This was my best friend's widow and I was falling in love with her. We tried to stay apart but it was apparent to us and to all around that we were in love. William's parents were so very kind. They insisted we should move on with our lives. They only asked that the baby would carry William's name and surname. The birth certificate shows him as Billy's father. Which is as it should be. I never adopted him because of their request."

Tina remembered the name on the child care role: William Andrews. Her eyes flashed with an unreasonable anger towards Jerry. "So, Billy's last name was not Williams? Then what was it?"

"Andrews. William Justin Andrews."

Tina's heart fell and the air went out of her anger. She mumbled to herself, "Well, that explains a lot of things."

Katie looked at Tina with raised eyebrows.

"When we were researching the names of anyone who was enrolled at the Day Care Center, we discovered two Williams. We could not find where either of them had checked into the center that morning. We assumed they had been fortunate to stay home that day. I suppose we were wrong. William Andrews was Billy." Tina's heart pounded against her chest. It was difficult to breathe.

Jerry continued, "Yes, and William Brownlee was Billy's best friend." Jerry paused and laid his head again on the back of the couch, looking up at the ceiling. Tina waited for him to compose himself enough to continue.

Katie and Barry slipped quietly out of the room and Tina could hear them in the kitchen, obviously preparing some sort of food. It dawned on her that she never had lunch. She and Jerry had a special day planned. Well, this certainly was turning out to be special.

She sat silently, staring at the carpet and thinking. There seemed to be nothing to say and yet their entire lives were hanging on what happened next. After a few minutes, she felt calm enough to speak. "One thing I still don't understand. If Justin is Billy, as you seem to think, why did he tell me that his name was Justin? He obviously went by Billy. I mean, even at two or three he should have known his name."

The corners of Jerry's mouth unexpectedly turned slowly into a small smile. "Let me explain. The two Williams were best friends. William Brownlee was the first close friend Billy had ever had. Remember, they were barely three years old. William Brownlee's parents had recently divorced and his daddy started bringing him to the Center. He went by Billy as well, and like I told you earlier, the two of them bonded immediately. They thought it was so funny that they both had the same name and before too many days, the teachers realized they had to give someone a nickname. The teachers agreed to call each boy by his middle name—Justin and Lamar. At home he was Billy but he understood that at the Center he was Justin. That is probably why he told you his name was Justin. He was at the center when he met you."

"But, why no DNA? I mean, DNA will show family relations. You could have taken a sample from his grandparents and solved everything. The more I think about what you are saying, the less sense it makes. I really thought I knew you, but you are acting like a crazed man right now. I am sorry you are hurting, but this is all a bit ridiculous. I mean, come on." As soon as the words were out of her mouth she regretted them. She should apologize, but for some reason she just could not.

"I know, I know how it sounds and I am sorry. I regret now that I decided against the DNA. But, at the time, his grandparents had just lost their daughter to cancer only a few months before the explosion. The ordeal was very difficult on both of them. By the time I was awake and able to investigate, Billy was already buried and they had suffered through weeks of grief. I could not bring myself to open them up to any false hope. Not to mention the expense and ordeal of digging up what we thought was Billy's body. From what they told us, it was horribly burned. I was just so certain that Billy was gone and his grandparents I'm sure had no thought of doing a DNA test themselves. They were in such an awful place during that time.

Every time you talked about Justin my heart would pound but I thought it was just his age and the circumstances that took me back to the explosion. Until I actually saw him at your house, I had no idea it could possibly be Billy. Can you understand? Can you forgive me and let me have the chance to do the DNA test and be absolutely certain? At this point, his grandparents are stable enough to understand and agree. I am certain they will grasp at any possibility."

Katie and Barry walked back into the living room with a platter of sandwiches and a bowl of chips along with the best cup of coffee Tina had tasted in a long time. Tina explained what Jerry had told her while they were in the kitchen. For a few minutes they ate in silence except for an occasional remark about the shock of it all. The strained atmosphere prevailed until finally, Tina turned to Jerry and resignedly agreed to the DNA testing.

"I will take both children to their pediatrician as soon as possible. Baby Girl's results will be mailed to Mr. Johnson personally. Would you like for me to ask him to coordinate Justin's as well?"

"Yes, thank you. Tina, I feel like my heart is being ripped right into two pieces. If Justin should turn out to be Billy, it will be a miracle from God that changes not only my life but his and our entire family. On the other hand, I know it will bring pain to you. After all you have done and been through with the children, I never want to cause you any kind of heartache. I want to do all I can to make this easier."

Jerry's eyes implored her to understand. Finally, all his resolve to maintain control over his emotions shattered and deep sobs shook his body. Tina pulled him over to her shoulder, much like he had done her earlier. There was a somber heaviness in the room as they watched this broken man lay aside all semblance of control. In a voice filled with pain he tried to explain.

"In my heart I know it is Billy. I knew it on the day I met him, but it seemed too good to be true. I thought my mind and my heart were just seeing what I so desperately wanted to see. I mean, he has changed so much. And I guess I thought he would recognize me if it was really him. It is all so unbelievably overwhelming.

The last time I saw him, he was a chubby little guy with a shock of white hair. My little towhead. When I saw him at your house he was a tall, thin, little boy with dark hair and freckles across his nose.

The eyes looked like Billy, but everything else was different. I was in shock, my heart, everything inside me went blank for a minute. Then after I got myself together, I was sure it was my imagination.

All day with him, I kept telling myself I was crazy. The pain of everything was just below the surface that day. Such a beautiful day and yet all the time, my heart was breaking all over again. I was determined to see the photos you took, just to see if it made things any clearer. But then, mom and all of that went down."

Even the air in the room was filled with grief. There was a heaviness and dread that mocked Tina. Justin could be Billy. Jerry could take him. His pain was evident, and yet, her pain was there too. She needed to know the truth of it all, and yet, as always, she wanted to delay that truth as long as possible. Justin was her son now.

"You know, Tina, legally, you probably have as much right to him as I do. I never adopted him because his grandparents were opposed to it. They desperately wanted to keep the connection between Billy and their son. It seemed a small thing to ask since they had lost so much and yet had accepted me into their hearts. I did have a power of attorney from Marcy that gave me legal rights to act on her behalf and that included decisions over Billy."

So, there it was. Tina found a small comfort in remembering he had not adopted Justin. Who knew whether he would be better off with her than with Jerry? Who was to say he, as a single man, who wasn't even his biological father was any better than she to raise him? This made everything a bit more acceptable. Billy—or Justin—was happy where he was. He had suffered too much for his age. Perhaps, just perhaps, he would need to stay right where he was. Jerry could visit him any time he wanted to.

No one moved or spoke. Tina barely breathed. Jerry sighed deeply. "All I want to do is hold him. Just hold him. But, I have restrained myself until I knew what to do. Then, this morning with Melinda, I saw the photo you took that day. And there, in the background, was Billy. He was stumbling out of the building. And I knew. Oh, God! I knew my son was alive. There he was." And again the sobs overtook him.

Barry had been quiet the entire time. Suddenly, Tina looked over to him for comfort. It was a habit from long back. He slowly stood and walked over to where she sat, kneeled down in front of her and took both her hands. "Tina, since the very beginning, we have known this day could come. At first, you prayed for it to come, really prayed. Remember? But, as time passed Justin and Baby Girl became a part of your heart. We all understand, at this point your lives are intertwined and it is impossible to imagine your life without them. We all understand and agree, it's overwhelming to say the least. For now, can we just wait on the DNA results and pray God helps us all with whatever happens?"

Jerry sat quietly agreeing with everything Barry said. After a moment, he looked at Tina and almost apologetically, began, "Tina, there is more."

The anger that flashed inside surprised even her. "What?"

"It isn't about Billy, or Justin. It's about Melinda."

Silence. Then finally, "Go on."

"Melinda told me about your meeting and that you do not remember her. But, get this, I may remember Melinda from the day of the explosion. I have been focused on Billy in my mind but now that I stop and think about it, I have a vague memory of seeing a lady carrying a baby that day.

It's all fuzzy, but I remember I was interviewing a prospective employee that day. Since the person I was replacing didn't know about it, I decided to interview at the hotel. It's a longshot, but what if Melinda was one of the ones I was interviewing? My calendar is backed-up online every night. The entries from four years ago have been archived but they should still be available. I have promised Melinda I will go back and see if I have any information on my calendar that may help her."

Tina held her breath. This was more than she could absorb. Jerry had been meeting with Melinda on the day of the explosion? He saw Baby Girl? "I . . . I don't really know what to say. Of course, it would be wonderful if you can help." Even as she forced a tight smile at Jerry, her heart screamed no.

By the time Jerry and Barry left that evening, Tina was emotionally and mentally exhausted. Both of her babies in one day. After four years of searching, after finally starting the adoption proceedings, after all of that, she may well have lost both of them in one day. She and Katie sat on the sofa with a cup of hot tea and rehashed all that had been said and the possible consequences that could be coming their way.

"It's preposterous to think Justin could be Jerry's son. What in the world is he thinking? I cannot even wrap my mind around the idea. It's crazy, Katie. Don't you think it's nuts?"

Katie looked quietly at Tina over the rim of her cup. "I have no idea, Tina. No idea at all. But, he seems pretty sure. And his story makes sense. Doesn't it?"

"I don't know. Maybe a little. I guess I was a little mean to Jerry, huh?"

Katie gave Tina a look and replied, "A little?"

"Well, look, Justin was old enough to remember a few bits about his daddy and he never recognized anything about Jerry." Tina remembered back to the man Justin had seen in the parking lot four years ago. Admittedly, the guy looked a lot like Jerry. Tall and thin with brown hair. It had not been his dad, but Justin was convinced when he first spotted him that it was. Jerry fit that description. So, why did he not recognize Jerry now? Could four years make that much difference? She thought back to stories she had read of missing children coming home. It was true, at times they were scammed by someone who lied about being their child. Justin was so very young, perhaps it was possible. On another note, how would Justin handle being told that his daddy was alive? She was his mom now and the Brogans were his family. How much trauma could a child take?

Tina's heart was in an upheaval. "And, what about Baby Girl? What if Melinda Simmons is her mother? We know nothing about her, except that she has definitely been traumatized. I could never turn Baby over to her. She may not even be in her right mind. If the DNA test is positive, will the courts mandate that I turn my sweet Baby Girl over?"

Again and again, she and Katie covered every possible scenario but each time they came back to the same point. All they could do was to wait for the test results. And pray. *Oh, God. Please. What will happen now?*

CHAPTER EIGHTEEN

The Answers

Back in Chickpea the following morning, Tina explained everything to her parents. There were questions and frustration and disappointment, but in the end, they agreed it was time to discover the truth. True to Brogan tradition, Mom called everyone and invited them over for dinner that evening, explaining it was important for all of them to be there if possible. First food, and then a family meeting. Standard procedure.

After a delicious meal, the older grandchildren took the little ones outside with Pepsi while the adults remained around the long dining room table. Mom and Tina cleared the dishes and refilled drinks before her dad finally suggested they get started.

Once again, Tina went over the details of the past few days, including Jerry's story about Billy being Justin and her fear of Melinda being Baby Girl's mother. Becca interrupted her before she had time to explain. "What is Billy's last name then?"

Tina nodded at her sister. "Andrews. He was—or is—William Justin Andrews. So that explains the names on the Day Care list."

It took quite a while to go over the details and say what she needed to say, what with the questions and outbursts from all of her family. The entire clan had fallen in love with Justin and Baby Girl. The thought of losing them at this point was not something any of them wanted to imagine. However, in the end, they too understood that the time had come to uncover the truth. Either way, they knew the Lord would guide them every step of the way. The evening ended with family prayer, hugs all around and promises to continue to pray as Tina walked through this painful time.

Out on the porch, Tina waved goodbye to each one as they pulled out of the drive. The last to leave was Lottie. Sweet Lottie, who had worked tirelessly on the mediation photos, babysat whenever she could and opened her young heart to two children she claimed as her own niece and nephew. She walked over and hugged her Aunt Tina. With tears running down her cheeks, she promised to do whatever she could to help and most of all to hold Tina and the children before the throne of God. Her Lottie loved God and was not timid about speaking it. Tina knew she would do just as she promised.

Lord, thank you for my family. What would I do without them?

As soon as she spoke, she knew that Justin and Baby Girl needed their families too. And their families needed them. It was a bitter pill to swallow.

Dr. Wilson listened intently to Tina's explanation about needing the DNA tests. He was already aware of the situation and the pending adoption, so the tests were expected. It would only take a moment to swab each child's mouth. She did not need an appointment.

Monday morning Tina sent a note to school with Justin that she would pick him up at lunch. He and Baby Girl—or John and Jane—as the official records indicated, were both enrolled at Live Oak Baptist Church School. Justin was in the second grade and stayed until 3:00 each day, but Baby was in pre-K so she was released at noon. The plan was to drop by the doctor's office for the test and then spend the afternoon together.

After leaving Dr. Wilson's office, they drove to

Chick Fil A where Tina ordered three meals to go. As they drove to the park in the center of town, Baby Girl bounced in her car seat and sang. The song was an original and had to do with puppies. Apparently, they had seen a short film this morning about puppies. Justin rolled his eyes and laughed at his sister, which made the song last even longer. At the park, Justin helped his mom find an open picnic table and together they spread out the food. Baby Girl wanted to play, but Mom insisted they eat first. Tina had come a long way as a mom. Gone were the days when pleading eyes and smiling faces could change her mind. Well, mostly gone.

After lunch, she found a bench swing close to the slides with the sun peeking through above at just the right angle. The air was fresh, the breeze was soft, and up above white fluffy clouds moved gently across the sky. It would have been a perfect day if not for the knot in Tina's heart. She did her best to shake off the gloomy feelings and watched as Justin and Baby maneuvered up and down the slide together. Justin was very protective and caring over his baby sister. They had been thrown together in a time of tragedy and had not been separated since that day. How would they deal with being torn apart? It had been a long time since Justin had asked about his father. Tina wondered if he even remembered him.

If things started coming together—or falling apart—depending on your perspective, she would have a hard time explaining to Justin. He was a mature seven year old whose heart had been sensitized by tragedy. He was, however, still a seven year old.

Baby Girl tumbled off the end of the slide before Justin could grab her. She stood crying, wiping her eyes with her hands while Justin wiped the dirt off her little dress. Tina could not help but smile as she walked that way. How Baby Girl loved her dresses. Most of the girls in her class wore jeans or capris to school, but not Baby. She asked for dresses every morning. Baby was all girl, no doubt about that. Tina picked her up and thanked Justin. Normally, Baby came home at noon, ate lunch and took an afternoon nap. Today was fun and exciting but her little body was demanding its rest.

As soon as Tina picked her up, Baby laid her head on her shoulder, inserted thumb in mouth and sucked her way into a peaceful sleep. Her long legs draped so far down Tina's side they bumped her knees. *When did she get so big? And that thumb. Gracious, it's time to deal with that.*

Tina settled on the swing with Baby wrapped around her, lying against her chest. Such a simple thing, to hold a sleeping child. Something Tina had done for several years, something she normally took for granted. But today, here in this sunny park with sounds of children playing filling the air, here on this day, it was not taken for granted at all. No, this time Tina cherished the tenderness and held the mood close in her heart, fighting the tears and thanking God for one more sweet time of love from Baby.

Justin was happily running in circles with a newfound friend. *Look at him, Lord. Look at what you have done. He was so frightened, terrified really. For days he barely spoke except to ask for Daddy. And you gave him to me, a young, inexperienced girl living alone, trying to make a name for myself in the photography business. I was just as terrified as he was. Look at us now, God. Look what you've done. And this sweet Baby Girl was not even old enough to know what was happening. But still, in her sleep she would cry and awake calling "mommy." And now, she is content, loved and happy. How can we uproot them again? How can we do that to them?*

Which is better, Lord, to stay with a family that is not their blood relatives or be traumatized again to reunite with their real parents? And if it's Jerry, then he isn't the real dad either. But, the grandparents. That's a different story. There has to be an answer somewhere in the middle. What are we going to do, Lord? What are we going to do? Groaning inwardly, Tina reminded herself that it was not up to her to find the answer. God would have his way, whether through the parents or the courts, his will would be done.

After a while, Justin tired of running and wandered over to where she sat holding Baby Girl. Tina handed him a bottle of water from her bag and gave him a quick one armed hug. He plopped down on the swing next to her and looked up at his mom with smiling eyes, a dirty, freckled face and a grin that showed a gap where he had lost his first tooth. She thought of the saying that her heart had somehow moved outside her body and sat next to her on the swing. This precious boy was oblivious to anything other than a perfect day at the park. Tina inhaled a deep breath, let it out slowly, and looked heavenward for help.

"Justin, do you remember when you first came to live with me?"

"Yes, Ma'am, I remember. I remember the fire and you saved me. My daddy was there and then he was gone and you and Barry were there. That was a long time ago. I don't remember much, but I remember you. Your hair was very red." At this he broke into a silly giggle and was up and off again to find his friend.

For the rest of the week, Tina stayed close to home and to the children. Thankfully, Ms. McGowen left them alone. She was relieved too that Jerry stayed away and did not call. The possibility that Jerry could be Justin's father put him in a different light. There were too many decisions on the table to even take time to think about their friendship. Her mind could not go beyond learning the truth from the DNA tests. She suspected Jerry felt the same way.

Friday afternoon, Tina and her mom were rocking on the front porch, watching Justin and baby Girl playing a game of tag with Pepsi. The barking, the giggles, the squealing—it was the sound of happiness. Her cell phone rang and Mr. Johnson's name appeared on the screen. Tina showed it to her mom before slipping into the house to answer. "Hello, Mr. Johnson."

"Tina, I am glad I caught you. We have the results. Would you like to hear them over the phone or wait and drive in on Monday?"

"Have you told Melinda and Jerry? Are they with you?"

"No, I called you first and I will abide by your decision whether to wait until you are all together."

Tina drew in a ragged breath and let it out slowly. Over the sound of her pounding heart, she managed to say: "I want to hear it now."

Mr. Johnson cleared his throat, breathed loudly into the phone, and continued. "Tina, it appears that Melinda Simmons is Baby Girl's mother. The test shows over 98% probability that she is the parent."

Tina sat down weakly on the sofa. Staring into nothingness, she fought back the tears and tried to speak past the lump in her heart. After several minutes, Mr. Johnson continued. "Of course there are several legal issues to consider before any permanent changes can be made. We will talk in depth about that when you come in. This will give you a few days to wrap your mind, and your heart, around the news."

Tina finally found her voice and tried to speak but she could only nod in agreement.

Mr. Johnson continued, "Tina, I can only imagine how difficult this is for you. As we go forward, I want you to understand that I represent you first. You are my client. I will act as an advisor or as legal counsel, whatever you desire."

Dad came in through the backdoor and tousled her hair as he passed through to the front porch. Her sweet daddy had no idea that her world was crumbling around her. As soon as he was out front to watch the children, Mom came in and sat next to Tina. One look at her daughter's face was all she needed to know the answer. "Baby Girl," was all Tina could whisper.

Tina continued her conversation with Mr. Johnson. "Thank you, sir. I have no idea what I should do at this point, but I know I need your help. Is there an answer on Justin?"

"I am conflicted on this one, Tina. The test sample, as you know, came from grandparents and that without their knowledge. We must be very careful with this one. It is a little more difficult to be certain in such cases, but the lab results indicate there is a 90% chance that they are family."

The tears flowed freely and silently as she made arrangements to meet with Mr. Johnson early Monday morning. They agreed that he would not give the results to Jerry or Melinda until after that time. Tina was aware how painful this was for Melinda and for Jerry, but she had to put the children's welfare first. They must move very slowly and carefully before starting a process that would change their lives.

Her next call was to Katie and then to her extended family, taking special care to talk to Lottie personally. The following weekend was bittersweet. After a thousand questions and a thousand conversations in her mind, Tina admitted she had no choice. It was time to move forward. Achingly, painfully, forward. Her daddy offered to ride with her to the appointment and after thinking it over, she agreed it was a good idea. Once again, she thanked God for the amazing turnaround in her daddy. He was a wise man and she needed his strength right now.

CHAPTER NINETEEN

Upheaval

At 9:00 Monday morning, Tina sat in Mr. Johnson's office with her dad on one side and Mr. Johnson behind his desk. She and her dad had left Chickpea before six in the morning, stopped for a quick breakfast and then drove into Atlanta for the meeting. Neither Jerry nor Melinda would be invited to join them until Mr. Johnson had time to review the entire test results with Tina and her father and to answer their questions.

She and her dad agreed it would be best for Mr. Johnson to act as her legal counsel in all matters pertaining to the guardianship of the children. Tina prayed she would have the right attitude when Jerry and Melinda were advised of their answers. She understood they were the rightful and legal parents, and yet, she felt like the mom. After signing all the necessary legal affidavits in front of a notary, Tina and her dad were asked to wait in a separate room while Mr. Johnson talked with Melinda and Jerry.

Melinda was the first to meet with Mr. Johnson. Jerry's meeting followed. After over an hour, Mr. Johnson's secretary summoned Tina and her dad back into his office. Jerry and Melinda had been asked to wait in the conference room for now. Mr. Johnson looked tired this morning. The usual twinkle was missing from his eyes and his handshake was replaced by a gentle arm around her shoulders when she entered the room.

"Tina, both Jerry and Melinda understand and appreciate your circumstances. They also both agree that we should all move very slowly with a plan for returning the children to them. They want to ensure the move is as easy on the children as absolutely possible. And Jerry, especially, is very concerned about you. He knows how much you love his son and does not want to cause you undue grief."

Tina felt a slight relief and relaxed a little in her chair. Her dad reached over and took her hand. It was good he was here with her. She had known this would be tough, but at this point, even breathing was difficult. Her heart would not slow down and the dizziness that came periodically made it hard to concentrate on what was being said.

"Tina, did you understand what I said?"

"I am sorry, sir, but no, I did not hear you."

Mr. Johnson looked at her dad for a moment before continuing. "Tina, do you need to take a break and get back to this after lunch?"

"No, thank you, I need to hear everything now. I am just having a little trouble concentrating. I keep thinking of Justin and Baby Girl. How will they ever handle such a trauma? I am the only Mama Baby has ever known. And Justin has been with me so long, he barely remembers his daddy."

"I understand. And so do the others. Each of them has told me how very much they appreciate you and your family. They feel indebted to you in many ways for the love and time you have showered on their children. However, you must remember, dear, they are parents who have longed for and missed their children for four years."

Tina nodded. "I understand."

Next, Mr. Johnson explained they would need to contact Children's Services and explain the situation.

"May I do that with Ms. McGowen?"

"Of course you are welcome to talk with her, but it also needs to come from me. There are legal steps we need to follow. Let's be certain we do it exactly right. In cases like this, DFACS will normally continue to monitor the children for at least a year before returning full parental rights to the parents. Regular visits, inspections, sessions with child psychologists, all will be routine until everyone involved is confident the children are adjusting to their new homes. Trust me, Tina, we all want what is best not only for the children, but for you as well. We cannot of course know all that is happening in your heart, but we know you well enough to know you are hurting. I am sorry for that.

Be assured, no one is going anywhere right now. You are the legal foster parent and that will not change overnight, plus both parents are in agreement to move slowly. It is of utmost importance to cause the children as little pain as possible.

Is there anything else you would like me to cover? Do either of you have questions?"

Tina looked over at her dad. "What are you thinking, Daddy"

"I am thinking that I have never been more proud of you nor more concerned for you than I am right now. But, as for what Mr. Johnsons has explained, I think we both understand well enough for now."

Tina nodded in agreement.

Mr. Johnson stood and shook hands with both of them. "We will of course be in close touch as things play out. Now, if you are ready, we should meet with Jerry and Melinda."

Holding onto her daddy's hand, Tina followed Mr. Johnson out the door and across the hall to the conference room. Jerry stood when she entered. It was apparent he had been crying, as had Melinda Simmons. He immediately stepped forward and hugged Tina. The others stepped back as the two hugged and cried together. Tina's heart was broken and confused, but as she stood there with Jerry holding her, she felt a tinge of his joy and knew this had to be done. There was no other way.

Melinda, on the other hand, held back and only nodded uncertainly at Tina. The woman was obviously overwhelmed and struggling to get a grip on the reality of what was happening. This was not just a matter of finding her daughter, but of finding herself. After covering the basics of what would happen next, Mr. Johnson agreed to contact DFACs on their behalf before he politely excused himself. Daddy stayed by her side while the four of them discussed the children.

As expected, Melinda was anxious to see her child. And as expected, Tina was reluctant to allow that. Finally, they agreed that Melinda would visit the house, perhaps stay overnight, but she would not reveal her identity to Baby Girl at this point.

Melinda agreed and plans were made for her to visit on Wednesday. Tina needed a day first to talk with Ms. McGowen and take care of any requests she may have. She seriously needed time to absorb all that had transpired in the last few days.

After Melinda left, Tina's dad slipped out to let her and Jerry have time to talk. "Tina, I do not know what to say. I hoped and prayed for this to be true, but in all honesty, in some ways I still thought my imagination was running away with me. The results are conclusive but my heart is still trying to understand. When I think of four years lost when you were looking for me and never knew it was me you were looking for. So much pain could have been avoided."

"I don't know what to say either, Jerry. I don't know how I feel; but that is not important. What is important is Justin. And Baby Girl. How will they handle this? Can you even begin to imagine what this will do to them? I am the only mom they know. We are all adults. We can understand what is happening, but they are just babies really. How in the world will they ever adjust? My heart is breaking for them."

Jerry stared intently into her eyes. His own eyes were filled with pain. "My heart breaks in so many ways, Tina. The entire situation is like something out of a movie. How could I have not known for sure the first time I saw him? Why did I not look at the photos earlier? How could the coroner have made such a horrible mistake? Who is the child we buried? It goes on and on with no answers.

I know they will both be traumatized over this. I hurt for both of them. Not just Justin, but Baby Girl too. However, as hard as it will be, it is four years out of a lifetime. Four years seems a long time now, but when he is an adult, it will seem like a brief season in his memories."

Tina's heart fell to the floor. A brief season in his memories? She knew that was true in a sense, but it was a life altering season and she prayed Justin never forgot his time with her.

Jerry took her hand, "Remember, the day Melinda and I looked over the mediation photo book? I thought I remembered seeing her right before the explosion. When I checked my backup calendar files, I discovered that I had an appointment with a Caroline Matthews that morning at the hotel. Apparently, we were hiring but the individual being replaced was not aware so we were giving interviews at the hotel. There was an application on file under that name, complete with a snapshot and an address. Unfortunately, when we checked, it was an apartment that had long ago been rented by someone else. Melinda—or Caroline—and I met with the landlord but records from four years ago have been stored in a warehouse and we have not yet been able to view them. The application she completed for us showed her as divorced with one child. The references listed were all out of state. Melinda is trying to locate them, but none appear to be relatives."

CHAPTER TWENTY

Justin

Justin had met Jerry, and knew him as his mom's friend, so it would not be unusual for him to visit. Neither of them wanted Jerry to be there at the same time as Melinda, so they agreed he would visit on the following Friday. She and Jerry both promised to work together and make this transition as smooth and painless as possible. For now, Jerry would still be his mom's friend with no mention being made of him being Justin's daddy.

The next weeks were like a roller coaster ride for all concerned. Melinda and Jerry were regular visitors at the Brogan home in Chickpea. Tina was aware that her relationship with Jerry was changing. They were the same two people who had enjoyed each other's company for months, and yet, they were different. Both of them walked on eggshells most of the time. Jerry could see that she was fragile, and she could sense the thinly veiled excitement in him. It made for a precarious situation. In the midst of such turmoil, any thoughts of developing a deeper relationship were dismissed. To call this time poignant for Tina would be a gross understatement.

Justin warmed to Jerry quickly and they spent many afternoons together at the park with Pepsi or hiking down country roads with the BB guns. Jerry had trouble restraining himself but he waited until the legal ramifications had been discussed and settled before asking Tina to allow him to tell Justin the truth. He had been more than patient; for her sake as well as Justin's, but it had been weeks and he was understandably anxious to officially be known as "Daddy." It was a moment she had hoped for years ago, but now, she could barely nod her head in agreement. Both she and Jerry thought it best that she be present when Jerry broke the news to Justin.

And so, on a Saturday morning, sitting on Tina's front porch with Pepsi lying at his side, Justin heard the news that Jerry was actually his long-lost father. At first he did not respond and she thought perhaps the shock was too great. She and Jerry looked at each other and waited. After a few moments, Justin looked up with tears running down his little face and answered, "I hoped it would be you, but I didn't think it could be true." Then in an instant, he was in Jerry's lap and both were sobbing. Tina slipped into the house and left them alone.

After a few minutes, they walked into the living room. Both had happy, red, smiling eyes. Tina could not help but be happy for them. Justin immediately walked over and hugged her. "Will you still be my Mama?"

"Oh, honey! I will always be your mama. Even if there comes a time when you get another mama, I will still be your Tina mama!" Wrapping her arms around her son, she held him so tightly he finally told her he couldn't breathe.

Grandma Joan and Grandad stood with tears in their eyes, watching their daughter giving the biggest gift of her life. The gift of unconditional love to this little boy. Grandma walked over, pulled Justin away and knelt down in front of him. She wrapped him in a big hug. "You will have another name of course, but you will always be a Brogan and you will always be my grandson. That will never change." Grandad joined the group hug and slowly the tears turned to laughter.

Baby Girl ran over and jumped on Justin's back, which threw him off balance and into Joan, who fell on her backside. Grandad laughed loud as Justin and Baby Girl dramatically fell over as well. After the commotion died down, Justin sat on the couch, snuggled down between Tina and Jerry. He politely listened to the grownups talk. He was so serious, with a sensitivity that surpassed his age. Every few minutes, he reached up to one or the other and patted their face, or hugged them. He was obviously completely overcome with all that was going down. Who could blame him?

Tina could see the wheels turning in his mind. Although she wanted him to open up about what he was feeling, she was hoping maybe he would do it privately with her. No such luck. Justin turned his sweet face towards Jerry and asked, "Daddy, will you live with us now?"

Of course he would think that. He was seven. The idea of leaving her had not even entered his mind. Another part of Tina's heart broke as she held him again in a tight hug and explained that no, Jerry would not live with them, but he should not worry about that right now. "Everything will come together very nicely. Wait and see. Right now, let's just thank God for bringing your daddy back to you."

Later, after nighttime prayer, Justin looked at his mom with serious eyes. "What about Baby? Where is her daddy?"

Tina's parents were gracious to both Jerry and Melinda, allowing them to visit whenever possible. After a while, however, the extra cooking, cleaning and entertaining were becoming difficult for her mom. Tina helped as much as she could, but Joan was bearing the brunt of most of it while Tina entertained and mediated between the children and their new parents. Something needed to break soon. Jerry had told Justin's grandparents about their grandson and although they too had been patient, they were bursting to see him. Ms. McGowen agreed to an overnight visit at Tina's convenience. Jerry was delighted and wanted to go immediately. At his request, Tina accompanied him to Tennessee for the first visit.

With the impending separation getting closer every day, Tina determined to enjoy this time with Jerry and Justin. The drive up was pleasant. Jerry and Justin talked while Tina relaxed and visited places in her mind. Places she had not been in a while—Justin's little couch-bed, the trips to Piedmont Park, the day they brought Pepsi home—the chewing. At this she laughed out loud and both guys looked at her questioningly. She related the story of Pepsi's chewing fits and Justin joined in the laughter. Justin had wanted Pepsi to accompany them to Tennessee but with only a few days before delivery, the trip would be too difficult for her.

Tina had to admit, she missed the close friendship that had once been between Jerry and her. He was a gentle, loving man who had endured great loss and managed to keep—or at least regain—his faith in God and in life. Once again, she put this relationship in God's hands. Only He knew if their relationship was a casualty of circumstances or a seed that would grow and bloom.

Jerry suggested lunch and Tina and Justin agreed they were hungry as well. The bar-b-que hut looked a bit suspicious from the parking lot, but once inside they were greeted with smiling faces and warm smells of good food. The waitresses knew Jerry by name. Apparently, this was a regular stop on his way up north. They made over Justin and Tina and served up free dessert in honor of the occasion. Afterwards, with only an hour or so left on their journey, the conversation quieted and Justin dozed off in the back seat.

"Tina, I very much appreciate you coming with me. I know my in-laws, they are a loving group of folks, but they can be a tad overbearing at times. I am concerned that Billy may be overwhelmed and need you close. Please give me a signal if things get too rough for you. They have all missed Billy so very much. Who knows what they have planned."

"It's OK, Jerry, we will be fine. I wanted to come to be with Justin especially the first time he sees everyone. You are right, I am still his mom." As soon as the words were out of her mouth, she regretted them. "Please forgive me, Jerry. That wasn't meant to be offensive, just habit, you know."

"I understand completely. He has been with you for almost four years. And although no one can ever replace her, he has actually been with you longer than he was with Marcy. In his eyes you are his mom and that is a beautiful thing for him." Once again, like so many times in the past weeks, Jerry thanked her for taking care of his son, for loving him and providing for him. "At times I imagine Marcy looking down and smiling to see Billy and me back together. I know she has been close to both of us the entire time." Tina smiled and reached out affectionately for his arm. She appreciated his gratitude, but every time he voiced it, she remembered that Justin was leaving.

Shortly after passing through Chattanooga, they turned off onto a two lane highway and headed west. Jerry explained that his parents were just south of Chattanooga and asked if she would be willing to visit with them at some point. Because of his mother's health, he had not mentioned taking Billy to see them yet. Twenty minutes later they pulled into an older, well-groomed subdivision with large yards and beautiful trees. The house was located in a cul-de-sac with a backyard that faced the golf course.

Before they could climb out of the car, the front door opened and Grandma and Granddaddy stood on the porch, shading their eyes from the sun and squinting to be sure it was indeed their grandson. Grandma was dressed in white capris, a tee shirt, and sandals. Her white hair was fashionably styled in a bob with subtle highlights. Granddaddy actually wore shorts and flip flops and sported a golf-course tan that was impressive. It was obvious that grief had taken its toll on both of them, yet they appeared to be in good health. Tina wondered if perhaps Jerry had been mistaken in thinking they could not endure the pain of a DNA test and legal proceedings when he regained consciousness after the explosion. Perhaps it was Jerry that could not endure it.

Jerry had asked them to go slow with Billy and they were trying, but as Tina neared the porch, she could see the tears streaming down four wrinkled cheeks. Once inside, the grandparents could not hold off any longer. They showered her son with kisses and hugs while Justin reluctantly soaked up the attention like any seven year old boy. Once the excitement calmed a bit, Jerry introduced Tina.

Grandma grabbed her in a bear hug. "Oh, dear. I am so very glad to finally meet you. I don't know you, but I feel I do. How can we ever thank you for all you have done for our boy? When I think of where he could have ended up without you taking him in. He could have even been left in that shelter. Or an abusive foster home. Dear God, it breaks my heart to know he has been so close all along and we never knew it. But, that is all over now. Thank you my dear. Thank you so very much! How can we ever repay you?"

Tina was beginning to understand what Jerry meant. "My time with Justin has been the most rewarding and loving time of my entire life. I thank God every day for allowing me to be his mama for these last four years. You owe me nothing. Nothing at all."

Grandma seemed a little taken aback. "Yes, of course. He is such a loving child. Of course, Marcy will always be his real mother, but we are so very thankful he had you to step up and care for him. I am sure he loves you dearly."

Awkward. After a pause, Grandma took Justin by the hand and led him into the kitchen. She offered every kind of cookie imaginable before Tina stepped in and suggested two would be enough for now.

While Justin enjoyed the cookies with a big glass

of milk, both Grandma and Granddaddy took great pains to let her know over and over how very much they appreciated her taking care of Billy these four years. They even offered to reimburse her financially. Tina was surprised at that, but she declined, explaining that Jerry had everything covered. There was no need to go into detail about that being part of the legal agreement. She had not expected nor requested financial recompense but Mr. Johnson and Jerry both insisted.

Later in the afternoon the extended family started showing up. Cousins, aunts, uncles, family friends—everyone was thrilled to see "Billy" again. Tina sat quietly observing the interaction from a comfy chair in the corner of the large, open living room. Occasionally, Justin would look her way to ensure she was still close. She would respond with a nod, an encouraging remark or a wink, just to help him relax and enjoy his time.

Grandma walked over to the bookshelf and pulled out a large photo album. Tina's stomach tightened just a little when she explained she wanted Justin to see photos of his "real" mom. It all happened so quickly, Tina had no time to prepare herself or her son. Suddenly, Justin was looking face to face at his mom. Everyone and everything in the room froze for a moment. Some looked cautiously at her from the corner of their eyes as others squatted beside Justin.

The look on grandma's face as she showed her grandson picture after picture of him with his mom—her only daughter—was almost too intimate for Tina to witness. Then, suddenly, everyone was talking at once about Justin as a toddler. His older cousins told stories of him as a baby and how they had pulled him around in the little red wagon. Justin was surrounded by strangers and everyone was talking at once. He looked up at Tina with fear and confusion shining in his eyes.

Was she the only person in the room who saw what was happening? Didn't any of these people understand how traumatic this was for a seven year old boy? Tina stood and started towards him but Jerry saw the look as well and reached down to pick up his son. He suggested they all go outside for a few minutes. Slowly, the room cleared. Jerry sat Justin down and turned towards the door. Justin took that opportunity to make his break straight for Tina. He crawled up in her lap and wrapped his arms around her neck. There he sat, his long legs dangling to the floor and his face hidden in her shoulder. "Mommy, I want to go home." He had not called her mommy in a long time.

Driving home the next day, Justin fell asleep in the backseat and Jerry took the opportunity to apologize for his in-laws. "They are so excited to see him. It is bizarre for them to think that he doesn't remember his time here. I promise, I will talk with everyone and help them to understand we must go very slowly with Billy . . . Justin."

"I know it is a hard thing for any of us to understand. I just want to be sure we keep Justin's feelings uppermost in every decision. This is the third life altering event in his short life. He must have time to process all that is occurring."

Jerry drove silently for a while. Tina was lost in her own thoughts. She understood this was monumental for Jerry and his family, but it was even more so for Justin. After a while Jerry broke the silence. "I overheard your conversation with my mother-in-law regarding finances. I appreciate you not going into detail about our agreement."

Tina nodded and changed the subject. She suggested he could sign Justin up for baseball this summer. Jerry was thrilled to do just that. Frankly, she was not all that thrilled, but little by little she was letting go. It had to be done, she knew that. The remainder of the ride was fairly quiet, with Justin sleeping most of the way and Tina lost in thought. That turned out to be a good thing because when they pulled into the drive about four o'clock that afternoon, they were met with much excitement. Pepsi had delivered six puppies—all by herself!

Justin was thrilled although he was a little sad he had not been there to see it all. Honestly, Tina was more than a little glad they were not present for the birthing process. Pepsi was settled in the garage on a large blanket; food and water close by, receiving guests like the hero she was.

When Justin walked in, Pepsi thumped her big tail against the blanket and raised her head as if to say, "Look what I did!" She allowed Justin to hold the puppies and Baby Girl could pet them as long as Justin was still holding. The camera came out and laughter filled the air while Tina clicked away. Pepsi was obviously quite proud of herself and her new family. Mom informed them the German Shepherd had shown up for a viewing that morning but was not invited to remain.

After a while, everyone except Justin, Jerry and Tina wandered into the house for snacks. Tina sat with Justin and explained how to treat the puppies. She wanted him to understand that Pepsi would be up and running around before he knew it. His little eyes were misted over as Tina talked about how fragile the babies were. He very tenderly picked up and examined each one before returning it to Pepsi's side.

Pepsi yawned and closed her eyes, trusting Justin with her family.

Jerry had sat quietly while Tina instructed Justin on proper puppy handling. Now he took her hand and stared solemnly into her eyes. "Tina, I know this is all happening so quickly—too quickly for you, I'm sure. But, please, I do not want to lose our friendship during the process."

Tina's heart beat a little faster and she returned his look with the same solemnity. "Me neither, Jerry, me neither."

CHAPTER TWENTY-ONE

Baby Girl

Melinda and Baby Girl were not as easy to understand or to accept as Jerry and Justin. Baby Girl had always been outgoing and loving to anyone who came to visit, so the fact that she and Melinda had fun together was no surprise. But other than playtime, Melinda was reluctant to take part in any of the duties pertaining to Baby Girl. She never asked to bathe her, or tuck her in, or prepare her food. Tina was perplexed and not quite sure how to handle it.

The ruling from DFACS was that Melinda would visit on a regular basis for at least three months before she could take Baby to her home for a visit. Since she was still under the care of a psychiatrist and on several medications, her doctor had to sign a release as well. Her apartment sounded nice, but it was a small one bedroom in Atlanta. That meant two hours away from Tina. If Melinda needed help it could become a problem. Tina wondered why she had not taken some of her money from the settlement and moved to a larger place—one that had room for her daughter. It was yet another red flag that perhaps she was not all-in to the idea of caring for her daughter.

Finally, after many visits, Tina decided it was time to have a heart to heart with Melinda. For one thing, she had never mentioned anything to Tina about discovering her real name—Caroline Matthews. And for another thing, she seemed content to visit Baby Girl here without any mention of taking the next step. Baby still had no idea who Melinda was. Actually, neither did Tina. The next Wednesday when Melinda arrived for her visit, Tina summoned her courage and drew her aside.

"Melinda, could we talk privately for a while?"

"Certainly. Can Baby Girl come along?"

"I would rather it be just us if you don't mind. We could sit for a spell on the front porch."

They sat in the rocking chairs with a glass of cold lemonade and a small plate of mom's chocolate chip cookies. After a time of small talk, Tina leaned up in her chair and looked Melinda directly in the eyes.

In her best calm voice, she started, "I don't want to upset you, Melinda. I understand you are in a very difficult place. I cannot even imagine. But, ummm, I am in a hard place too—we all are here."

Melinda sat staring straight ahead. Tina wondered if she had even heard her. Leaning back in her chair, Tina began again. "I hope it is OK, but Jerry told me about discovering your real name. I was just wondering why you never mentioned it."

"Because, Caroline Matthews is no longer my name. It took months to legalize my new name. Changing everything back now seems pointless unless I can connect it with my family."

"Yes, I can see that. Have you made any progress on finding the references listed on Jerry's employment application?"

"No. None of the addresses are valid anymore, nor the phone numbers. Plus I have no idea what connection I have with them. The relationship only shows *Friend*."

Melinda shifted in the chair, took a deep breath and blew it out slowly before continuing. "Actually, Mr. Johnson's office was able to locate a birth certificate issued to Caroline Denise Matthews. The date could very well be my birthdate. They are researching the names listed as mother and father, but so far they have not been able to locate them."

"Melinda! That is wonderful news. I thought you would be thrilled. Are you hesitant to believe it is you?"

"No, that isn't it. I do believe it is me. But not being able to locate the parents brings me to another dead end. And . . . well, there's more. Using the information from my birth certificate, they discovered a birth certificate issued to Elizabeth Denise Matthews. I am shown as the mother and the address is the same as listed on the application."

Tina squealed and jumped to hug Melinda. "That's wonderful news! Baby Girl has a name and a birthdate and you have more proof that you are her mommy. And her daddy? You have that now too. This is wonderful!"

Not only did Melinda not return the hug, nor share in the excitement, she looked positively stricken. "No," she said, "the father's name was not listed. On that line was one word: *Unknown*. Can't you see? This makes everything so much worse. At least when I didn't know the truth, I could imagine a happy family. Now I have nothing—not even hope."

Tina eased back in her seat, stunned. "You have Baby Girl—Elizabeth Denise. You have her. And you have God. And you have all of us to help you. You are not alone, Melinda."

They sat rocking without speaking for a while.

Tina was disturbed by Melinda's reaction to discovering her identity, but without having walked in her shoes, she had no idea how to even begin to console her. *Lord, give me the words. Melinda obviously needs help—from you mostly.*

Mom walked out onto the porch and joined them. Her question took both women by surprise. "Melinda, do you think you are ready to care for Baby Girl by yourself?"

Tina loved her mom's way of just telling it like it was. She hated to have it put to Melinda so bluntly, but time was slipping by without much progress. They were all beginning to feel the frustration of being caught between two worlds.

"No, I don't. Why do you think I have let Tina continue to be her mom? To bathe her, feed her, dress her? I don't even know my own child in the way both of you know her. I am still so broken inside. And every time I gain a bit of knowledge from my past, it kicks me down further."

Mom reached over and squeezed Melinda's hand. She reassured her that they were in this together. They would figure it out. In the weeks following their talk, Melinda began making attempts to be more involved with the daily routine of caring for Baby Girl. But, once again, it was Tina's mom who solved the dilemma. One Friday in late July, Melinda was visiting for the weekend. Justin had gone with Jerry to visit his grandparents. This would be his first full weekend without her and Tina's nerves were raw thinking about her son being alone with the family vultures. Yes, she knew that was not fair, but she remembered the lot of them swarming around Justin, everyone talking at once. For the hundredth time since they left yesterday, Tina asked God to take care of Justin.

Melinda, Tina and her mom were sitting at the kitchen table enjoying a glass of iced tea when her mom threw out an amazing idea. "Melinda, I understand that you have settlement money to live on, but wouldn't you like a job as well? I mean, I have no idea how much money you have, but even with good investments, it will not last forever."

"That's true. I have actually been looking in Atlanta, but with my situation here up in the air, I am reluctant to make a commitment."

"Yes, I understand. But, have you considered moving to Chickpea? Ms. McGowen called this morning to check on everyone and in the conversation she mentioned the DFACS office is hiring. It is a full time position here in the local office. I believe it involves accounting. Anyway, it may not be a bad idea. That way, you would be close to us if you needed help with Baby Girl."

She could see the wheels turning in Melinda's head. Perhaps this would work. She would, however, need a place to live. *And please, Lord, not here. That would be too much for all of us. Except of course, for Baby Girl, she would love it.*

Her mom was one step ahead of her. "There is a small house for rent just a few miles from here, right in downtown Chickpea. It is an older home but pretty with a small fenced yard. The area is very safe and it is only a few blocks from the church where Baby Girl goes to school. Well, where she went last year."

To Tina's relief, Melinda was very interested and by afternoon they had viewed the vacant house and made an appointment with Ms. McGowen for a job interview.

CHAPTER TWENTY-TWO

The Inevitable

The interview went well for Melinda and within a week, she was hired by Children's Services. She moved into her new house in Chickpea the first of August and this weekend Baby Girl was going for her first overnight visit. Her little bag, packed with an assortment of stuffed animals, games and a photo of her and Tina along with her prettiest pajamas, had been sitting by the front door since early that morning. Tina had secretly added her Sunday necessities to the bag and hung her dress close by. The plan was for Melinda to take her home Saturday evening and meet them at church Sunday morning.

Melinda and Baby Girl were bonding nicely. They had talked with her several times, but Baby did not understand the concept of Melinda being her mother. It was a difficult situation to say the least. No one wanted her to feel abandoned by Tina and the Brogans, but as the weeks wore on, it was apparent that living in limbo was not a good idea either. Beth, as she was now called, was almost five years old. Tina had shown the photo of her with Melinda the day of the explosion and then photos of her in Tina's apartment a few weeks later, hoping to help her put the pieces together. That had helped in her mind but her heart still clung to Tina.

Justin's grandparents had agreed Jerry would have sole custody, but requested that he live in TN if possible. Jerry was in the process of finding employment and housing in the area. Late one Sunday afternoon, Jerry and Justin returned from another visit to TN. Tina knew when they walked in the door that something was up. Sure enough, Justin came immediately over and hugged her. Standing up, he smiled and said, "I love you. You will always be my Mommy. You are the best Mom ever!" With that he bounded up the stairs to his room and the X-Box.

Looking at Jerry with a raised eyebrow, Tina waited for the explanation she knew was coming. Clearing his throat, Jerry came over and sat next to her on the couch. "Tina, you know how I feel about you and all you have done for Justin and for me. You are an amazing lady. You saved my son's life. If you had not taken him into your heart and your home that day, he would be in foster care somewhere and I would never have known he was alive. We owe you, Tina. We can never repay what you have done for us."

"What is this about, Jerry?"

"There is no easy way to say this. I believe it is time for Justin to move back home with me. It's been months since we discovered the truth. We have built a relationship based on mutual love. His grandparents are elderly and they want to see him as much as possible. They deserve that."

Tina looked away to hide her tears. After a few moments of silence, she turned to Jerry with a calm façade. "I thought we agreed to take our time."

"Yes, you are right, we did agree to that. You know I am trying my best to make this as easy as possible for all of us, but Tina, he is my son and he knows that now. We talked about moving this weekend. I think he is ready. School starts in two weeks up there and it seems like the logical time to make the move. You know of course, he—hopefully both of us—will always be a part of your life, your family. We will visit anytime he or you ask. And you are always welcome there. Think about it Tina, I have missed my son for a long time."

Jerry continued, "This weekend, I—we—found the perfect house. It has three bedrooms, two baths and a full basement, perfect for Justin and his friends to hang out as he gets older. It is in a cul-de-sac, two miles from my in-laws. Billy loves it. We would need to fence the backyard for Pepsi and the one puppy we are taking, and update the kitchen. Of course new carpet, painting etc., but, if all goes as we hope with our cash offer, the place should be ours within a couple of weeks. If not, we can stay with his grandparents until we get it ready. I have a second interview with a law firm there early Monday morning."

Jerry reached over and took her hand and very gently continued, "Everything seems to be falling into place now. Not next year, Tina, but now."

Tina choked back the tears as she looked out the window and ignored Jerry. Finally, after minutes of silence, she felt that nudge deep in her spirit. Jerry was right, it was time. It would never be time in her opinion, but for Jerry, for Justin and apparently for God, it was time. Slowly she turned and met Jerry's eyes. She nodded. That was all she had. Sometimes there are no words that work. This was one of those times.

The plans were laid out one by one, day by day. Justin seemed to understand as much as he could what was happening. The entire Brogan family was reluctant to let him go and yet they too knew it was time. There were long, emotional talks with Justin. There were tears and promises and hugs—lots and lots of hugs. Justin tried to explain to Baby Beth (who she wanted to be called now) what was happening, but since he did not really understand himself, the talks always ended with him saying he would always be her big brother.

Tina and Beth visited the new house in TN. Beth was a little confused when told she would not be living there. And neither would Tina. It was all too much for her five year old mind, but she was such a trusting little girl, she just accepted it. Everything was fun for Beth. She sang her way through life with a smile and dimples.

One Saturday afternoon they were standing in the middle of the kitchen going over granite samples when Jerry suddenly laid them on the counter and drew her into his arms. At first Tina resisted out of habit, but then she relaxed and reminded herself there was no reason not to be romantic with Jerry. She laid her head gently on his chest and breathed in the scent of him, allowing her heart to relax there in his arms. Jerry kissed the top of her head and whispered, "I have wanted to do this so many times. I know things are complicated, but can we still explore the possibility of us?"

After that day, things were gentler between them. Their playful banter returned and she was able to laugh at his attempts to put together a house from scratch. His choices were surprisingly tasteful and Tina enjoyed shopping and arranging Justin's new home. At times she had to reign in her own thoughts about what Justin needed. Jerry was blatantly spoiling him with game consoles, his own T.V. and pretty much anything he asked for. "Oh, boy, Jerry, you are going to have to back down on this or you will be sorry later."

Jerry laughed and shook his head. "I have waited too long to spoil him. I have a lot of catching up to do. But, for you, I will tone it down a bit. I promise."

The move went more smoothly than anyone expected. For the first week, Justin called every day. Tina suspected it was more to check on her than anything else. He was conforming to his new life just as he had done when Tina took him home almost five years ago. Her awesome little boy.

Tina cried every day the first week. It was impossible to even consider living the rest of her life without Justin. At times it was difficult to even get a deep breath. Jerry had asked her to decorate the guest room in a way that pleased her and now he gave her an open invitation to visit whenever possible. She went on Saturdays and stayed over until Sunday when possible, but that meant leaving her mom with Beth and Melinda. Occasionally, she took Beth with her, but Melinda made her feel guilty when she did that. The days stretched into weeks, but God was faithful and by the end of the month, she managed an ever so slight consideration that perhaps God's will was perfect. If not in this life, then at least in the next one. It would take a long time for Him to fill the empty place left in her heart and life, but at least she acknowledged that He was capable of doing that.

After Justin moved out, Beth began to understand more what was happening. There was a subtle shift in her attitude, almost as if she was slowly saying goodbye. Tina was saddened and proud of her girl, all at the same time. Her overnight visits with her mother increased to a full weekend. Melinda was able to arrange her work schedule and went for lunch at the school a couple of days a week. It was an emotional time for all of them. But, in the end, it was Beth who announced one day that she wanted to stay with Mommy Melinda.

Her eyes were solemn as she looked into Tina's face and stroked her cheek. "I love you mommy. You are my first mommy. But, Mommy Melinda is very lonesome. And you have Grandma and Granddaddy here with you. I think I need to go stay with Mommy Melinda now. Is that OK? I mean, we talked about it. I even asked God about it. He didn't answer me like he does you, but he made my heart feel good about it. Is that how he talks?"

Tina thought her heart would fall right out on the floor. She could not speak over the lump in her throat and struggled to keep the tears at bay. She didn't want to upset Baby Girl or make her think she was wrong to want to go. She also did not want her to think she would not be missed. In the end, all she did was pick her up and hold her as tight as she could. She held Baby Girl in her arms until her heart slowed. And then she hugged her again.

"Beth" promised to call every day, to visit every week and to always remember to say her prayers at night and to never stop loving Mommy Tina or Grandma Joan or Granddaddy or Lottie . . . on and on in her little girl voice she proceeded to name each and every Brogan relative.

It was at that moment Tina understood for the first time that the bond between a mother and her child can withstand every obstacle imaginable. Even at such a young age, Beth instinctively knew her mother. Tina thought of her own mom and the closeness they shared. Her mom knew things about her that no one else understood, even though Tina hated to admit it, it seemed her mom could see straight into her heart.

Beth was Melinda's daughter, nothing could change that. And nothing should. God had given Beth to Melinda. He had loaned her to Tina for a few short years, but Melinda would always be her true mother. It was time for Tina to accept that and begin her own journey to return to wholeness. Wholeness. She had once thought she understood that, but now, it was only a word. A distant phenomenon that she had yet to achieve. Wholeness meant you were whole—with no pieces missing. She had parts of her heart missing. She was not whole. She wondered if she would ever be again.

That night Tina and Baby snuggled for a while until Baby Girl fell asleep. Gingerbread, the puppy Melinda had agreed for Baby to keep, slept peacefully at the foot of her bed. Tina stood and surveyed the scene. So beautiful. So perfect. Then Tina went into her own bedroom and cried—tears of thankfulness, sorrow and love—pure love for two children who had filled her heart in ways she could never have imagined. A week later, Tina and her mom packed up Beth's favorite things and drove her to Melinda's house. She insisted on leaving some of her clothes and toys at Tina's for when she visited.

Her new room at Melinda's was decorated just the

way she requested, complete with a princess poster and glow-in-the dark stars on the ceiling. Over in the corner was a small doggie bed with a pink cushion and chew toys. Tina laughed, remembering her own naivety when Pepsi was small and she thought chew toys would keep her from chewing the furniture. Ha—that was a joke.

On the dresser were photos Tina had taken of Melinda and Beth, but also photos of Justin, Tina and Baby Girl. There was a scrapbook Tina made for Baby with photos of all the Brogan clan, taken over the last few years. And over on the wall above Gingerbread's bed was a large photo of Pepsi and all her pups. That was a special touch. Melinda had taken great care to create a space where Baby Girl—Beth—would feel comfortable, loved and secure. As Tina walked out of the room, she noticed the stencil right above the light switch: *Beth's Room*. That was fitting. Beth lived here now, but Baby Girl would always be Tina's and would forever live in her heart.

Going back into the empty house was more than Tina could endure, so they picked up Granddad and drove over to the next small town for dinner at the family buffet. Sitting there with their food barely touched, they looked for all the world like three lost souls, not sure what to do next. The following days were pretty much the same. It was strange how the final move had knocked them down, even though they had known it was coming for weeks. When Justin moved out, there were a lot of tears, but they still had Baby Girl. The house was still full of silliness and busyness. But now, after she left, there was nothing. Emptiness has a loud voice.

Tina sat on the porch swing and moved slowly back and forth while she petted Chipper, the tiny Pepsi look-alike she had kept. Smiling, she remembered the pact they made before Justin left. Baby Girl had sat very still while Justin explained that each of them would have one of Pepsi's pups. They would always remain family and now Pepsi's family would be a part too. Of course, Justin took Pepsi as well as Bernice. Bernice—what a peculiar name for a seven year old boy to choose for his puppy, but he had heard the name on a movie and thought it to be the perfect fit for his new doggie.

Justin had held Bernice, Baby Girl held Gingerbread and Tina held Chipper while Pepsi lay in the middle of the circle. Justin read a proclamation stating that they would always be family and so would the puppies. Justin signed first, and then Baby made a big B of which she was very proud. After Tina signed, each puppy paw was dipped in food dye mixed with water and pressed onto the paper. Pepsi was the last to place her "seal" of approval. Later, Tina presented each child with a framed copy of their pact along with a "family" photo. It was all very legal and as Justin explained, binding forever.

Tina remembered looking up at Jerry and asking, "do we maybe have a budding lawyer on our hands?"

There were so many memories in her heart. So many unexpected hurdles they had overcome. With tears streaming unhindered down her cheeks, she held Chipper close and explained that they were a family. "It doesn't matter if we are not really blood, in my heart we are family, you know?" Chipper curled closer to her tummy, as if in approval. Tina knew it made no sense whatsoever to talk to a dog, but there she sat in the porch swing—all alone except for Chipper—and she cried and talked and cried some more. "They are really gone. They won't ever live here again. Oh, they will visit, but only for a few days. This isn't home to them anymore." She held the little puppy close to her heart and let the tears drop on its head while she explained how badly her heart ached and how much she missed them. Puppy eyes looked up adoringly at Tina as if he understood completely. "Oh, Chipper, it hurts so bad." Once again, the smothering feeling overcame her. The hole in her heart seemed to open wider and wider the longer she sat there.

Justin had been right. He was only seven years

old and yet he understood they needed an ongoing connection. He had thought up the pact and that each one should have a puppy. How did he think of such a precious thing to do? He was the child and she had been the mom and yet here she sat, talking to a puppy and believing that he understood because he was part of this strange, disjointed family of hers. And all because a seven year old understood her need before she did.

Tina moved through the next few weeks with little enthusiasm. Her reason for living had been hijacked and along with it, her joy. It didn't help to remind herself that God was in control or that the children were happy. None of that mattered to her wounded heart. Life stood still. Tears were a normal part of her day and came unbidden at the simplest thought of Justin or Baby Girl.

Weeks passed and then months. She visited Jerry and Justin as often as possible and saw Beth on a weekly basis. Jerry repeatedly asked for more of her heart but she could not rise to that level of intimacy right now. It was all she could do just to get through each day. She knew it was time to rejoin life and resume her career, but every time she picked up her camera she remembered the many photo shoots with Justin and Baby Girl. Her creative juices were blocked. Normally, photography would open her mind and help her to move forward when things in life were stagnated, but now, the camera held no interest for her. Would she ever heal? After a while, the daily phone calls from Justin and Baby tapered off to every few days, and then weekly. It gladdened her heart, though, that each one still called her any time there was an out of the norm occurrence in their life—whether good or bad. Thankfully, both Melinda and Jerry accepted the fact that she was still the first go-to in an emergency. She was still Mom.

Finally, slowly, Tina began to open up once again to life. It did not come easily, and it did not happen smoothly, but it did happen. Her career had suffered because her heart was not open to anything creative, but one day an offer from the Atlanta Aquarium caught her attention and lured her out of the gloom and back to business.

Wandering through the aquarium and scoping out photo opps helped until she started identifying with the sea life held prisoner behind glass cages. How sad to be able to look out at all the people but not be free themselves. This slip into despair was a new level even for her. Tina found a bench positioned close to the sea lions, laid her camera beside her and sat watching their movements.

They were chasing one another, climbing up and down the rocks, clapping their hands and overall enjoying their day. She realized that even though they looked imprisoned, they were actually exactly where they belonged and were most likely very content to enjoy their beautiful surroundings. She, on the other hand, was spending her days grieving and walking backwards. Again, the voice came softly to her heart, *I will never leave you, Tina.* It was like cool water on a hot day or warm honey on a sore throat. *Thank you, Father.*

Since then, life has been easier and even conversations with Jerry are a little less awkward. At times they even managed to talk about things other than Justin. Perhaps, just perhaps, healing was possible after all.

CHAPTER TWENTY-THREE

A New Season

Tina and her Mom sat on the couch, drinking coffee and replaying the events of the past few months. It had been almost a year since the children left. The house was unbelievably quiet for a while, but slowly she and her parents developed a new routine. Tina tried to keep busy with her photography, but coming home to the two empty bedrooms was still uncomfortable.

Both children kept in touch and visited fairly often. They were safe with their new families and appeared to be doing well. Justin played baseball and then football. The Brogan clan made a road trip to watch him play and meet his "new" family. Melinda and Baby joined them as well. They would always be brother and sister in their hearts. Nothing and no one could change that. It was a healing weekend for all of them. Since then, Justin and Jerry had been to Chickpea a couple of times. Once, he brought a cousin to visit. And of course, Pepsi always made the trip.

She was feeling more and more comfortable visiting in TN. She and Jerry were in complete agreement to keep things at a respectable distance and normally had cousins over on the nights she spent in the guest room. Jerry was very clear to all the family that Tina was there as Justin's mother.

Jerry would definitely love for them to be together and Tina was not opposed to exploring the idea, but it would take time. For now, Justin and Jerry needed to be free to reestablish their bond. She explained to Jerry that she could not interfere with that. He agreed but asked that she at least keep her heart open for the possibility of a long term relationship with him. He still called for advice when he was unsure of how to handle a situation with Justin. Not only did that help Tina feel close to Justin, it kept her heart in tune with Jerry as well.

Beth visited more often since she was closeby. It was heartwarming to see the change in Melinda once she and Beth were safely together again. She was working with the DFACS office and continuing to search for her extended family. Unfortunately, at this point, every lead had been a dead end.

To everyone's surprise, Melinda had been able to locate the soft spot in Ms. McGowen's heart and they formed a close friendship. As it turned out, the older lady lost her only child, a daughter, in an automobile accident years earlier. She was not able to forgive the drunk driver who hit her. Had the daughter lived, she would be about Melinda's age now. How sad that she had endured such pain all these years.

Tina turned to look at her mom. "So, what happens now? Where do I go from here? Sometimes I feel like my life has been derailed and will never get back on track. I am twenty-seven years old and I live with my parents. I have money to move out, but honestly, I have no desire to do that. Will my life ever be normal again, mom?"

Pulling Tina's head over to her shoulder, Joan wrapped her arms around her daughter and squeezed. "Oh, honey! Yes, of course it will." Tina started to pull away, but mom's hug felt so good, she relaxed into it.

"Tina, I have watched you over these past few years grow from a strong-willed young girl to a mature, loving woman. I know your heart is broken, but, honey, it will heal. Do you know how I know that?"

Sniffing and reaching for a tissue, Tina sat up next to her mom and breathed deeply. "How, Mom?"

"Because love has broken your heart. Your heart is not broken by fear, grief or loss, but by love. You loved these two children with all your heart. You were willing to surrender your plans, your very life to God's will in accepting them. You did not have to do that. No one made you, but your heart could not reject His will or their need. This was a season of sacrifice, dear. Granted, you received much in return, but still, it was you who surrendered your will to His."

Tina sat trying to soak up the full meaning of what her mom was saying. She had not looked at it that way. In her mind, she had fought with God every step of the way. It seemed to her that she met every change with resistance and arguing.

"Tina, listen to me, you struggled at times, sure, but in every instance you bowed to Him. This was a season," her mom reminded her again. "And now, that season is over and you need to take what you have learned and use it to help you go forward. You did what He asked, and now you are ready for the next season in your life. Anytime the Lord takes us through a challenge, there is an opportunity to learn. Think about it, Tina. You have new and amazing insights, revelations, places in Him, places you have discovered in your own heart. All these are treasures you will take away from this time with the children. And most of all you have a new place of intimacy with Christ that was forged in the furnace of his fire. He loves you greatly or he would never have trusted you with his precious children."

Tina remembered the scripture God dropped in her heart a few weeks before the children came to live with her. It was in Isiah. "Hold on, mom, I remember something." She picked up the Bible from off the coffee table and turned to Isaiah. She had marked it in red, Isaiah 45:3.

She read it aloud for her mom,

I will give you the treasures of darkness,
Riches stored in secret places,
So that you may know that I am the Lord,
The God of Israel, who summons you by name.
(NIV)

"Yes," her mom said, "I know that verse well. It has spoken to me many times. In many ways, this has been a time of secret places and at times, darkness. Wouldn't you agree? So, what are your treasures?"

Tina thought about that for a moment. "You are right, there have been times of darkness over the past few years. It was dark at first. There were times I fought against keeping them, but my heart always surrendered. When Barry left, I was ready to give up, and again when Ms. McGowen first appeared. When we moved back to ChickPea I hated losing many of my clients and laying down my dreams of being a photojournalist. Oh, I know now that I can still do that, but at the time I was certain my career was over. None of that though was as difficult as when the parents showed up and I had to say goodbye and let them go.

Isn't it interesting—I tried so hard to get rid of the kids, but in the end, they were the very ones that I wanted more than anything else."

"I know, dear, I know. My heart hurt for you, but I knew the Lord was doing something deep inside you and I couldn't interfere."

"But, Mom, the most amazing part of it all, is the way God revealed Himself to me. Over and over, He took me to places I didn't know existed. The end of that verse talks about Him giving us treasures in dark times so we will know who He is. But the thing is, I cannot explain in words how I know Him now. Some of the revelations are beyond human expression. It is like once I *accepted* the kids and let go of my career and my dreams, it became easier. I think if a person wants to walk with God and follow His direction, it is imperative to open up and accept what He brings. Don't get me wrong, backing off my career and then moving back to Chickpea was more difficult than you will ever know. However, once I did that, things began to fall into place in my heart.

It wasn't just the doing of it, but the acceptance of it in my heart. You know, moving on without bitterness. Accepting that this was my path and coming to the point where I could walk it with a good attitude was the trick. Now, accepting that it was my path to walk when He removed the kids—well, that was a different thing. That was so much worse. You know how long I grieved before God could bring me out of my cave."

Tina laughed and continued. "Mom, those sea lions will never know what they did for me that day. Isn't it neat how the Lord can and will use anything at his disposal to get His point across?"

Mom sighed deeply and hugged her daughter again.

"Thank you mom. Thank you for everything you did to help. I absolutely would not have made it without you and dad."

They sat quietly, enjoying each other's company and the fact that words were not always necessary.

Tina looked at her mom and smiled. "You asked me what I have learned through all this. I do have treasures. Wonderful, amazing treasures. They are hidden in my heart where only God can see, like my private treasure chest. Some I cannot put into words, some are too intimate to share, but they are all revelations of his love that He showed me along the way. I suppose my greatest treasure is the realization that no matter where I go or what comes into my life, He really will never leave me. I have been in some rough places lately but He has been there every step of the way. In such a powerful way, I know who He is now. He is everything I need. That's who He is.

And, in many ways, I have learned how to be a friend. There were times when I was so down or lonely or confused that I could not talk to anyone. I could not pray. My heart would just be numb. It was at those times He would show up and sit with me. He never preached to me or quoted scripture, He just sat with me. And, the best thing was, He had this way of holding my heart. You know, from the inside out. He would hold me and hold my heart and even though nothing changed on the outside, on the inside I was better. I could go again. You know, I could get up and go again.

I think that's what a real friend does. I suppose it is human nature to want to fix things, to say something encouraging, but with Jesus, His presence was my answer. It's like we were such close friends, we did not need to talk. Kinda like us, you know? I am so glad I was at the right place that morning. I would not change one thing."

The back door opened and they heard Dad's footsteps coming through the dining room. "Here you are. What's for dinner?"

Mom laughed and shook her head. "Aren't you glad that in the midst of upheaval, some things never change?"

After dinner the three of them sat around the kitchen table talking. As usual, the conversation turned to her future. Mom was thoughtful for a moment before she spoke. "Tina, have you thought about moving back to Atlanta?"

Tina laughed. "Trying to get rid of me?"

"No, you know better. But it has been a while now since the children moved and they are both settled in their new lives. What about you? Remember how much you enjoyed living in the city? The last time we were there, we noticed a new condo building going up close to your old apartments. You could afford one now. And with the business Mr. Johnson is throwing your way, it would be much more convenient. And, of course it would be closer to TN. That is, if you are interested in that."

"Oh, mom. You are too funny. But, yes, I am definitely interested in being closer to TN."

Dad spoke up, "Tina, please do not take this wrong. You know how much we love you and that you will always have a home with us. No matter your age or circumstances, our home is your home."

"Yes, of course I know that, Daddy. But, what are you saying?"

"We haven't mentioned it yet because we wanted you to have all the time you wanted to regroup, but, your mom and I have decided it's time for us to pamper ourselves a little. We want to travel. And . . . if it is OK with you, we are ready to book that cruise you promised."

Tina was thrilled for her parents. "If anyone deserves pampering, it is you two. It is absolutely fine with me. Let's book it!!"

For a moment, they were all three laughing and talking at one time. After the excitement settled, Tina and her mom cleaned the dishes and started into the living room. Dad stepped between them, took his wife by the hand, and excused them. As they made their way upstairs, Tina could hear her dad doing his happy dance, "Yep . . . going on a cruise!" and wait . . . was her mom giggling?

Tina stepped outside to her favorite spot on the front porch and sat thinking. Her time here was over . . . again. She had come through a difficult time and she had not only survived, she was stronger than before. In the midst of it all, she had discovered secrets . . . and treasures.

Tomorrow I will call about the condo. Katie will be happy to have me back in time to help with her and Barry's wedding. After all, a Maid of Honor should be close by. Thoughts of the wedding brought thoughts of Jerry and Justin. "Perhaps I should keep the door open with Jerry. After I have time to travel, buy that condo, and make a name for myself in Atlanta. Perhaps then. Who knows?"

Lord, thank you for interrupting my life. I realize the explosion and the tragic losses many suffered was not your doing in any way. Still, you took the remnants and brought new life. You do not waste anything, but use all that comes our way to enlarge and grow us. Thank you for my treasures.

Early Monday morning Tina was on the phone inquiring about the new condos her mom had mentioned. Just as she finished her call, Mr. Johnson beeped through. "Good morning, Mr. Johnson."

"Good morning, Tina. Do you have a few minutes to discuss a possible new assignment? Even if it involves a good bit of travel?"

Tina smiled and nodded at her phone. "Absolutely, I am all ears!"

Mr. Johnson laid out the details of the proposed assignment. By the time the call ended, Tina's brain was zooming with plans, ideas and pure excitement. The client was presently living in Georgia, but was originally from France. Tina's task would be to investigate his former life in France. She would visit the places he did business, the places he lived, former colleagues and of course take photographs. It sounded more like a job for a private eye than a photojournalist. But hey, whatever the Lord was bringing, she was up for. And France! One of the Associates from the law office would accompany her and act as interpreter when needed. That made Tina feel a bit safer, knowing she would not be wandering around France alone, but she did hope there would be days when she could do just that.

Two weeks later, she arrived at the Atlanta airport at 4:30 A.M. Everything was in order. Her bags were checked, reservations were made for several towns in France, her bank account sported a nice advance and she had a company charge card. When Mr. Johnson said it was a chance of a lifetime for her, he was not lying.

Tina settled into her seat and took a deep breath. First class all the way. Next stop, France!

Afterword

In Georgia alone there are over 11,000 children in foster care ranging from newborn to 18. They are removed from their homes because they are not safe, or their parents cannot care for them. They leave behind most of their clothes, toys, stuffed animals, friends, school, relatives, even the grocery store they are used to, and worse, many times siblings. They are lost, scared and none of what is happening is their fault nor do they have any control. The first thing they experience in this new life is their case worker, the second is their foster family. Having a loving, supportive, patient, and understanding foster family could be the single most important thing to determine if a foster child becomes a statistic

(⅕ become homeless at 18, under 3% get a college degree, 80% have signs of depression) or a well-adjusted successful adult. Often foster homes are too far away, too crowded, or can not take all siblings together. More people becoming foster parents helps alleviate all three of those issues. If a child can go to a stable environment when they first come into care, they can become a part of a family, make friends, join activities, do well in school, be a "normal" kid to an extent. However if they have to be moved because they are too far away or they are trying to get siblings back together or they have conflict with one of the many other foster kids (who have their own issues and insecurities) in the home, those connections and things that signify a normal life can not exist. With every home move, there is usually a school move which generates gaps in education, a doctor and/or counselor change, new classmates, new teachers and coaches and the child is no longer around for the season of the sport or activity they hoped to do so eventually they don't even try.

As a volunteer who works with foster children, I have seen a lot of heartbreaking situations. Imagine a 6-year-old who comes into care with his baby sibling due to his mom's drug abuse and incarceration. He is placed 4 hours from his home because there are no placements nearby. Within 6 months, he and his sibling have been moved 3 times for a variety of reasons (none of which they created) and are on their second caseworker. Fast forward 9 years. They are still in care. The baby who was placed in a foster home she could stay in ended up being adopted and doing well. The 6-year-old was moved around between family members and foster homes and is now an angry 15-year-old with no real support system and no direction. While caseworkers work hard to do the best for the children, they are so overloaded and their hands are often tied. Children need stability and most of the time that comes in the form of a foster home for however long they need it.

Consider fostering a child in need, you could literally save a life. In Georgia, each county has informational sessions. You make no commitment, just get information and if it is something you can do, they will give you the next steps. The sessions are even online. Go to dfcs.georgia.gov or call 1-877-210-kids. For other states just google the state and foster parenting.

Rhonda Wyatt

Thank You!

My heart is so full of love for all those who helped and encouraged me. My children are always there for me and I appreciate them so very much. Two of them, Kerry Morris and Kathryn Bowden, are also authors and their input is invaluable. My retired teacher-son, Kenny Morris, has a bird's eye for things that do not line up. And of course, my niece, Rhonda Frizzell. Once again, her critique was spot on. My grandson, Tyler Morris, stepped up to help me design the book cover. Aren't families the best?

Most importantly, you, my dear reader. I hope you enjoyed Tina's story. Please consider posting a comment on Amazon. I would love to hear your feedback.

About the Author

Marie Dias writes with the humor, love and reality of a Southern lady. Expect heartwarming stories of strong women who face real life with courage and determination mixed with love and vulnerability.

She is constant in two things: her love for Jesus Christ and her love for family. Marie resides in Newnan, GA. She enjoys photography, crafting and of course, writing.

Made in the USA
Columbia, SC
15 April 2023

ab102ba3-6804-4811-a833-fb8bf8fb7a60R01